To Christianna Brand
With grateful thanks
For all her help and encouragement

And appetite, an universal wolf,
So doubly seconded with will and power,
Must make perforce an universal prey,
And last eat up himself.

Troilus and Cressida
Act 1, Scene 3

Foreword
by John Nettles

Twenty years ago, a producer came to see me where I was working up in Stratford-upon-Avon. He was clutching a bunch of books by Caroline Graham about the adventures and exploits of a Detective Chief Inspector Tom Barnaby who worked for Causton CID. 'We want to make a television series out of these novels,' he says, 'and we would like you to play the part of the DCI. What do you say?' At the time, I thought that after playing a policeman in Jersey, I was not about to play another one in Causton. But the producer, Brian True-May, had come a very long way to see me, so I politely agreed to read the books and get back to him with a decision.

Reading the books that summer in Stratford was my first introduction to the world of Caroline Graham and Detective Chief Inspector Barnaby. And what a happy experience it was! The books are wonderful. I found Tom Barnaby quite fascinating; he's an ordinary, decent man who continually finds himself in extraordinary and often indecent circumstances, yet he still makes time to tend his garden and endure his wife Joyce's appalling cooking with an almost god-like equanimity. And, of course, he loves his daughter Cully (the only girl with that name in the known universe) to distraction, like most dads love their daughters. He has no obvious faults or tics, injuries or addictions, depressive illnesses, failing relationships. He doesn't even own an antique car, the usual badge of a television detective. Tom Barnaby is a four-square, well-mannered Englishman and I love him for that. After reading Caroline Graham's books, there was no question. I knew that I had to play him . . .

There began *Midsomer Murders*, one of the most success-ful British cop shows of all time, shown in every country and every territory known to man. Around the world, Tom Barnaby is celebrated as the top English cop.

The television shows are great, but, good as they are for the viewer, they are not as good as the original books can be for the reader, because when you read the book you can make up your own pictures of the characters, and they are the per-fect creations for *you*. But there is something else that makes the Barnaby novels better than their television counterpart: the variety and depth of the characterisation, to say nothing of the complex and satisfying plotting.

On television, because of the need to tell a story quickly, the novels have to be simplified; the characters are less rounded, and many fascinating details left out. In the books, Barnaby is a much more interesting character than we managed to convey in the television series. His style of non-confrontational, even conversational, interrogation that is so quietly absorbing in the books does not work on the box, which demands a noisier, more muscular approach from a copper. Likewise with Troy, the character you see on the screen is quite different from how he appears in the books. In the novels, Troy is an amazing creation, as far removed from Tom Barnaby's character as the North Pole is from the equator. The character was softened and made more attractive to a TV audience. It is true there were hints of his original red-top attitude, but they weren't ingrained or obvious enough to be character defining. In fact he became a lovable character in the television show and it must be said that, despite the simplification involved, Troy remains one of the best-loved characters in Midsomer.

In Caroline's novels, unlike the television series, the size of the social canvas is vast, with a huge variety of characters from all social classes: the lords and ladies; the poor; the young; the old; the disadvantaged; the indulged; the psychotic; the deranged; the loved and the unloved. The lives of all these characters are inti-mately and entertainingly delineated and explored, the murder mysteries are character led, in a way that the television versions are, very often, not – the television plots concentrate almost exclusively on the exotic methods of murder rather than the character of those who commit them. They have succeeded on this level beyond all expectation, but there is always a price to pay for turning books into a television series. Very often, the human interest is lost in the pursuit of ever more lurid and some-times ludicrous plot lines; and while the results of this chase can be as entertaining as they are popular, something essential to good whodunnit storytelling is undoubtedly lost.

But despair not! In Caroline's books you will find that humanity restored, the drama therefore more real and the satisfaction absolute. Enjoy!

John Nettles
July 2016

Prologue

She had been walking in the woods just before teatime when she saw them. Walking very quietly although that had not been her intention. It was just that the spongy underlay of leaf mould and rotting vegetation muffled every footfall. The trees, tall and packed close together, also seemed to absorb sound. In one or two places the sun pierced through the closely entwined branches, sending dazzling shafts of hard white light into the darkness below.

Miss Simpson stepped in and out of these shining beams peering at the ground. She was looking for the spurred coral root orchid. She and her friend Lucy Bellringer had discovered the first nearly fifty years ago when they were young women. Seven years had passed before it had surfaced again and then it had been Lucy who had spotted it, diving off into the undergrowth with a hoot of triumph.

Their mock feud had developed from that day. Each summer they set out, sometimes separately, sometimes together, eager to find another specimen. Hopes high, eyes sharp and notebooks and pencils at the ready they stalked the dim beechwoods. Whoever spotted the plant first gave the loser, presumably as some sort of consolation prize, a spectacularly high tea. The orchid flowered rarely and, due to an elaborate system of underground rhizomes, not always in the same place twice. Over the last five years the two friends had started looking earlier and earlier. Each was aware the other was doing so; neither ever mentioned it.

Really, thought Miss Simpson, parting a clump of bluebells gently with her stick, another couple of years at this rate and we'll be coming out when the snow's on the ground.

But if there was any justice in the world (and Miss Simpson firmly believed that there was) then 1987 was her turn. Lucy had won in 1969 and 1978, but this year . . .

She tightened her almost colourless lips. She wore her old leghorn hat with the bee veil pushed back, a faded Horrockses cotton dress, wrinkled white lisle stockings and rather baggy green-stained tennis shoes. She was holding a magnifying glass and a sharp stick with a red ribbon tied to it. She had covered almost a third of the wood, which was a small one, and was now working her way deep into the heart. Ten years could easily pass between blooms but it had been a wet cold winter and a very damp spring, both propitious signs. And there was something about today . . .

She stood still, breathing deeply. It had rained a little the evening before and this had released an added richness into the warm, moist air – a pungent scent of flowers and verdant leaves with an undernote of sweet decay.

She approached the bole of a vast oak. Scabby parasols of fungus clung to the trunk and around the base was a thick clump of hellebores. She circled the base of the tree, staring intently at the ground.

And there it was. Almost hidden beneath flakes of leaf mould, brown and soft as chocolate shavings. She moved the crumbs gently aside; a few disturbed insects scuttered out of the way. It gleamed in the half light as if lit from within. It was a curious plant: very pretty, the petals springing away from the lemon calyx like butterfly wings, delicately spotted and pale fawny yellow but quite without any trace of green. There were no leaves and even the stem was a dark, mottled pink. She crouched on her thin haunches and pushed the stick into the ground. The ribbon hung limp in the still air. She leaned closer, pince-nez slipping down her large bony nose. Tenderly she counted the blooms. There were six. Lucy's had only had four. A double triumph!

She rose to her feet full of excitement. She hugged herself; she could have danced on the spot. Nuts to you Lucy Bellringer, she thought. Nuts and double nuts. But she did not allow the feelings of triumph to linger. The important thing now was the tea. She had made notes last time when Lucy had been out of the room refreshing the pot and, whilst not wishing to appear ostentatious, was determined to double the choice of sandwiches, have four varieties of cake and finish off with a home-made strawberry water ice. There was a large bowl of them, ripe to bursting, in the larder. She stood lost in blissful anticipation. She saw the inlaid Queen Anne table covered with her great aunt Rebecca's embroidered lace cloth, piled high with delicacies.

Date and banana bread, Sally Lunn black with fruit, frangipane tarts, spiced parkin and almond biscuits, lemon curd and fresh cream sponge, ginger and orange jumbles. And, before the ice, toasted fingers with anchovies and Leicester cheese . . .

There was a noise. One always had the illusion, she thought, that the heart of a wood was silent. Not at all. But there were noises so indigenous to their surroundings that they emphasized the silence rather than disturbing it – the movements of small animals, the rustle of leaves and, overall, the lavish ululation of birdsong. But this was an alien noise. Miss Simpson stood very still and listened.

It sounded like jerky, laboured breathing and, for a moment, she thought that a large animal had been caught in a trap, but then the breathing was punctuated by strange little cries and moans which were definitely human.

She hesitated. So dense was the foliage that it was hard to

know from which direction the sounds came. They seemed to be bouncing around the encircling greenery like a ball. She stepped over a swathe of ferns and listened again. Yes – definitely in that direction. She moved forward on tiptoe as if knowing in advance that what she was about to discover should have remained forever secret.

She was very close now to the source of the disturbance. Between herself and the noise was a tight lattice of branches and leaves. She stood stock still behind this screen then, very carefully, parted two of the branches and peered through. She only just stopped a sound of horrified amazement passing her lips.

Miss Simpson was a maiden lady. Her education had in many respects been sketchy. As a child she had had a governess who turned puce and stammered all through their 'nature' lessons. She had touched, glancingly, on the birds and the bees and left the human condition severely alone. But Miss Simpson believed deeply that only a truly cultivated mind could offer the stimulus and consolation necessary to a long and happy life and she had, in her time, gazed unflinchingly at great works of art in Italy, France and Vienna. So she knew immediately what was happening in front of her. The tangle of naked arms and legs (there seemed in real life to be far more than four of each) were gleaming with a pearly sheen just like the glow on the limbs of Cupid and Psyche. The man had the woman's hair knotted around his fingers and was savagely pulling back her head as he covered her shoulders and breasts with kisses. So it was that Miss Simpson saw her face first. That was shock enough. But when the woman pushed her lover away and, laughing, scrambled on top of him, well . . .

Miss Simpson blinked, and blinked again. Who would ever have thought it? She eased the parted twigs back together and, holding her breath, gently let them go. Then she stood for several minutes wondering what to do next. Her mind was a mass of conflicting thoughts and emotions. She felt shock, intense embarrassment, disgust and a very faint flicker, instantly and resolutely suppressed, of excitement. She felt as if someone had handed her a ticking bomb. Having, by force of circumstance and natural inclination neatly sidestepped all the mess and muddle of selection, courtship, marriage and the resulting clash of arms, Miss Simpson felt singularly ill equipped to handle it.

A prim irritation started snagging the edge of her mind. A 'tsk' almost escaped her lips. In the middle of a wood of all places. When they each had a perfectly good home to go to. They had spoiled what should have been a really wonderful day.

Now she somehow had to get away as silently as she had approached. She studied the ground thoughtfully. She must avoid snapping even a twig. And the sooner she moved the better. For all she knew they might almost have come to . . . well . . . whatever point it was people came to.

And then the woman shouted. A strange terrible cry, and a bird flew up from the thicket right into Miss Simpson's face. She cried out in her turn and, full of shame and horror at the thought of discovery, turned and started to run. Seconds later she tripped over a tree root. She crashed heavily to the ground but panic drove out any feeling of pain. She scrambled to her feet and ran on. Behind her she heard a lumbering, crashing sound and realized they must have jumped up and torn the branches aside to see what was happening. They would recognize her. They must. She was only a few yards away. Surely, naked, they wouldn't pursue?

Her eighty-year-old legs responded to demands that hadn't been made on them for years. Flying up behind her at odd angles like freckled sticks, they carried her, in an incredibly short space of time, to the edge of the wood. There she rested against a tree, listening and panting, her hand on her flat, agonized chest, for almost five minutes. Then she walked slowly home.

Later that evening she sat on the window seat looking out over the darkening garden. She pushed the casement wide, breathing in the fragrance from nicotiana and night-scented stocks planted directly beneath the window. At the end of the lawn was the faint white blur, almost blue in the dusk, of the beehives.

Since her arrival home almost three hours ago she had sat thus, unable to eat, becoming more and more aware of the pain in her shin, and less and less certain of what to do next.

Everything was changed now. They knew that she knew. Nothing could alter that. Would that it could. She would have given anything to put the clock back to yesterday. It was her own vanity that had got her into this mess. Wanting to crow over her friend; wanting to win. Serve her right. She sighed. All this castigation didn't solve a thing.

She wondered if they would come and see her, and turned cold at the thought. She imagined the awful, three-cornered conversation. The hideous embarrassment. Or perhaps they wouldn't be embarrassed? To be able to frolic about in the open like that argued a certain brazen confidence. Perhaps she should take the initiative and approach them. Assure them of her continuing silence. Miss Simpson's fastidious soul was repelled by the idea. It would look as if she was forcing further intimacies that they may well not want. How strange it was, she thought, to be suddenly handed a startling new piece of information about two people one thought one knew well. It seemed to colour, almost cancel out, all her previous knowledge of them.

She shifted slightly, clenching her teeth against the pain from her bruised leg. She recalled wistfully the moment she had discovered the orchid and how much fun it would have been making the celebration tea. She could never tell Lucy now. Everything seemed grubby and spoiled. She eased herself off the window seat, went through the kitchen and entered the perfumed stillness of the garden. A few feet away her favourite rose, a Papa Meilland, was about to flower. Last year the buds had been struck by mildew but this year all seemed well and several dark, glowing scrolls hinted at the glories to come. One looked as if it would be fully open by the next morning.

She sighed again and returned to the kitchen to make her cocoa. She unhooked a spotless pan from one of the beams and measured out the milk. She had never felt more keenly the truth of the saying 'a trouble shared is a trouble halved'. But she had lived in a small village long enough to know that what she had discovered could safely be discussed with no one – not even dear Lucy, who was not a gossip but who had absolutely no idea of concealment. Nor the people one would normally have regarded as natural confidants such as her own solicitor (now on holiday in the Algarve) and, of course, the vicar. He was a terrible gossip, especially after the Wine Circle's monthly get-together.

She took an iridescent fluted cup and saucer (she had never been able to adapt to the modern fashion for hefty mugs), put in a heaped teaspoon of cocoa, added a little sugar and a sprinkling of cinnamon. She could tell her nephew living safely in Australia, but that would mean writing it all down and the very thought made her feel slightly sick. The milk foamed up to the saucepan's rim and she poured it into the cup, stirring all the time.

Sitting in her winged chair Miss Simpson sipped a little of the cocoa. If no individual was to be trusted surely there were organizations one could talk to at times like this? Never friendless in her life, she cast around in her memory for the name of a society which helped those who were. She was sure there had been a poster in the offices where she had gone to argue about deductions from her pension. A man holding a telephone and listening. And a name which had struck her at the time as faintly biblical. Inquiries would know. Thank goodness everything was automatic now: nothing would have got past Mrs Beadle on the old post office board.

The girl knew immediately what she meant and connected her to the Samaritans. The voice at the other end was most comforting. A little young, perhaps, but kind and sounding genuinely interested. And, most important, assuring her of complete confidentiality. However, Miss Simpson, having given her name, had hardly begun to explain the situation when she was interrupted by a sound. She stopped speaking and listened. There it was again.

Someone was tapping, softly but persistently, at the back door.

PART ONE

SUSPICION

Chapter One

'There's something very wrong here and I expect you to do something about it. Isn't that what the police are for?'

Sergeant Troy observed his breathing, a trick he had picked up from a colleague at Police Training College who was heavily into T'ai Ch'i and other faddy Eastern pursuits. The routine came in very handy when dealing with abusive motorists, boot-deploying adolescents and, as now, with barmy old ladies.

'Indeed we are, Miss . . . er . . .' The sergeant pretended he had forgotten her name. Occasionally this simple manoeuvre caused people to wonder if their visit was really worth the bother and to drift off, thus saving unnecessary paperwork.

'Bellringer.'

Chiming in, thought the sergeant, pleased at the speed of this connection and at his ability to keep a straight face. He continued, 'But are you sure there's anything here to investigate? Your friend was getting on in years, she had a fall and it was too much for her. It's quite common, you know.'

'Rubbish!'

She had the sort of voice that really got up his nose: clear, authoritative, upper upper middle class. I bet she's ordered a few skivvies around in her time, he thought, the noun springing easily to mind. He and his wife enjoyed a good costume drama on the television.

'She was as strong as an ox,' Miss Bellringer stated firmly.

'As an ox.' There was a definite tremor on the repetition. Jesus, thought Sergeant Troy, surely the old bat wasn't going to start snivelling. Mechanically he reached for the Kleenex under the counter and returned to his breathing.

Miss Bellringer ignored the tissues. Her left arm vanished into a vast tapestry bag, trawled around for a bit then reappeared, the hand gripping a round jewelled box. She opened this and shook a neat pile of ginger-coloured powder on to the back of her wrist. She sniffed this up each nostril, closing them alternately like an emergent seal. She replaced the box and let out a prodigious sneeze. Sergeant Troy grabbed resentfully at his papers. When the dust had settled Miss Bellringer cried, 'I wish to see your superior.'

It would have given Sergeant Troy a great deal of pleasure to say that none of his superiors was on the premises. Unfortunately this was not the case. Detective Chief Inspector Barnaby had just returned from holiday and was catching up on some files in his office.

'I won't keep you a moment,' said Troy, horrified to find the word madam lurking at the end of the sentence.

As he knocked on Barnaby's door and entered, Troy kept his face expressionless and his ideas regarding Miss Bellringer's degree of senility firmly to himself. The Chief could be very terse at times. He was a big, burly man with an air of calm paternalism which had seduced far sharper men than Gavin Troy into voicing opinions which had then been trounced to smithereens.

'Well, Sergeant?'

'There's an old – elderly lady in reception, sir. A Miss Bellringer from Badger's Drift. She insists on seeing someone in authority. I mean someone apart from myself.'

Barnaby lifted his head. He doesn't look as if he's had a holiday, thought Sergeant Troy. He looks tired. Not very well either. The thought did not displease him. The little bottle of tablets which Barnaby carried everywhere was on the desk next to a beaker of water.

'What's it about?'

'Her friend has died and she's not satisfied.'

'Who would be?'

The sergeant rephrased his question. It was obviously going to be one of the Chief's sarky days. 'What I meant, sir, was that she's convinced there's something wrong. Not quite straightforward.'

Chief Inspector Barnaby looked down at his top file: a particularly unsavoury case of child molestation. It would be a pleasure to postpone reading it for a while. 'All right. Show her in.'

Miss Bellringer settled herself in the chair that Sergeant Troy drew forward and rearranged her draperies. She was a wondrous sight, festooned rather than dressed. All her clothes had a dim but vibrant sheen as if they had once, long ago, been richly embroidered. She wore several very beautiful rings, the gems dulled by dirt. Her nails were dirty too. Her eyes moved all the time, glittering in a brown seamed face. She looked like a tattered eagle.

'I'm Chief Inspector Barnaby. Can I help you?'

'Well . . .' She eyed him doubtfully. 'May I ask why you're in mufti?'

'In what? Oh' – he followed her stern gaze. 'I'm a detective. Plain clothes.'

'Ah.' Satisfied, she continued, 'I want you to investigate a death. My friend Emily Simpson was eighty years old and because she was eighty a death certificate has automatically been issued. If she'd been half that age questions would have been asked. A post mortem carried out.'

'Not necessarily, Miss Bellringer. That would depend on the circumstances.'

It had been years since Barnaby had heard such an accent.

Not since his early days of going to the pictures. In the post-war years films had been full of clean-cut young Englishmen with straight up and down trousers, all sounding their As like Es.

'Well the circumstances here are very strange indeed.'

They didn't sound all that strange, thought Barnaby, picking up a notepad and pen. Apparently his visitor's friend had been discovered, lying on a hearthrug, by the postman. He had needed a signature for a parcel and, not getting any reply to his knock (except the frantic barking of a dog) had peered through the sitting-room window.

'He came straight to me . . . he's been our postman for years you see . . . knew us both and I telephoned Doctor Lessiter –'

'That's your friend's GP?'

'He's everyone's GP, Inspector. Well, all the elderly in the village and those without transport. Otherwise it's a four-mile trip into Causton. Well – I hurried over, taking my key, but in the event it wasn't necessary because . . .' – Miss Bellringer lifted a compelling annunciatory finger – 'and this is the first odd thing – the back door was unlocked.'

'Was that unusual?'

'Unheard of. There have been three burglaries in the village recently. Emily was most particular.'

'Everyone has a lapse of memory sometimes,' murmured Barnaby.

'Not her. She had a fixed routine. Nine p.m. check time with the wireless, set her alarm for seven, put Benjy in his basket then lock the back door.'

'And do you know if her alarm was set?'

'No. I looked specially.'

'Then surely that simply indicates that she died before nine p.m.'

'No she didn't. Died in the night. The doctor said.'

'She may have died in the night,' the inspector continued gently, 'but lost consciousness several hours before.'

'Now here's the clincher,' said Miss Bellringer, eagle bright, as if he had not spoken, '*what about the ghost orchid?*'

'The ghost orchid,' repeated Barnaby evenly, thirty years of dealing with the public standing him in ineffably good stead. Miss Bellringer explained about the contest.

'And in the afternoon after my friend died I went for a walk in the woods. Silly really, because of course I simply got rather upset. I found myself half looking for the orchid then realized that it didn't matter any more whether I found it or not. And this brought Emily's death home to me in a way that seeing her . . . lying there . . . hadn't.' She looked across at the inspector, blinked several times and sniffed. 'That must sound a bit peculiar.'

'Not at all.'

'And then I found it. But you see Emily had found it first.' Responding to Barnaby's raised eyebrows she continued, 'We had a stick with a ribbon to mark the spot. Hers red, mine yellow. Now' – Miss Bellringer leaned forward and Barnaby, so intense was her regard, only just stopped himself doing the same – 'why did she not come and tell me?'

'Perhaps she was saving it. As a surprise.'

'No, no,' she said, irritated by his apparent inability to grasp the situation, 'you don't understand. I've known Emily for nearly eighty years. She would have been overwhelmed by excitement. She would have come straight to me.'

'She may already have felt ill and been anxious to get home.'

'She has to pass my gate to get there. If she'd been ill she would have come in. I would have looked after her.'

'Did you see her at all on that day?'

'Saw her bringing Benjy back from his walk about two o'clock. And before you ask, they both looked as fit as fleas.'

She looked around the room in a lost yet hopeful manner, as the newly bereft sometimes do. Unable to accept the empty space, half expecting the dead person to reappear. 'No' – she focused her gaze firmly on the inspector, 'something happened after she saw the orchid and before she returned to the village, to put the discovery out of her mind. And it must have been a pretty big something, believe you me.'

'If what you say is true, are you suggesting that the shock killed her?'

'I hadn't really got as far as that.' Miss Bellringer frowned. 'But there is one more thing . . .' She rummaged furiously in her bag, crying, 'What do you make of this?' and handed him a scrap of paper on which was written: Causton 1234 Terry.

'The Samaritans.'

'Are they? Well, they may give succour but they certainly don't give information. Couldn't get a thing out of them. Said it was all confidential.'

'Where did you find this?'

'On her little table, tucked under the telephone. I can't imagine why she would have rung them up.'

'Presumably because she was worried or depressed and needed to talk to someone.'

'To total strangers? Fiddlesticks!' Hurt lay behind the snort of disbelief. 'Anyway our generation didn't get depressed. We soldiered on. Not like today. People want tranquillizers now if the milk goes off.'

Barnaby felt his innards twang aggressively and shifted in his chair. The brief flicker of interest her story had aroused died away. He felt irritated and impatient. 'When did your friend actually die?'

'Friday the seventeenth. Two days ago. I've been stewing about it ever since. Knew there wasn't much to go on, y'see. Thought I'd probably be told I was talking a load of nonsense. Which of course I was.'

'I beg your pardon?'

'Young man at the desk. Said at her age it was to be expected and hinted that I was wasting his valuable time. Not,' she added caustically, 'that he seemed to be doing very much.'

'I see. No, all complaints and inquiries are investigated. Our opinion on their veracity is quite irrelevant. Who is the next of kin in this case?'

'Well . . . I am, I suppose. Neither of us had any near relations. Odd cousins and aunts long since popped off. She had a nephew somewhere in the Antipodes. And I'm her executor. We left everything to each other.'

Barnaby made a note of Miss Bellringer's name and address then asked, 'You're in charge of the funeral arrangements?'

'Yes. She's being buried on Wednesday. That doesn't leave us with much time.' Suddenly they were in the realms of melodrama. 'You know, I can't help being reminded of *The Case of the Vanishing Orchestra*. The circumstances are really quite –'

'You read detective fiction, Miss Bellringer?'

'Avidly. They're a mixed bunch, of course. My favourite is –' She broke off and looked at him sharply. 'Ah. I see what you're thinking. But you're quite wrong. It's not my imagination.'

Detective Chief Inspector Barnaby rose and, after a preliminary flapping of garments, his companion did the same. 'I shouldn't worry about the funeral, Miss Bellringer. These things can always be postponed if it proves to be necessary.'

In the doorway she turned. 'I knew her, you see, Emily.' Her fingers tightened on the bone handles of her bag. 'All this is totally out of character. Believe me, Chief Inspector, there is something very wrong here.'

After she had left Barnaby took two tablets and swished them down with some water. He leaned back in his chair and waited for them to work. It seemed to take longer and longer. Perhaps he should start taking three. He loosened his belt and returned to the child molester's file. A photograph grinned up at him: a sunny-faced little man who had had three previous convictions, then been given a job as a primary school caretaker. He sighed, pushed the folder away and wondered about Emily Simpson.

It was his belief, forged by thirty years of looking and listening, that no one ever acted out of character. What most people thought of as character (the accumulation, or lack of, certain social, educational and material assets) was shallow stuff. Real character was revealed when these accretions were stripped away. It was the chief inspector's belief that anyone was capable of anything. Strangely enough this did not depress him. He did not even regard it as a pessimistic point of view but rather as the only sensible one for a policeman to hold.

However, Miss Simpson had done several things on the last day of her life that someone who had known her closely since childhood had never known her do before. And that was odd. Odd and interesting. Detective Chief Inspector Barnaby had made a note of the Samaritans' number and took hold of the phone. But first there was the little matter of Miss Bellringer's reception to be dealt with.

He pressed the buzzer and said, 'Send Sergeant Troy in here.'

Chapter Two

There was no joy from the Samaritans. Barnaby had not expected that there would be. Clam tight as usual. Which was why after a second, later telephone call he presented himself at their tiny terraced house behind Woolworth's at seven p.m. looking worried.

An elderly man sat behind a desk with two telephones. The receiver of one was clapped to his ear. He covered the mouthpiece and whispered, 'Please sit down' to Barnaby, then continued listening, nodding gravely from time to time. Eventually he replaced the receiver and said, 'You're the person who rang hoping to see Terry?'

Barnaby, who had thought the elderly man might have been Terry, nodded. 'That's right. We talked on Friday.'

'And you are . . . ?' He was turning back the pages of a log book.

'I'd rather not give my name,' said Barnaby truthfully.

The phone rang again, and almost simultaneously a middle-aged woman and a young girl came out of a room nearby. The couple shook hands. Barnaby turned to the woman who murmured 'Good evening' and left. The girl waited expectantly. The man at the desk smiled and made a sign bringing her and Barnaby together.

She was slim and pretty, with a fall of shiny, fair hair. She had on a neat checked dress and a necklace of little silver beads. Barnaby compared her to his own daughter who, on her last visit home, had been wearing shredded jeans, an old leather breastplate and her hair in a sequinned crest.

'We can talk in here.' The girl led him back into the room. There was a comfortable armchair, a banquette against the wall and a pine table with a jar of marguerites. Barnaby took the banquette. 'Would you like some coffee?'

'No thank you.' He had entered the building with no plan, prepared to play it as it came. For all he knew Terry might have been a tough old pro like himself. Blessing his good fortune, he smiled gravely at her and produced his warrant card.

'Oh! But we're . . . I can't . . . what do you want?'

'I understand you were the person who spoke to Emily Simpson last Friday evening?'

'I'm sorry.' She sounded a bit firmer this time. 'But we never discuss clients with anyone. Our service is completely confidential.'

'I appreciate that of course,' replied Barnaby, 'but in the case of a death –'

'A death! How dreadful . . . I'd no idea she was suicidal. I've only been a volunteer for a few weeks . . . I'm still training, you see . . .' The words tumbled out. 'If only I'd known . . . but the other two Sams were interviewing and on the other line and I thought I could handle it . . . Miss Simpson I mean –'

'Hold on, hold on.' She looked younger by the minute and on the verge of tears. 'As far as we know there's no question of suicide. But there may be suspicious circumstances.'

'Oh? What sort of circumstances?'

'So I would like you to tell me, if you would, what you remember of the call.'

'I'm sorry. I can't do that. I'd have to check –'

'I've spoken to your director Mr Wainwright and I can assure you that in this case the rules can be waived.' He gave her a fatherly smile.

'Well . . . I don't know . . .'

'You wouldn't wish to obstruct a police inquiry?' A hint of sternness entered the smile.

'Of course not.' She glanced at the slightly open door. Barnaby sat patiently, guessing that in a moment she would recall the helpful gesture with which the Samaritan at the desk had introduced them. Her face cleared. She said, 'I do remember Miss Simpson's call. We only had about three that evening . . . but not word for word.'

'That's all right. As much as you can. Take your time.'

'Well, she said something like "I've got to talk to someone. I don't know what to do." Of course an awful lot of people start off like that . . . then I asked her if she'd like to give her name because you don't have to and some clients would rather not, but she did. And I encouraged her, you know . . . and waited.' She added with rather touching self-importance, 'A lot of our work is just sitting and waiting.'

'I understand.'

'Then she said, "I've seen something. I feel I've got to tell someone about it."'

Barnaby felt his concentration tighten. 'And did she say what it was?'

Terry Bazely shook her head. 'She did say it was unbelievable.'

Barnaby thought that didn't signify. Elderly spinsters of both sexes were inclined to think the mildest spot of chicanery unbelievable if letters to the local press were anything to go by. They nearly always started: 'I was absolutely amazed to see/hear/observe/experience . . .'

'But then someone came.'

'What?' He leaned forward.

'She said she had to go – there was a knock at the door and I said we'd be here all night if she wanted to ring back, but she didn't.'

'How do you know?'

'I checked in the book when I arrived.'

'And she hung up before she answered the door?'

'Yes.'

'She didn't say which door?'

'No.'

'Did you hear a dog bark?'

'No.'

'And that's all you remember?'

She looked distressed, fretting her brows, afraid she had disappointed him. 'I'm afraid so . . . at least . . .' A long pause, then she said, 'I'm sorry.'

Barnaby got up. 'Well thank you Miss –'

'Bazely. But I'm always called Terry. We only use Christian names here.'

'Thank you. You've been extremely helpful.'

She opened the door for him. 'There was something else . . . I know there was.'

He thought there probably was. She didn't look like the sort to make something up just to please. 'It'll probably pop into your mind when you're at work or doing the washing up. Give me a ring if it does. Causton Central.'

'Even if it doesn't seem important?'

'Especially if it doesn't seem important. And' – he closed the door – 'you do understand that all this is completely confidential. Not to be discussed even with your colleagues?'

'Oh.' Doubt flooded back. She looked more worried than ever. 'But . . . I shall have to put your visit in the book.'

'Just enter me,' smiled Barnaby, opening the door again, 'as an unnamed client worried about a death in the family.'

It was almost nine o'clock. Detective Chief Inspector Barnaby sat at the dining-room table facing a plateful of leathery strips, black and shiny as liquorice, surrounded by coils of yellowish green paste.

'Your liver and greens are spoiled, dear,' said Mrs Barnaby, implying that there had once been a time when they were not.

Tom Barnaby loved his wife. Joyce was kind and patient. She was a good listener. He always talked when he came home, usually about work, knowing her discretion was absolute. And she would look as interested and concerned at the end of half an hour as she had at the beginning. She was, at forty-six, ripely pretty and still enjoyed what she called, with a nudge in her voice, 'a bit of a cuddle'. She had brought up their daughter with affectionate firmness, doing most of the things parents were supposed to do together by herself because of his job, and with never a word of complaint. The house was clean and comfortable and she carried out lots of boring chores in the garden willingly, leaving all the creative and interesting bits to him. She could act very well and sing like the lark ascending and did both, *con brio*, in the local amateur operatic and dramatic society. Her only flaw was that she could not cook.

No, thought Barnaby, as a particularly resilient bit of liquorice sprang up and hit the roof of his mouth. It was not just that she couldn't cook, it was much, much more. There was between her and any fresh, frozen or tinned ingredient a sort of malign chemistry. They were born antagonists. He had observed her once making a tart. She didn't just weigh and handle materials, she squared up to them, appearing to have some terrible foreknowledge that only an instant and combative readiness could bend them to her will. Her hand had closed over the shrinking pastry ball with a grip of iron.

When Cully was about thirteen she had persuaded her mother to go to cookery classes and, on the evening of the first lesson, she and her father had stood at the gate gripping each other's hands, hardly able to believe their good fortune. Mrs Barnaby had set off carrying a basket of good things covered with a snowy cloth like a child in a fairy tale. She had come home three hours later with a small leather mat thickly studded with currants, crunchy as bits of coal. She had gone a few more times then given up – out of, she explained, kindness to the teacher. The poor woman, never before having experienced failure on such a monumental scale, had started to get terribly depressed.

Chief Inspector Barnaby rearranged his paste and strips and finished telling his wife about Miss Bellringer and Miss Simpson.

'It's an intriguing story, darling.' Mrs Barnaby lowered her knitting, an exquisite puffball of silky creamy wool. 'I wonder what she could have seen?' Her husband shrugged. She was not deceived by the casualness of the gesture. 'I suppose your next step will be to talk to the doctor?'

'That's right.' Barnaby laid down his knife and fork. You could ask just so much from ordinarily tempered cutlery. 'Probably after his evening surgery, so I might be late again. Don't worry about keeping anything hot. I'll eat out.'

'You may go in now.'

Barnaby had turned up, at Doctor Lessiter's suggestion, at eleven the following morning. He entered the consulting room to find the doctor seated behind his desk and as busy as a bee. All through their conversation his fingers were never still: fiddling with pencils, tidying a stack of pharmaceutical literature, pulling down his cuffs or just drumming away on his blotter. He glanced quickly at the chief inspector's warrant card.

'Well ... er ... Barnaby' – he handed it back – 'I can't give you long.' He didn't invite the other man to sit down. The chief inspector explained the reason for his visit.

'Don't see any problem there. Elderly lady, bad fall, too much for her heart. A very common problem.'

'I assume you attended Miss Simpson at some time during the two weeks before her death?'

'Oh yes indeed. You can't catch me out, Inspector. The death would have been reported otherwise. I know the law as well as you do.'

Leaving this unlikely possibility aside, Barnaby asked, 'For what reason?'

'She had a touch of bronchitis. Nothing serious.'

'She didn't die of bronchitis, surely?'

'What are you implying?'

'I'm not implying anything, Doctor Lessiter. I'm simply asking you a question.'

'The cause of death, which occurred several hours before she was discovered, was heart failure. As I've already stated. The bruise was a large one. She must have fallen quite heavily. This sort of shock can be fatal.'

'I can see that would be the natural deduction –'

'Diagnosis.'

'– and that you would not be looking for anything untoward. Perfectly natural under the circumstances. But if you could cast your mind back for a moment was there nothing which perhaps' – he searched for the most tactful phrase – 'didn't quite fit?'

'Nothing.'

But there had been a brief hesitation. And a note in the doctor's voice that ran counter to the strong negative. Barnaby waited. Doctor Lessiter puffed out his cheeks. His head was as round as a turnip and his cheeks the colour of russet apples. His nose was reddish too and thin crimson threads fanned out over his eyeballs. Lurking behind the acceptable aroma of soap, antiseptic and strong mints the chief inspector thought he could detect a whiff of whisky.

Doctor Lessiter's hands took a break and rested on his pot belly. When he spoke his tone was judicial, implying that he had finally decided that Barnaby could be trusted.

'Well . . . there was something . . . oh hardly worth mentioning, really. There was rather a funny smell.'

'What sort of smell?'

'Umm . . . like mice.'

'That's not surprising in an old cottage. Especially if she didn't have a cat.'

'I didn't say it *was* mice. I said it was like mice. That's the nearest point of comparison I can make.' Doctor Lessiter rose, a fraction unsteadily, to his feet. 'And now you'll have to excuse me. I have a very busy day ahead.' He pressed the buzzer and moments later Barnaby found himself in the open air.

The surgery was behind the house, a splendid Victorian villa. He walked down the long gravel drive and entered a narrow lane bordered by hawthorn and cow parsley. It was a lovely sunny day. He broke off a bit of hawthorn and chewed it as he walked. Bread and cheese they had called it when he was a lad. He remembered biting into the sweet green buds. It didn't taste the same now. Bit late in the year, perhaps.

Badger's Drift was in the shape of a letter T. The cross bar, called simply the Street, had a crescent of breeze-block council houses, a few private dwellings, the Black Boy pub, a phone box and a very large and beautiful Georgian house. This was painted a pale apricot colour and almost smothered on one side by a vast magnolia. Behind the house were several farm buildings and two huge silos. The post office was a two-up two-down, no doubt suitably fortified, called Izercummin, which doubled as the village shop.

Barnaby turned into the main leg of the T. Church Lane was not as long as the Street and ran very quickly into open country – miles and miles of wheat and barley bisected at one point by a rectangular blaze of rape. The church was thirteenth-century stone and flint, the church hall twentieth-century brick and corrugated iron.

As Barnaby strolled along he felt more and more strongly that he was being watched. A stranger in a small community is always an object of keen interest and he had seen more than one curtain twitch as he passed by. Now, although the lane behind him appeared to be deserted, he felt a spot of tension develop at the base of his neck. He turned. No one. Then he saw a rainbow of light bobbing near his feet and looked up. In the loft window of an opulent bungalow close to the Black Boy a prism of light flashed and a face turned quickly away.

Miss Bellringer lived in a small modern house at the end of the lane. Barnaby walked up the narrow path of pea shingle encroached by a tangle of luxurious vegetation. Rhododendrons, laurel, hypericum, roses all running amok in all directions. On the front door was an iron bull's head and a notice in a clear plastic envelope which read KNOCK LOUDLY. He knocked loudly.

Immediately a voice yelled: 'Don't do that!' There was a heavy bang as if a piece of furniture had fallen over, a shuffling sound, and Miss Bellringer opened the door. She said, 'I'm sorry, it's Wellington. Do come in.'

She led the way into a cluttered sitting room and started to pick up a pile of books from the floor. The chief inspector crouched to help. All the books were very heavy. 'They will climb, you see. I don't know who first put the idea about that cats are sure footed. They can never have owned one. He's always knocking stuff about.'

Barnaby spotted Wellington, a solid cat the colour of iron filings, with four white socks, on top of a grand piano. The name seemed apt. He had a face like an old boot, squashed in, tuckered and rumpled. He watched them re-stacking the books. He looked secretive and ironical. A cat who was biding his time.

'Please' – Miss Bellringer waved an arm, just missing a group of photographs – 'sit down.'

Barnaby removed a pile of sheet music, a painted terracotta duck and a tin of toffees from a wing chair and sat down.

'Well, Chief Inspector . . .' She sat opposite him on a Victorian love seat and clasped her knees (she was wearing copper-coloured knickerbockers), 'What've you found out?'

'Well,' echoed Barnaby, 'there was certainly something troubling your friend.'

'I knew it!' She slapped a brocaded thigh, sending up a little puff of dust. 'What did I tell you?'

'Unfortunately there seems to be no way of discovering what it was.'

'Tell me what happened.'

As Barnaby described his meeting with Terry Bazely he glanced around the room. It was large and crammed from floor to ceiling with books and ornaments, dried flowers and plants. Three of the shelves held old Penguin crime classics with the green and white covers. There was a huge primitive stone head in the fireplace, magnificent Quad and Linn high-fidelity equipment, and a Ben Nicholson, festooned with cobwebs, hanging near the french windows.

'And what do we do now?' She gazed at him, clear-eyed and expectant, sitting forward on the very edge of her seat, ready for anything.

Barnaby found he was resenting her confidence. She seemed to regard him in the light of a conjuror. But his feelings about the case (if case there proved to be) were vague and nebulous. He had no rabbit to produce. He was not even sure he had the hat. 'There's nothing you can do, Miss

Bellringer. I shall ask the police surgeon to have a look at the body. I shall need your permission for that –'

'Of course, of course.'

'If he sees no need to proceed further that will probably mean an end to the matter.' He had expected her to be downcast at this remark but she nodded with vigorous approval.

'Excellent. Brown's is the undertaker. Kerridge Street. I'll write a note.' She did this quickly, using a broad-nibbed fountain pen filled with Indian ink, and heavy smooth cream paper. She handed him the envelope, saying, 'I mustn't keep you. You'll let me know the outcome? And very well done, Detective Chief Inspector Barnaby.' Barnaby covered his mouth with his hand and coughed. As they turned towards the door Miss Bellringer picked up one of the photographs in a barbola frame. 'Here is Emily. She was eighteen then. We'd just started teaching.'

Barnaby looked at the faded sepia print. It was a studio portrait. Lucy was standing next to a jardinière which held a potted palm. Emily sat on a stool. She was looking straight at the camera. Smooth fair hair coiled into a chignon, wide-apart eyes, her mouth firm. Her calf-length skirt and white blouse looked very crisp. Lucy was smiling broadly. Her bun of hair was lopsided and the hem of her skirt dipped slightly. One hand rested protectively on her friend's shoulder.

'What did you teach?' Barnaby handed back the photograph.

'My special subject was music. And Emily's English. But we taught almost everything else of course. One did in those days.' She accompanied him to the front door. 'School's gone now. Converted into flats. Full of horrible people from London.'

'By the way' – on the point of leaving Barnaby turned – 'was your friend ever troubled by mice?'

'Good heavens, no. The place was as clean as a whistle. Emily loathed mice. There were pellets everywhere. Good day to you, Chief Inspector.'

Chapter Three

'I don't suppose Doctor Bullard's on the premises?'

'Actually he is, sir,' replied the desk sergeant. 'Been giving evidence at an inquest this morning then he went over to Forensic.'

From behind a glassed-in panel Policewoman Brierly called: 'I saw him go across the yard for lunch.'

The canteen lay at the end of a large quadrangle. Everyone at the station moaned endlessly about the food which, to the chief inspector's tortured palate, seemed positively Lucullan. They should try eating chez Barnaby, he thought, loading up with shepherd's pie, soggy chips and livid mushy peas. That'd soon shut them up. He added a mincemeat slice and looked round, spotting the doctor alone at a table by the window.

'Hello, Tom,' said Doctor Bullard. 'What brings you to these desperate straits?'

'What brings you?' said Barnaby, sitting down and tucking in.

'My wife's at her Ikebana class.'

'Ah. I wanted to talk about something, actually.'

'Talk away,' replied the doctor, pushing aside the wreckage from a devilled haddock and considering a castle pudding.

'An old lady had a fall and was found dead the next morning by the postman. Not, sadly, all that unusual. But she saw something, probably in the woods near her house, the afternoon before that distressed her considerably. So much so that she rang the Samaritans to talk about it but before she could say much someone came to the door. And that's all we know.'

'So . . . ?' Doctor Bullard shrugged. 'Slightly more unusual.'

'I'd like you to have a look at her.'

'Who signed the death certificate?'

'Lessiter. Badger's Drift.'

'Ohhh . . .' George Bullard blew out his cheeks and placed the tips of his fingers together. 'Well, it won't be the first time I've trodden on his hand-made two-tones.'

'What d'you think of him?'

'Come on, Tom – you know better than that.'

'Sorry.'

'God, they don't call these castle puddings for nothing, do they? This one's completely impregnable.' He stabbed at it then added, 'I can tell you what's common knowledge. That he has a lot of private patients and a pretty upmarket lifestyle. A definitely scrumptious second wife and a very unscrumptious daughter who must be about the same age as my Karen. Nearly nineteen.'

'Can you look at the body this afternoon?'

'Mm. I've got a hospital call at three, though, so we'd have to go straight away.'

There were only two funeral parlours in Causton. Brown's was thought to be the more select. The other was the Co-op. Brown's front window was padded with crumpled satin in the very centre of which was an urn of shiny black basalt holding several lilies. Engraved on the urn was: Til the Dawn Breaks and Shadows Flee Away. Parked in a space adjacent to the building was a new silver Porsche 924, sparkling in the sunshine.

'Beautiful.' Doctor Bullard stroked it appreciatively. 'Nought to sixty in nine seconds.'

Barnaby imagined himself jammed into one of the low seats. The red and black chequered upholstery seemed to him hideously unattractive. He realized that he would always be, philosophically as well as incrementally, a middle-of-the-range-family-saloon man. 'I'd no idea these fellows were so well paid,' he said, pushing open the glass-panelled door.

'No short time either,' replied the doctor jovially. 'The one thing you can always be sure people are going to do is pop off.'

The bell rang with subdued and appropriate gravity. It disturbed only one occupant: a young man, almost colourless in appearance, who flowed through some deep velvet curtains at the back of the room. He wore a black suit and had a pale skin, pale straight hair, pale hands and pale, hard-boiled lemony eyes, like acid drops. About to give them extreme unction, he took a second look and rearranged his expression. 'Doctor Bullard isn't it?'

'That's right. And you're . . . don't tell me . . . Mr Rainbird?'

'Got it in one,' the young man beamed. His eyes didn't change. He seemed to beam through his skin. 'Dennis the menace,' he added, apparently serious. He turned inquiringly to the doctor's companion.

'This is Detective Inspector Barnaby. Causton CID.'

'My . . .' Dennis Rainbird gave the chief inspector a slippy glance. 'Well, you won't find any naughtiness here. We're all as good as gold.'

Barnaby handed over the note from Miss Bellringer. 'We'd like to see the body of Emily Simpson, if you'd be so kind.' He was watching the other man's face as he spoke. There was an expression almost immediately suppressed, of unnaturally intense curiosity laced with excitement.

'Toot sweet,' cried Mr Rainbird, looking at the note then whisking off behind the curtains. 'Always ready to help the force.' He spoke as if it was an everyday occurrence.

They stood by the coffin. Barnaby gazed down at the gaunt, white-clad corpse. She looked very neat and dry as if all the vital juices had drained away not recently but years ago. Impossible to believe there had ever been a clear-eyed young girl with a smooth chignon.

'Hundreds of wreaths back there. She was ever so popular,' opined Mr Rainbird. 'She taught my mum, you know. And all my aunties.'

'Yes. Well, thank you.' Barnaby received a bridling, slightly truculent glance which he calmly returned, then Mr Rainbird shrugged and melted away.

Doctor Bullard bent over Miss Simpson. He lifted the ringless hands, felt the skin beneath her feet, pulled the gown aside and pressed his hand on her ribcage. Rigor mortis had long passed and the thin chest gave under his thumbs. He frowned and felt some more.

'Something wrong?'

'Lungs are badly congested.'

'He was treating her for bronchitis.'

'Hm.' Using both thumbs he pushed back her eyelids. 'When did she die?'

'Three days ago.'

'You don't know what he was giving her?'

'No. Why?'

'Look at this.'

Barnaby peered at the yellow dead eyeballs. The pupils were the size of a pinhead. 'Struth. What do you think, then?'

'I think you should have a word with the coroner.'

'And ask for a PM?'

'Yes.' The two men exchanged a glance. 'You don't sound surprised.'

Barnaby realized he was not surprised. Perhaps Miss Bellringer's confidence had not been misplaced after all. He said, 'I'll let him know what's happened so far. Who do you think will do it?'

'Eynton I expect. Our chap's gone to Crete for a month.'

'All right for some.'

'Give me a call when the report comes back, would you? I'd be interested to hear what they find.'

It came back Thursday morning. Barnaby rang Doctor Bullard who turned up shortly before noon. He read the report. Barnaby watched his face with some amusement. It was, as they say, a picture. Bullard laid the report down.

'*Hemlock*?'

'Hemlock.'

The doctor shook his head. 'Well, it's certainly a collector's item.'

'It's out of the ark, George. The Medicis. Shakespeare. That Greek chap.'

'Socrates.'

'That's him. I mean these days it's usually Valium or Mogadon washed down with half a pint of vodka.'

'Or something handy from the garden shed.'

'Quite. If you're going to use coniine there must be far easier ways than boiling up a distillation of that stuff.'

'Oh I don't know,' the doctor demurred. 'It's not usually available over the counter. You can't just pop into Boot's and buy a boxful.'

'How does it work?'

'Gradual paralysis. Plato describes the death of Socrates very movingly. Feet, legs, everything gradually going cold. He took it very well. A real Stoic.'

'So whoever gave her the stuff – if someone gave her the stuff – had to sit there and watch her die.'

'That's about it. Poor old soul. Not a pretty thought.'

'Murder never is.'

Doctor Bullard scanned the report again. 'Apparently she hadn't eaten for some time. That would speed up the process. No seeds in the stomach, which would argue a distillation.'

'Yes. I rang Pathology about that just before you came. They say it's soluble in alcohol, ether or chloroform.'

'Not in water?'

'No.'

'That means, for it to look like a natural death, she must've drunk it?'

'I should say so,' agreed Barnaby. 'Anything else would have been too risky. Even an eighty-year-old lady can put up quite a struggle if someone's pushing a chloroformed pad over her face. Things might have got knocked about. Ornaments smashed. The dog would have kicked up a hell of a racket.'

'This explains the engorgement of the lungs.' Doctor Bullard tapped the paper. 'A bit excessive even for a bronchitic. Of course we shouldn't be hard on old Lessiter. It'd be an unusual doctor who checked for symptoms of coniine poisoning in what looks like a perfectly straightfoward, if unexpected, death. All the same,' he grinned, 'I wouldn't mind being a fly on the wall when you tell him.'

Chapter Four

'There's no need to drive as if you're auditioning for *The Sweeney*, Sergeant.'

'Sorry, sir.' Troy slowed down sulkily. What on earth was the point of being in the force with all the dreary forms and typing and gormless people endlessly asking you gormless questions if you couldn't occasionally put your foot down, start the siren and drive like the clappers. And he was still smarting after the criticism (totally unwarranted in his opinion) that had been dished out a couple of days ago. He knew the rules as well as anyone, but how many officers followed up and investigated every single piddling thing that came their way? Just his luck the old bag had dropped him in it. And now here they were running around in ever-decreasing circles just because some other old bag had snuffed it. The only pleasurable thing about the whole affair was that Detective Chief Inspector frigging Barnaby was going to come out looking an even bigger fool than when he went in. Happily ignorant of the contents of the post-mortem report, Troy turned into Church Lane and parked outside number thirteen.

Barnaby found Miss Bellringer chopping up fish in her untidy kitchen. Wellington sat on top of the fridge watching the knife rise and fall, his punchball face suffused with satisfaction.

'He won't eat tins,' said Miss Bellringer, reasonably

enough. Then, 'I understand there's been a post mortem.'

Barnaby could not conceal a look of surprise. He had been brought up in a village not much larger than Badger's Drift and knew how efficient the grapevine could be, but he was impressed at the speed with which this item of news had been disseminated. Proceeding in the first instance, he supposed, from the undertakers. 'That's right. There's an inquest tomorrow. Would you be prepared to identify Miss Simpson?'

'But' – she turned pale, resting her knife on the board – 'why?'

'After a post mortem it's necessary.'

'But . . . can't you do that?'

'I'm afraid not. I didn't know her, you see.' He paused. 'I could ask Mr Rainbird.'

'No, don't do that. Horrible little wart.' An even longer pause. 'All right – if someone has to I'd rather it was me.' Wellington made a protesting 'mmr' and she started chopping again.

'Then the coroner will issue a certificate and your friend can be buried.'

'Thank God. Poor Emily.' She banged the plate down on the floor and opened a carton of cream. She poured some into a stone dish and set that down as well. 'This cat's arteries must be well and truly furred up by now. Fur inside and out. Ha!' She gave Wellington an affectionate nudge with her boot. 'But he does love it so.'

'You said you had the key to Miss Simpson's cottage.'

'That's right. Do you want to look round?'

'Just briefly. There'll be a more thorough investigation tomorrow.'

'Ohh . . . does that mean . . . ?'

'I'm sorry. I can't really go into that at the moment.'

'Of course. You're quite right to chide, Chief Inspector.'

She pressed a finger to her lips. ' "Silent was the flock." Do you admire Keats?'

'If we could go as soon as possible?'

She took a Burberry cape from a hook behind the door and flapped her way into it. They made their way down to the front gate, Miss Bellringer kicking aside a supplicant cotoneaster. 'We used to have an excellent relationship, these plants and myself. I left them alone and they left me alone. Now everything's getting out of hand. Look at all that fluffy stuff. I thought a shrubbery was supposed to be ideal for people who didn't care for gardening.'

'They need an occasional cutting back,' advised the chief inspector, whose herbaceous borders were the envy of Arbury Crescent.

Sergeant Troy watched them cross the road – the tall man in the light grey summer jacket and trousers and the shabby ancient frolicking alongside looking like an old English sheepdog caught up in a canvas sack. Not, Troy thought, that clothes were anything to go by. He remembered his mum cleaning for old Lady Preddicott who always looked as if she dressed in Oxfam rejects. And he remembered wearing her grandson's castoffs: ludicrously expensive clothes from the White House and Harrod's when all he longed for was jeans and a Batman T-shirt.

Two children and a woman with a shopping trolley stopped opposite the car and stared at him. He leaned back, relaxed yet keen eyed, holding the steering wheel with a negligent hand. Riding shotgun. Then Barnaby turned and beckoned. Pink with annoyance Troy scrambled out of the Rover, checked the lock and hurried after the others.

Beehive Cottage was just a few yards further up the lane on the opposite side from Miss Bellringer's house. It was perfection. The sort of house that turns up on This England calendars and tourist posters. The exile's dream of home.

The house was neatly and imaginatively thatched, with a second roof, like a scalloped apron, over the first. The windows had leaded panes. A herringbone brick path crumbling with age and edged with lavender and santolina curved around to the back door. Here were hollyhocks and pinks, delphiniums, thyme and mignonette. An immaculate lawn stretched away from a flagstoned area. At the bottom of the lawn, half hidden by a huge *viburnum bodnantense*, were two beehives. Barnaby, after his first shock of pleasure, stood for a long moment in silent appreciation. The garden settled round him as gardens will. Indifferent and harmonious; consolingly beautiful.

'What a wonderful scent.' He approached a nearby rose bush.

'That was her favourite. Don't know what it's called.'

'It's a Papa Meilland.' Barnaby bent his head and inhaled the incomparable fragrance. Sergeant Troy studied the sky. Miss Bellringer produced a large iron key and opened the door. Telling Troy to stay where he was, Barnaby followed her into the house.

The first thing they saw when they entered the kitchen was a wooden shelf which held a sacking apron neatly folded, a clean trowel and a kneeling mat. Miss Bellringer turned quickly away into the centre of the room then cried: 'Phroo . . . what a ghastly smell.' She moved towards the sink.

Barnaby cried: 'Don't touch anything, please.'

'Oh.' She stood stock still like a child playing statues. 'Because of dabs, you mean?'

There was certainly an overpoweringly musty odour in the air. The chief inspector looked around. Everything was beautifully clean and tidy. There was a jam jar of parsley on top of the fridge. A vegetable rack holding a few potatoes, and a couple of apples in a cloisonné bowl.

'Have you been back here since the body was removed?'

She shook her head. 'I can't bear it without her.'

'Did you notice the smell before?'

'No. But my olfactory equipment isn't too lively. Emily was always grumbling about it. Urging me to sniff this or sniff that. Complete waste of time.'

'But you would have noticed, surely, if it had been as strong as this?'

'I suppose so.' She started to move unhappily about, frowning with distress. 'Good grief.'

'What is it?'

'Here's the explanation. Who on earth could have brought it in?' She indicated the jar on the fridge. Barnaby approached and smelt it. The mousey odour made him want to sneeze.

He said: 'Isn't it parsley?'

'My dear man – it's hemlock.'

'What?'

'There's a fieldful of it down by the old railway lines.'

'It looks like parsley. Do you think your friend mistook –'

'Good heavens, no. Emily had a lovely little parsley patch. Next to the walnut tree. Grew three sorts. You can forget that idea. Anyway – it wasn't here the morning she died.'

'Are you sure?'

'Pretty sure, yes. I didn't go round taking an inventory, you understand.'

'And the cottage has been locked up since?'

'It has. And' – she anticipated his next question – 'I have the only spare key. The front door was kept bolted on the inside. It opens directly on to the lane. Emily never used it. Don't you realize what this means, Chief Inspector?' She seized his arm excitedly. 'We've found our first clue!'

'Is this the sitting room?' Barnaby moved away, ducking his head.

'Yes.' She followed him. 'There are just these two rooms downstairs.'

'Was this door open the morning she was found?'

'No. Closed.'

A grandfather clock ticked slumbrously in the corner. There was a small inglenook fireplace and beams decorated with brasses, a chintz-covered three-piece suite, a Queen Anne table and two diamond-paned cabinets full of plates and figurines. One wall was solidly packed with books.

The interior of the cottage was so precisely what the exterior led one to expect that Barnaby had the disturbing feeling that he had stepped on to a perfect period stage set. Surely any minute now a maid would enter, pick up the heavy black Bakelite telephone and say, 'I'm afraid her ladyship is not at home.' Or a cream-flannelled juvenile would ask if there was anyone for tennis. Alternatively there was the crusty old colonel: 'The body was lying just there, Inspector.'

'I beg your pardon?'

'Just here.' Miss Bellringer was standing in front of the empty fireplace.

'Could you show me exactly?'

'Do m'best.' She frowned at the hearthrug then lay down, kicked aside the Burberry revealing a glimpse of eau-de-nil celanese knickers, and curved herself into a helpful comma. 'Her head was about here – is that all right?'

'Yes. Thank you.' To himself Barnaby cursed the delay. No pictures. The corpse tidied neatly away. The scent stone cold.

'Of course.' Miss Bellringer got up very slowly. 'Doctor Lessiter must have – oh thank you, Chief Inspector – must have moved her during the examination.' She watched Barnaby walk over to the cabinets and take a closer look. Some of the plates were exceptionally beautiful, gleaming with the touch of gold.

'Meissen in there' – Miss Bellringer nodded to the left –

'and the other's Coalport. Although there's a couple of pieces she brought home from France. We used to bicycle to the sales years ago. Picked up all sorts of snips.'

Between the cabinets a little piecrust table held the telephone and a stack of books. Palgrave's *Golden Treasury*, some Jacobean plays, *The Adventurous Gardener* and the Mermaid edition of *Julius Caesar*.

'She loved her Shakespeare. Shakespeare and the Bible. Food for the mind and comfort for the soul.' *Julius Caesar* lay open on top of the pile next to a magnifying glass. 'She adored the theatre too. We used to go a lot when she could still drive. Topping times they were. Absolutely topping.' She produced a large khaki and crimson silk handkerchief and blew her nose.

They went upstairs. Only one bedroom was furnished. A narrow, virginal bed, wallpaper sprigged with forget-me-nots, faded velvet curtains. All as sweet and innocent as a liberty bodice. The spare room was used for storage. There was a vacuum cleaner and a stack of boxes, also several carboys of home-made wine, some cloudy, some clear, one or two hiccuping quietly.

'She was planning to bottle the honeysuckle this weekend. It's a bit like a Sancerre, you know.'

They retreated down the narrow staircase and returned to the kitchen. Barnaby said, 'There must be a bottle open somewhere. She drank something alcoholic before she died.'

'You could try the cold larder.' Miss Bellringer indicated a blue door at the end of the kitchen adding, a second too late, 'Mind the step.'

He pitched forwards into semi-darkness. What light there was had a greenish tinge, being admitted through the leaves of a cherry laurel which was pressing against a largish window covered with wire mesh of the type used in an old-fashioned meat safe. It had a simple catch fastening which was broken. Barnaby took his handkerchief, seized the catch, pulled the window open and carefully closed it again. There was more than enough room for a reasonably slender person to climb in.

The larder had low stone shelves holding lots of bottles and jars. There was chutney and spiced apricots in tall jars and opaque whitish honey with flowered labels and last year's date. A large bowl of luscious scarlet strawberries. And jams and jellies: liquid fruit, dark and translucent. She salted runner beans too, just like his mother had. Close to the door was a half-empty bottle of wine. Elderflower 1979.

Barnaby opened the back door and beckoned Troy, saying, 'I need you to take a statement.' They re-entered the sitting room and sat down, Miss Bellringer looking slightly apprehensive and very serious.

'Now,' began Barnaby, 'I'd like you to –'

'Just a moment, Chief Inspector. You haven't said . . . you know . . . anything may be taken down and used in evidence . . . all that . . .'

'This is just a witness statement, Miss Bellringer. It's not necessary in this case, I assure you.'

That was the trouble with members of the public, thought Sergeant Troy. Watched a few so-called police dramas on the telly and thought they knew it all. Sitting out of his chief's line of vision, he allowed his lip a slight curl.

'If you could tell me what happened from when you first arrived.'

'I came into the kitchen –'

'Was the postman with you?'

'No. After he'd spoken to me he went off on his rounds. I opened the back door and hurried in here and found her where I showed you.'

'Did you touch the body at all?'

'Yes. I didn't move her but I . . . I held her hand for a moment.'

'And did you touch anything else?'

'Not then. Doctor Lessiter arrived and examined her . . . he moved her, of course. Then he rang the mortuary to ask for a car . . . well a van it was actually, to take her away. He explained about the death certificate and asked who would be handling the funeral arrangements. I said I would and while we were waiting for the van to arrive I'm afraid' – she blushed regretfully at Barnaby – 'I'm afraid I tidied up a bit.'

'What exactly did that involve?'

'There was a cup of cocoa on the telephone table. And an empty wine glass. Which struck me as a little odd.'

'Why was that?'

'Emily never drank alone. It was one of her foibles. I believe she thought it rather dissolute. But anyone could get her to bring a bottle out. The merest hint would suffice. She made wonderful wine. It was the only thing she was vain about . . .' She covered her face with her hands for a long moment then said, 'I'm so sorry . . .'

'Don't worry. Just carry on when you're ready.' Of course if it was murder they were talking about there would be only one glass. The other would have been carefully washed and replaced in the cupboard.

'There was a milk pan in the kitchen,' continued Miss Bellringer. 'I washed everything up and put the things away. I knew how she'd feel, you see. Dirty pots and people coming into the living room. She was always most particular. I expect I've done the wrong thing.' Guilt made her sound aggressive. When Barnaby did not reply she carried on, 'Then I emptied the refrigerator. Some lamb and milk. A few bits and bobs. Half a tin of Benjy's food. Actually I gave him that. He hadn't had breakfast, you see.'

'Where is the dog now?'

'Trace's farm. You must have seen the place. End of the village – pale orange job. They've got half a dozen already so one more won't notice. I've been to see him a couple of times but I shan't go again. It's too upsetting. He just comes trotting out hoping it's Emily. She'd had him thirteen years.'

'Didn't you hear him bark? On the evening of her death?'

'No, but he was very good like that . . . for a Jack Russell. As long as he knew the people, of course. With strangers it was different.' She smiled at Barnaby, the significance of the last two remarks not registering. 'And he slept in the kitchen, so with the sitting-room door closed he'd simply think she'd gone to bed.'

'To return to Friday morning . . .'

'That's about it, really. Once the van had gone I switched off the electricity, took the dog lead from behind the kitchen door, locked up and off we went.'

'I see. I shall have to keep the key now, I'm afraid. I'll let you have a receipt in due course.'

'Oh.' He watched questions form in her mind and remain unasked. 'Very well.'

'You went straight to the farm then?' continued Barnaby. 'Not into the garden or shed at all?'

'Well . . . I had to tell the bees.'

'I'm sorry?'

'You have to tell the bees when someone dies. Especially if it's their owner. Otherwise they just clear off.'

Clear orf is right, observed Troy to himself. Clear orf her rocker. He flexed his fingers, deciding to omit this unlikely bit of potted folklore.

'Really?' said Barnaby.

'Goodness yes. Known fact. I struck the hive three times with the key, said "Your mistress had died", then left. Village people say you should tie something black around the hive as well but I didn't bother. They're a superstitious lot. Also I thought if I started messing about the bees might sting me.'

'Thank you. Sergeant Troy will read your statement back now and ask you to sign it.'

When this had been done Miss Bellringer rose, saying, rather wistfully, 'Is that all?'

'After lunch I'd like you to show me where the orchid was found.'

'Won't you have something to eat with me?' she asked, visibly perking up.

'No thank you. I shall get a snack in the Black Boy.'

'Oh, I shouldn't do that! Mrs Sweeney's food's notorious.'

Barnaby smiled. 'I expect I shall manage to survive.'

'Ahhh . . . I understand. You're in search of local colour. Background information.'

Using his handkerchief, Barnaby opened the door for her. As she turned to leave something caught her eye. 'That's funny.'

'What is it?'

'Emily's fork's missing. She always kept it on that shelf with her trowel and apron.'

'Probably in the garden.'

'Oh no. She was a creature of habit. Tools cleaned with newspaper and placed on her mat after use.'

'No doubt it will turn up.'

'Doesn't really matter now, does it?' She turned away. 'See you around two o'clock then?'

After she had left, Barnaby posted Sergeant Troy outside the front door and sank into the chintz sofa in the still, orderly room and listened to the ticking of the clock. He faced the two armchairs, their cushions now plump and smooth. In one of them had someone sat with a glass of wine, smiling, talking, reassuring? Killing?

There was little doubt in the chief inspector's mind. The hemlock in the kitchen was almost certainly a rather crude attempt to suggest that short-sighted Miss Simpson had picked a bunch in mistake for some parsley and so poisoned herself. A hurried afterthought once the news of the post mortem had travelled around the village.

He walked over to the piecrust table already covered in a thin film of dust and looked down at the books. The Shakespeare lay open on top of the pile. Julius Caesar, the noblest Roman of them all. Not to mention the most boring, thought Barnaby, remembering his struggles with the text over thirty years before. He had read no Shakespeare since, and a dutiful visit to an overly inventive production of *A Midsummer Night's Dream* in which Joyce had played Titania as an Edwardian suffragette, did nothing to make him regret the decision. He looked at the open pages, screwing up his eyes. He felt for his reading glasses, remembered they were in his other jacket and picked up the magnifying glass with his handkerchief.

Miss Simpson had almost reached the end of the play. Pindarus had brought the bad news to the battlefield. Barnaby read a few lines. None of it was in the slightest degree familiar. Then he saw something. A faint soft grey line in the margin. He took the book to the window and peered again. Someone had bracketed off three lines of a speech by Cassius. He read them aloud:

> This day I breathed first. Time is come round,
> And where I did begin there shall I end;
> My life is run his compass.

Chapter Five

All conversation ceased as Barnaby entered the Black Boy. Not that that was saying much. There was an old gaffer in the corner, only partly visible through drifts of noxious smoke; two youths with their feet on the bar rail; a girl playing the fruit machine. Mrs Sweeney, grey-haired and untypically flat-chested, had an air of being at bay rather than at home behind the counter.

Detective Chief Inspector Barnaby asked about food, refused one of Mrs Sweeney's home-made pies and settled for a ploughman's and a half of bitter. He was sure that curiosity as to the reason for his presence would soon produce some comment or other. However he was unprepared for the rapidity with which the nub of the matter was reached. He had hardly taken a sip of his beer (warmish and soapy) before one of the youths said, 'You're the fuzz 'ent you?'

Barnaby cut off a piece of cheese and made a movement of the head that could have meant anything.

Mrs Sweeney said, 'Is it about poor Miss Simpson?'

'Did you know the lady?' asked Barnaby.

'Ohhh . . . everyone knew Miss Simpson.'

The fumes in the corner cleared slightly and a rattle-snakish clatter could be heard. My God, thought Barnaby, the poor old chap must be on his last legs. Then he realized that the sound was caused by a collapsing wall of dominoes. 'She used to teach me in English,' the old man stated.

'That's right, Jake, she did,' agreed Mrs Sweeney, adding, in a whispered aside to Barnaby, 'and he can't read nor write to this day.'

'She was well liked in the village then?'

'Oh yes. Not like some I could mention.'

'What d'you want to know about her for?' said one of the youths.

'Yeah,' the other chipped in. 'She been up to something?'

'We're just making a few inquiries.'

'Do you know what I reckon?' said the first one again. He wore a T-shirt reading 'Don't Drink and Drive You Might Get Caught'. Beneath it a wodge of fat, leprously white and hairy, hung over his commando belt. 'I reckon she was a godmother. Gorra vice ring going over there. Slipping it in the honey.' They both guffawed. The girl tittered.

'That's not funny, Keith,' Mrs Sweeney said angrily. 'If that's the best you can find to say you can go and drink somewhere else.'

Barnaby listened for another half hour as more people came and went, but the verdict on Miss Simpson didn't change much. Very kind. Patient with the children. Ever so generous if there was a stall. Jam. Honey. Jars of fruit. Did lovely flowers for the church. That poor Miss Bellringer. Whatever will she do now? And what about Benjy? They pine, you know. And he's getting on. She'll be greatly missed. Sadly missed.

Even when it was shorn of the eulogistic flavour deemed obligatory in all statements about the recently dead, Barnaby was still left with the picture of a singularly nice human being. Mrs Sweeney's final remark seemed to sum it up neatly.

'Not an enemy in the world.'

The air was green and fresh as they entered the wood, yet

within minutes Barnaby felt a change. As the trees closed tightly over their heads the ripeness of the vegetation all around and underfoot assailed his nostrils with a rich and rotten scent.

Miss Bellringer was leading the way. She was carrying a shooting stick and keeping close to the chief inspector, as he had requested.

'It was just over there I think, by those hellebores. Yes – there it is.'

'Wait.' Barnaby took her arm. 'If you could stay here, please. The less trampling about the better.'

'I understand.' She sounded disappointed but stayed obediently where she was, opening her shooting stick and perching on the canvas strap. She called, 'More to the left' and 'Getting warmer' and 'Hotsy totsy' as he walked carefully around the patch of little green flowers. Then, when she saw him bob down, 'Perfect isn't it?'

Barnaby studied the orchid and the little stick with the red ribbon. Inanimate, the marker still seemed more alive than the ash-pale plant. There was something very touching about the neatly tied bow. He got up and looked round. As far as he could see the leaf mould in the immediate area, although scuffed about, probably by rabbits and other small creatures, revealed no more serious disturbance.

To the left of him was a tightly latticed screen of branches. Treading carefully, he looked at the ground. There were two quite deep indentations indicating that someone had been standing there for some considerable time. He noted where the broader part of the shoe had pressed, stood parallel and looked through the branches.

He was facing a hollow. Quite a large piece of the ground was flattened: bluebell leaves and bracken bent backwards and crushed. He walked around the screen and approached the rim of the hollow, where he crouched and studied the ground more closely, being careful not to step on the squashed area, which was quite extensive. Someone or something had certainly been threshing about a bit. On his way back to Miss Bellringer he saw on the ground an impression not clearly defined enough to be called an outline, as if a log or something heavy had briefly lain there.

'Thank you for showing me.' It was good to break out of the oppressive crowding trees into an open field. Lapwings wheeled overhead in a sky full of light and sun. 'Would you like to be taken to the inquest, Miss Bellringer?'

'Oh no. We have an excellent village taxi. I shall be quite all right.'

As they approached Beehive Cottage they saw that Sergeant Troy, watching watchfully, was now surrounded by a small but appreciative audience. Barnaby bade Miss Bellringer goodbye and crossed the road. He was immediately accosted by the youngest of the group.

'Woss he doing standing around like a wally?'

'Is he the police?'

'You're the police aren't you?'

'Why ain't he got a uniform on?'

'Now, son.' The words were chopped off individually through Troy's gritted teeth. 'Why don't you just move along? There's nothing to see here.' The suggestion sounded stale and had a mechanical ring. The group stayed put.

'I'll send someone to relieve you, Troy.'

'I'm off duty in half an hour.'

'You were, Sergeant, you were. Someone should be here by five.' A teenage girl with a toddler and a baby in a pushchair joined the group. Barnaby grinned. 'You should have a full house by then.'

The proceedings at the coroner's court the following day took no time at all. The remains of Emily Simpson had been identified, a short time previously, by her friend Lucy Bellringer, and were released for burial. The pathologist's report was read and the inquest adjourned to a later date pending further police inquiries.

PART TWO

INVESTIGATION

PART TWO

INVESTIGATION

Chapter One

Barbara Lessiter approached the cheval-glass in the corner of her bedroom. She had switched off all the lights with one exception, the ivory figurine by her bed. The light from this filtered through an apricot shade, casting a warm glow over her shimmering nightdress and brown, solarium-toasted skin. Little peaks of strawberry-scented mousse-like cream trembled on the tips of her fingers. She started to stroke her throat from the hollow at the base to the point of her chin, rhythmically, closing her eyes and smiling. Then, using both hands and more mousse she tapped all over her face. Oil for her eyes came last. French, forty-five pounds a pot, and it went nowhere.

She loved this ritual. Even as a young girl, years before it had been necessary, she had massaged and patted and knuckled and stroked with voluptuous satisfaction. It was hardly necessary even now, she told herself, secure in the light from the shaded lamp.

After she had finished her face she brushed her hair: fifty strokes from the crown to the tip. Glowing reddish-brown hair as rich and glossy as henna and egg yolks and conditioners could make it. She tossed her head back and smiled.

The movement caused a strap to slip from her shoulder. She came closer to the glass, touched her naked breast, touched the tiny purplish red bruises and smiled again, a smile of greedy reminiscence. Then she stood very still, listening.

Someone was approaching her door. She held her breath. There was a knock. It sounded tentative, almost apologetic. She waited, covering up her bare skin as if the door had been transparent. After a minute or two the slippered footsteps moved away. She breathed out, a long sated exhalation. She must let him in next time. It had been simply ages. And he'd been very good, considering. But God – what a contrast it would be . . .

She'd been born Barbara Wheeler in Uxbridge 'some time in the late fifties', she told people with coy deceit. Her father was a ganger on the railway, her mother a household drudge. They had five other children. Only Barbara was beautiful. They were packed into a terraced house flush to the pavement, with a concrete back yard. She shared a bedroom with two sisters, now household drudges themselves, defending her space and belongings with tigerish possessiveness. She had scorned their cheap clothes and cosmetics, holding her nose when they sprayed on their Californian Poppy from Woolworth's. She started stealing at fifteen – creams, perfumes and lotions, peeling off the price labels, knowing that no one at home would ever have heard of the brands.

After her sisters had been consumed into the local sweet factory she got a job as a filing clerk in a solicitor's office and, it seemed to her, a precarious toehold on the slippery slope that would lead her out of a slummish and ugly environment into the glossy perfection of middle-class life. A world where you didn't have to go to a park filled with screaming kids and snapping dogs to enjoy grass and trees but had them actually belonging to you, in your own garden. Where people washed their clothes before they looked dirty and men shook hands when they met whilst women brushed powdered cheek against powdered cheek in easy, meaningless display.

Barbara was not especially intelligent but she was shrewd and worked hard and quietly, keeping her mouth shut and her eyes alert. She started to take clothes from one of the larger department stores in Slough – choosing, as nearly as she could, styles resembling those worn by the elder partner's young married daughter. This stage of affairs continued until she was almost eighteen. She was still a virgin, partially because she'd never met anyone she fancied enough but mostly because she had some vague extravagant idea that to be able to offer virginity to a serious suitor might cancel out the debit of her shabby beginnings. She never mentioned them of course, but was constantly nervous in case the easy, upper-class patronage that she encountered in the office would somehow flush them to the surface.

Alan Cater, newly articled to the firm, started work there on her eighteenth birthday. He was tall, fair, had sharp blue eyes and smoked slim brown cigars. He had a red Cobra sports car and a watch that was the slimmest wafer of gold. He smiled a lot, especially at Barbara. He touched her too, only casually, nothing you could take offence at: a hand on her shoulder, an arm around her waist at the filing cabinet. She was rather shocked at the surge of pleasurable excitement she felt when he did this but said nothing, not realizing that her quickened breath and flushed skin gave her away.

One evening in midsummer he was late leaving the office. He was playing tennis straight from work and had gone into the cloakroom to change. Barbara never left before he did. She had graduated to dicta-typing, taking lessons in the evening, and was covering her machine when he came out in brief shorts and a white Aertex shirt. Everyone else had gone. He had stood looking at her for a long moment, first at her face, then everywhere else. Then he locked the door and told her he had been longing for this moment. Barbara had felt sick with excitement. He stood very close to her, said, 'Shall I show you what you do to me?' and guided her hand. As he opened her blouse, in the moments before she was completely swept away, Barbara saw them framed in the doorway of an old country church, herself in white of course, Alan in morning suit. There would be champagne afterwards and a three-tier cake, with some kept back for the christening.

'You're a lovely girl, darling.' He unhooked her bra. 'Come on – what's the matter? You're not going to pretend you're surprised?'

'My legs seem to be giving way . . .'

'That's soon solved. There's a settee in old Rupert's office. And a mirror.'

They walked there, arms entwined, leaving her blouse and brassiere on the typewriter. They lay on the settee facing the mirror and a net-curtained window looking on to the street. When she was quite naked Alan threatened to pull the nets back. This, which should have alarmed her, made her even more excited. He seemed to know exactly what he was doing. It hardly hurt at all, not like people said it did, it just seemed to be over so quickly. She wanted more and he gave her more. After an hour someone knocked at the outer door and he smiled, touching her lips with his finger. She was sitting straddled across his knees and saw a girl in a white tennis dress, her long hair tied back with a scarf, walk past the window. It was nearly nine o'clock when they finally left.

After this they met often, usually quite late in the evening, Alan explaining that he had to catch up with his studies first. He would drive out into the green belt and find a secluded spot or, if the weather was bad, they would use his car. She never took him to her tiny bedsitter and had already told him (to save awkward questions at invitation time) that she was an orphan. On the evenings they didn't meet she was restless, consumed with longing. He treated her very professionally in the office, occasionally winking at her when the coast was clear. Once, when they had been briefly alone, he had stood behind her chair and slipped his hand down her shirt.

Halfway through the winter she discovered she was pregnant. She had felt slightly anxious when telling him, as if it had been all her fault. She ended her confession by asking what his parents would say. He had looked disbelieving, incredulous and then amused for a moment, then given her a casual hug before saying, 'Don't worry. We'll sort something out.'

At the end of the week Rupert Winstanley had called her into his office and given her the address of a private clinic in Saint John's Wood and a cheque for a hundred and fifty pounds. She had never seen any of them again.

She had had the abortion, being too distressed and lonely to work out an alternative. She wouldn't now, of course. She'd drain the buggers dry. If she couldn't get their respect or admiration or love she'd make bloody sure she got their money.

She'd been home from the clinic about a month and working as a shelf filler at Sainsbury's when someone knocked at her door late one night. She opened it a crack. A man stood there smelling faintly of cologne and, more strongly, of beer. He wore a blazer with a badge, striped tie and grey flannels. He said, 'Hu . . . l . . . l . . o . . .' and eyed her up and down.

'What do you want?'

'I'm a friend of Alan's, actually. He thought we might . . . you know . . . get on . . .'

She slammed the door. Rage and pain and disgust boiled up in her. She stood very still as if moving might wound. The bastard! The pain ebbed away; the disgust rushed down the conduit of memory, redirected at Alan and his kind. Only the rage remained. She listened. No footsteps. He must be still there. She reopened the door. He gave her a sloppy smile.

She said, 'It'll cost you.' She watched the beery complacency slip a bit, and thought, so wrap that in your old school tie and stuff it.

'Oh . . . um . . . all right . . .' He made as if to step into the room. She put her foot in the gap. 'How much have you got?'

He fumbled with his wallet, pulling out notes, a driving licence, a child's photograph. 'Fifty pounds . . .'

Nearly a month's wages. She opened the door wide. 'You'd better come in then, hadn't you?'

And so it had gone. Recommendations. A friend of a friend. She'd never actually been without anyone. On the other hand she'd never really felt secure. The rent was always paid. She'd had some presents. Some very nice presents. A wolf coat from Harrod's, a vast colour telly, a holiday in Portofino when the man's wife was having a hysterectomy. But no security. No financial security, that is. Emotional security she had. None of them touched her. She would look down at them, as if from some high vantage point, huffing and puffing like saggy, impotent sea lions, and despise them all. She would never again let herself feel that sweeping golden rush of pleasure that had carried her so completely from the shores of sanity in the offices of Winstanley, Dennison and Winstanley over twenty years before. She couldn't even remember Alan's second name let alone his face.

And then she had met Trevor Lessiter. She had bumped into him, literally, in the food department at Marks and Spencers. Turning a corner in one of the aisles too sharply, their trolleys had locked antler-like in a metal clinch. She had immediately flashed him a radiant professional smile. He had been bowled over by the radiance and had quite missed the professionalism.

He was a funny little man with a round head, pepper and salt hair and a woolly scarf although it was quite a warm day. Expensive clothes, she thought, running a knowledgeable eye over his appearance, boringly old fashioned of course. The sort of man who carries his change in a purse. They pushed their trolleys round together. His was already over half full.

'Your wife must have given you a very long list.'

'No . . . that is . . .' he stammered, looking at her quickly then back to the shelves. 'It's my daughter's list . . . I'm a widower.'

With hardly a break in her step she said, 'Oh – how thoughtless . . . I just didn't . . .' She stopped walking then and looked straight at him. 'I'm so very sorry.'

They went for tea at a café over the Odeon. Barbara excused herself as soon as they were settled and retired to the Ladies' where she removed one set of false eyelashes and half her lipstick, and put on some more scent. They met for tea again, then dinner at a hotel on the bank of the Thames at Marlow. They drove down in his beautiful old Jaguar. The doors clunked when they closed and it had real leather seats. At the hotel there were candles in glasses and flowers floating in glass bowls. She was used to dining in out-of-the-way places, but not with men who didn't keep looking over their shoulders. He told her about his wife's accident and about his daughter. He said, 'I'd like you to meet her.'

This took some time to arrange. Weekends came and went and Judy always appeared to have something on. However eventually, at her father's insistence, a Sunday afternoon was set aside. Barbara dressed very carefully: a soft paisley dress and a light tweed coat. Hardly any makeup: just blusher, bronzer, soft lipstick and a light brown eye pencil.

The village was nearly thirty miles from Slough (thank God, she thought) and as they drove along she kept saying prettily, and only half falsely, 'I do hope she'll like me.'

And he, obtuse and self-deluding, said, 'Of course she'll like you. Why on earth shouldn't she?'

When he turned the car into the drive she thought at first that there must be some mistake. That he was calling on a wealthy patient or dropping in on some friends before taking her home. Lawns swept each side of the drive. There were trees and shrubs and flowerbeds. The house was a large Victorian villa with a turret and gables and (she discovered later) seven bedrooms. She felt cold as she got out of the car. Cold with longing and hope and fear.

She said, 'This reminds me of my father's house.'

'Oh. Where was that, dear?' She had never before mentioned her family.

'In Scotland. It went, I'm afraid, like everything else.' She looked up at the many windows and gave a heavy sigh, pulsating with remembrance and loss. 'He was a terrible gambler.'

'I hope you'll –' He checked himself. Barbara knew what he'd been going to say and cursed the unseen girl in the house. She had never got on well with women, never had a close woman friend. Well – she'd just have to play it as it came.

It came as an absolute disaster. The daughter had sat, lumpen and disapproving (that was my mother's favourite chair), dispensing tea and heavy damp wodges of home-made cake. Barbara tried to make conversation, the daughter either didn't reply or spoke only of times gone by when Mummy did this or Mummy did that or we all went . . .

Meanwhile Barbara looked around at the chintz-covered puffy sofas (two) and armchairs (five). At the bowls of flowers and washed Chinese rugs and beautiful mirrors and ornaments. And through the french windows a flagged terrace with urns of brilliant flowers leading to the shaven, incandescently green lawn, and prayed for the first time in years: Oh God – *please* make him ask me. She realized she was gripping the handle of her delicate cup with unnatural force and set it down very carefully.

Driving back in the car, he had said, 'She'll come round.' She wouldn't of course, thought Barbara. That sort never did. Frigid little bitch. With that granular complexion and a bum that nearly touched the ground. A born spinster. She'd be there looking after Daddy when she was ninety, never mind nineteen.

'Oh – do you think so, Trevor? I was so looking forward to meeting her.' Her voice shook a little. As he parked outside her flat she said, 'Would you mind coming in for a moment? I feel a bit down.' It was the first time she had issued such an invitation. He bounded eagerly out of the car and up the steps.

The flat was in Mancetta Road over a newsagent's in the centre of the town. She didn't offer him anything to drink, just flung her coat over a chair and slumped on the mock ocelot sofa, burying her face in her hands. Immediately he was beside her.

'Don't be upset.' He put a lumpy tweed arm around her shoulders. She turned to him, childlike in her sorrow.

'I wanted her so much to like me. I pictured us talking about clothes and makeup and things . . . I thought I could look after her . . . after both of you . . . I suppose you think that's silly?'

'Darling, of course not.' He suddenly became very conscious of the heaviness of her breasts, pressing into his shirt front. And the scent of her hair. He raised her chin and was touched to see tears in her eyes. He kissed her. For a moment her mouth parted eagerly under his, he even felt the tip of her tongue, then she gasped and pushed him away. She got up and crossed the room, turning to face him. She was panting.

'What must you think? Oh – Trevor. I don't know what it is . . . you're in my thoughts all the time . . . I should never have asked you up here.'

Then she was in his arms again. For a moment she let her whole body relax and press against his, noting that at least he was going to be able to do it when the time came. Another long kiss. His hand moved. She allowed herself one little cry of excitement before breaking away. 'What do you think you're –'

'Barbara . . . I'm sorry –'

'What sort of woman do you think I am?'

'Forgive me, darling . . . please . . .'

'Just because I love you – yes I admit it! I love you. Oh Trevor' – she started to cry again – 'you must go. It's all so hopeless.'

He went and was back again the next day. And the next. For three weeks he visited, agonized, tumefied, was refused entry, subsided, begged, pleaded, squirmed and writhed. The day he cracked, Barbara had been feeling so unhappy that she had not even bothered to dress and was sitting by the gas fire wearing an edge-to-edge peignoir.

They were married on the morning of 30 June 1982. The night before the wedding he stayed in the flat, experiencing transports of delight which he was to remember, with an increasing degree of resentful yearning, for the rest of his life. Then they drove off to Badger's Drift to break the news to Judy.

And now – Barbara let the strap slip and studied the bite again – she was putting it all at risk. A mixture of frustration and boredom had led her to take a lover. And what a lover. Only a few hours since they had parted, and she already wanted him again. For the second time she had slipped out along the golden stream. Her body felt things she hadn't allowed it to feel for years. She had been very, very careful, but for how long could the affair stay concealed? Yet she couldn't stop. He was as necessary to her now as breathing. She got into bed and lay for a moment experiencing again in memory the rhythmical movements of love, then slid into a deep and dreamless sleep.

Chapter Two

The cordoning of Miss Simpson's cottage caused more
interest than a whole platoon of Sergeant Troys. Half the
village seemed to be out, ignoring the patently untruthful
statement from an attendant constable that there was nothing
to see.

The scene-of-crime men worked deftly and methodically
through the whole house. Barnaby wandered about, went
into the garden. The bereaved bees thrummed in their hive.
He noticed without surprise that any unplanted ground was
already full of weeds. He returned to the back door and the
sweet scented arch of the Kiftsgate rose.

'We found this under some laurels near the larder window,
sir.' Barnaby was shown a garden fork already labelled and in
its polythene bag. 'Probably been used to fork over any
prints. Somebody's certainly been out that way.'

By lunchtime the men had finished. A car left, taking
information obtained to the forensic laboratories, the
cordons were removed and the team repaired to the Black
Boy for beer and sandwiches. Half an hour later they drove
out of the village to the beechwood. Most of the crowd had
by then given up, but Barnaby heard a woman on the pub
forecourt say, 'Run home, Robbie, and tell your mam they're
going down the lane.' A small boy shot off and, shortly after
they had parked on a layby near the beechwood, another
interested group had arrived.

In the woods the cordons enclosed a very large area. The scene-of-crime officers plotted it out, taking sections at a time for a fingertip search. Barnaby described his own movements and those of Miss Bellringer. The watchers pressed eagerly against the ropes, craning their necks. A man ducked underneath, saying, 'It's a free country, you know – we're not in Russia yet,' and was ordered back. A large woman with a golden retriever called: 'I'm sure Henry could help.'

Barnaby watched and kept out of the way. He realized he was becoming impatient. These things could not be hurried, but so much time was going by. Another day for the reports to come through. He had the feeling that everything was turning to dust in his hands before he'd even started. He beckoned to Sergeant Troy and hurried back to the car.

In fact it took less than twenty-four hours. Forensic never closed (except on bank holidays) and Barnaby had the scene-of-crime reports in his hands before lunchtime the following day. He read them through carefully and now sat facing a row of alert faces in one of the station's interview rooms.

'What we're trying to discover' – he swallowed his first tablet of the day with the remains of his coffee – 'is the whereabouts of all the inhabitants of the village, including any children who were not at school on the afternoon of the seventeenth, and also for that same evening – all right? There's a stack of pro-formas on the table over there. Allocation of addresses on the board outside.'

'At what point do we assume the afternoon to end, sir?' asked Sergeant Troy, who had already forgotten his earlier animadversions and was anxious to shine. 'Did anyone see her come back from the woods for instance?'

Barnaby looked at his sergeant. He had been quite aware of the man's previous unspoken scepticism and wondered at the ease with which attitudes and beliefs which proved inconvenient were sloughed as naturally as a snake's skin. He knew nothing of Troy's private life but suspected that relationships might be handled with the same insouciance.

'Well of course that would be very handy, but life is rarely so obliging. I think it would be best at this stage if you take the time in one block, from two p.m. to midnight. We know that Miss Simpson was alive at eight o'clock because she made a telephone call.'

'This person or people that she's supposed to have seen,' asked a young policewoman, 'how do we know they're from the village at all?'

'We don't for sure, but it was certainly someone she knew, and no car parked on the verges anywhere near the field which leads to the woods. And the only other place to park, the layby in Church Lane, is clearly visible from the last house. The owner was in his garden most of the afternoon and is quite convinced he saw no car. This means whoever it was walked there.'

'So we're looking for someone who doesn't have an alibi for part of the afternoon and some of the evening?'

'Probably. I'm inclined to believe a couple are involved. The report shows that a rug, a Black Watch tartan, had been laid on the ground.' He watched Troy give Policewoman Brierley a lewd wink and a nudge so sharp that she dropped her pencil. 'Also other bracken and plants outside the actual area where the rug was placed show signs of bruising which seems to indicate that it may be a favourite spot. One that the couple have used several times before.'

'Seems a bit incredible, sir.' Troy again. 'I mean that she could have been killed because she saw someone having it –' He cleared his throat. 'A bit old fashioned. We're in 1987 after all. Who expects fidelity these days?'

Barnaby, who had never been unfaithful in his life, said, 'You'd be surprised. People can still be divorced for adultery.

Disinherited. Relationships can be ruined. Trust destroyed.'
There were a lot of blank looks and one or two understanding nods. He got up. 'On your way then.'

'Handy they were seen in the afternoon, sir. So many people at work then, it'll make elimination easier.'

'We don't know when they were seen. It could have been seven o'clock. It's still light then.'

'Oh.' Troy drove carefully, keeping an eye on the speedometer. 'They could've walked over from Gessler Tye. It's not all that far. Get off their own manor.'

'Yes. We may have to spread out a bit.'

'Course even if it was a couple it doesn't mean they're both in it.'

That thought had already occurred to Barnaby. It was more than likely that one half of the couple was fancy free, with nothing to lose by discovery. It was also likely that, even if both had partners, only one had so much to lose that he or she would be prepared to kill rather than have the liaison exposed. And the loss need not necessarily be a financial one. Barnaby did not discount the possibility that Miss Simpson had been killed to avoid causing anguish to someone's legitimate partner. It was after all quite possible to love one's spouse dearly and still not be able to resist a roll in the hay. They entered Badger's Drift, passing two police cars already parked by the Black Boy. The house-to-house was under way.

Barnaby said, 'I shall be starting at the Lessiters'. That big house with the lions.'

Sergeant Troy gave a low envious whistle as he crunched up the drive and let himself go a bit by the front door, parking in a showy swirl of dust and gravel. Barnaby sighed and climbed out. He used the mock ancient knocker and, whilst waiting, studied the carriage lamps and a board, with an arrow pointing sideways, giving the doctor's surgery hours in Gothic, horror-movie script.

Barnaby was getting to know the surgery rather well. He had visited it again the previous day to inform the doctor of the post-mortem findings. The news had not been well received. Trevor Lessiter had looked at him incredulously, saying, much as George Bullard had done, '*Hemlock?*' and dropped like a stone into his chair. He then so far forgot himself as to indicate to Barnaby that he should also be seated. Even his fingers were temporarily stilled.

'And what put you on to that if I'm not being too inquisitive?' Already he was on the defensive.

'We were asked to look into the matter.'

'Who by? That loopy old hag down the lane, I shouldn't wonder.' He noticed Barnaby's slight change of expression and made a visible effort to calm down. 'It would have been courteous of you to let me know.'

'We are letting you know, sir.'

'I mean before this, as I'm sure you damn well realize.'

Approaching footsteps recalled Barnaby to the present. A girl opened the door. Remembering Doctor Bullard's description of a 'not so scrumptious' daughter, Barnaby immediately assumed that this must be she: short, not much over five feet, and dumpy. Her complexion had a thick, soupy texture and there was a fuzz of down on her top lip, her hair was coarse but full of vitality, springing up into a wiry halo around her head. She had large, rather beautiful hazel eyes which she blinked rapidly from time to time. This habit gave her a timorous yet slightly defiant demeanour: the sort of girl who made a career out of being insecure.

Barnaby stated their business and was admitted. He followed Judy Lessiter across the hall. Her legs, emerging from a shapeless pinafore dress, were really remarkable: hugely wide at the knees then tapering off into sparrow-thin ankles, like upended skittles. She pushed at the sitting-room door and went in, Barnaby close behind.

Doctor Lessiter looked up, then flung his *Telegraph* down with some annoyance. 'Good grief – I thought I'd seen the last of you lot.'

'Yes. I'm sorry, but this sort of inquiry is quite usual –'

'Turning the whole village upside down.'

'In the case of an unexplained death –'

'The woman picked some hemlock by mistake. There's a large field of it just beyond Church Lane. The seeds blow everywhere. Obviously some went into the garden and took root. I've never known such a palaver.'

'We are asking everyone in the village to account for their movements on the day in question. That is last Friday the seventeenth of July, afternoon and evening.'

The doctor gave an irritated little snort, threw his paper down and stood with his back to them, staring into the fireplace. 'Well . . . if we must. On my rounds in the afternoons . . . then in the even—'

'Your rounds are Tuesday and Thursday, Daddy.' Judy's tone was calm and reasonable but Barnaby thought he detected a rather unpleasant smile plucking the corners of her mouth.

'What? Oh . . . yes . . . sorry.' He picked up a magazine from the log basket and started to flick through it, illustrating his lack of concern. 'I was here, of course. Bit of gardening but mainly watching the final Test. What a game that was . . . superb bowling . . .'

'And the evening?'

'Still there, I'm afraid. A dull day really.'

'And your wife was with you on both of these occasions?'

'Part of the evening. She was shopping in the afternoon.'

'Thank you. Miss Lessiter?'

'I was working during the day. I'm a librarian. At Pinner.'

'And in the evening?'

'. . . here . . .'

Both policemen noticed the rather theatrical start of surprise the doctor gave at this remark, as no doubt they were meant to. Tit for tat, thought Barnaby.

'Well . . .' she elaborated, 'I did go out for a bit of a walk . . . it was such lovely weather.'

'Do you remember what time that was?'

'Sorry, no. I wasn't out long.'

'Where did you go?'

'Just down Church Lane, past the fields for about half a mile, then back.'

'Did you meet anyone?'

'No.'

'Did you hear or notice anything out of the ordinary when you were passing Beehive Cottage?'

'No . . . I think the curtains were closed.'

'And what time did you return?'

She gave a couldn't-care-less shrug.

'Can you be of any help here, Doctor Lessiter?' asked Barnaby.

'No.' The doctor had returned to the settee and reimmersed himself in his newspaper. Barnaby was just about to ask if he could see Mrs Lessiter when she appeared in the doorway behind him. He was made aware of this by a sudden change in the atmosphere. The doctor, after a glance over Barnaby's shoulder, started reading his paper with a degree of intensity which could only be feigned, Judy glowered at no one in particular and the blood heated up and zipped around under Sergeant Troy's almost transparent skin, staining it an unbecoming bright pink.

'I thought I heard voices.'

She dropped into the armchair by the window, put her feet up on a tiny footstool and smiled at the two policemen. She could have stepped straight out of one of his centrefolds, Troy thought, eyeing the ripe curves pressing against a terry-towelling jump suit, the tumbling hair and glossy fondant lips. Her slender tanned feet were in high-heeled golden sandals. Barnaby thought she was not as young as all that hard work and hard cash would have you believe. Not early thirties but mid, maybe even late forties.

In reply to his question she said that in the afternoon she had been in Causton shopping and in the evening she was at home except for a short period when she had gone out for a drive.

'Was that for any special purpose?'

'No . . . well . . . to be honest we'd had a little tiff, hadn't we, Pookie?'

'I hardly think our domestic squabbles are of any interest to the police, my dear –'

'I overspent my dress allowance and he got cross so I took the Jaguar and drove around for a bit till I thought he'd've cooled down. Then I came home.'

'And this was?'

'Was Miss Lessiter here when you returned?'

'Judy?' She frowned at the girl in an impersonal way, as if wondering what she was doing in the place at all. 'I've no idea. She spends a lot of time in her room. Adolescents do, you know.'

Barnaby could not think of the figure now lumpily taking up half a settee as an adolescent. The word implied not just a lack of confidence, ungainliness and a personality in a state of flux but fragility (if only of the ego) and youth. Judy Lessiter looked as if she had been born middle aged.

'You didn't stop anywhere, Mrs Lessiter? For a drink perhaps?'

'No.'

'Well, thank you.' As Barnaby rose he heard the flap of the

letter box. Judy heaved herself up from the sofa and lolloped out of the room. Her stepmother glanced at Barnaby.

'She's in love. Every time the post arrives or the phone rings we get a touch of drama.' Her shiny unkind smile included all three men. It said: isn't she ridiculous? As if anyone would. 'A dreadful man too, but devastatingly attractive, which makes things worse.'

Trevor Lessiter's knuckles whitened over the newsprint. Judy returned with a handful of letters. She threw one into Barbara's lap and dropped the rest down the inside of the *Daily Telegraph* chute. Her father clicked his tongue with annoyance.

When they left the house Barnaby stopped to admire a spectacular Madame le Coultre clematis climbing up the portico. Before he walked on he looked back through the window of the room they had just left. Barbara Lessiter, standing now, was staring out unseeingly into the garden. Her face was a mask of fear. As Barnaby watched she crumpled a letter into a tight ball and thrust it into the pocket of her suit.

'What's the matter, Stepmamma?'

'Nothing.' Barbara moved back to the armchair. She was longing for some strong black coffee. Everything was on a low table in front of the sofa. But she wouldn't trust her shaking hands.

'You're white as the proverbial sheet under all that plaster of Paris.' Judy stared at the older woman. 'You're not pregnant are you?'

'Of course not.'

'Of course not,' echoed Judy. 'You're well past it, aren't you?'

'Have you got a cigarette, Trevor?'

Her husband, not looking up from his paper, replied, 'There's some in a box on my writing desk.'

Barbara took one, tapping it so furiously on the lid it almost snapped. She lit it with a silver football and stood smoking at the window, her back to them. The silence, packed with unspoken animosities, lengthened.

Judy Lessiter directed her burning gaze at her father's paper shield. She would have liked to burn straight through it like a magnified ray from the sun. To see it brown and blacken and flake away, leaving a hole for his stupid astonished face to peer through.

It was now five years since that shattering day when they had both turned up on the doorstep with matching gold bands. He had been away from home the night before, telling her he was at the bedside of a dying patient. She had been unable to forgive him for this lie which she felt was utterly despicable. She wasn't even sure if she still loved him. Certainly her pleasure in observing his day-to-day discomfiture augured strongly against it.

From the very first she had resisted strongly Barbara's rather half-hearted suggestions about clothes and makeup and alterations to her room. She liked her room the way it had always been – old toys, patchwork quilt, school books and all – and found Barbara's suggestions on how to make it more feminine (ruffled curtains, soppy Pierrot wallpaper and oyster shag-pile carpet) quite nauseating. She was also, she told herself, far too intelligent to be taken in by the stupid magazines Barbara spent half her life reading. As if a new you could be found by starving the old you half to death then tearing the eyebrows out of what was left. But the motherly advice hadn't lasted long and Barbara had soon slipped into the daily routine that had continued ever since. Giving orders to the daily help, visiting her hairdresser, health club and dress shops and lying about the house studying what Judy called 'Harpies Bizarre and other gorgoneia'.

Judy was not happy. She had not been happy since the day her mother died. Not, that is, in the fearless uncomplicated way an only child of two loving parents is happy. But the unhappiness of the other two gave her a curious sort of comfort. And then there was Michael Lacey. Or rather there wasn't. And would never be. That was something she would have to keep repeating every time the little worm of hope wriggled in her heart. Not only because of his looks (even after the accident he still had the most wonderful face) but because of his work. A painter must be free. Only last week he told her he was going to travel; to study in Venice, Florence and Spain. Full of anguish she had cried, 'When, when!' but he had simply shrugged, saying, 'One day . . . soon.' Since her engagement his sister Katherine was hardly ever at home and Judy walked over to the cottage sometimes, cleaned up a bit, made some coffee. Not too often. She tried to space her visits widely with the secret hope that he might start to miss her.

Two weeks ago he had taken her arm and led her over to a window. He had held her chin and studied her face, then said, 'I'd like to paint you. You have amazing eyes.' He had spoken almost clinically, as if he were a sculptor and she a promising lump of stone, but Judy's heart had melted in her breast (A New You!) and her dreams, refurbished, gained in strength. He hadn't mentioned it again. She had walked over a few evenings ago, seen through the window that he was working and, lacking the courage to disturb him, crept quietly away. She had not returned, afraid that an unwanted visit might try his patience and bring about what she dreaded most of all, a definite dismissal.

Trevor Lessiter watched his daughter, miles away as usual, as he folded up his *Telegraph*. He wondered what she was thinking and how it was possible to miss someone so much when you saw them every day. He was glad she had not been driven, despite his wife's heavy hints, to find a flat in Pinner 'to be nearer work'. Judy did nothing now in the house. She who had always taken such a pride in polishing her mother's things and arranging flowers. Now whatever Mrs Holland couldn't manage got left. And whenever he and Barbara bickered (nearly all the time lately, it seemed), he saw a relish in Judy's eyes which he found deeply wounding. He knew she was thinking 'serve him right'. He looked at his wife, at the heavy breasts and narrow waist, and felt dizzy with lust. Not love. He recognized now that he no longer loved her, indeed wondered if he ever had, but she still had the power. So much power. If only he could talk to Judy. Try to make her understand how he had been driven, almost tricked, into marriage. Surely now she was herself in love she would understand. But he shrank from such an attempt. Young people were invariably disturbed, even offended, by revelations of their parents' sexuality. And her persistent indifference and unkindness were now provoking a similar reaction in him. Something he would not have believed possible a few years ago.

He remembered how, after her mother died, she would wait up for him to return from a night call and heat up some Ovaltine, then sit with him to make sure he drank it. She took all his messages neatly and accurately and listened to his patients rambling on with as much kindness as his wife would have shown. Looking across at her sad sulky face, it seemed to him that he had thrown away something of unique worth and replaced it with shoddy.

Barbara Lessiter felt the hard paper ball pressing on her thigh when she moved. She wondered, for the millionth time in the last five minutes, where the hell she was going to find five thousand pounds.

Chapter Three

'Where to now, sir?'

'Well, there's Mrs Quine in Burnham Crescent . . .'

'I thought the others were doing the council houses.'

'I'm doing that one, she's Miss Simpson's cleaner. Then there's that alarmingly smart bungalow and the next four cottages – and Trace's farm. Or rather, Tye House.'

'Expect to see a bit of rank, do they? Top people?'

'I can do without the mass observation, Troy. Just keep your wits about you and your eyes open.'

'Right, Chief.'

'And your pencil sharp. We'll start with the farmhouse and work down.'

There was a graceful iron white-ribbed fanlight with lacy curlicues over the main door. The magnolia was in fulsome bloom, great waxy cups in dark green saucers pressing against the windows. Sergeant Troy gave the brass pull a yank and, a long way away, a bell could be heard tinkling. Barnaby wondered if they had a glass and mahogany case in the kitchen with a row of little bells jerking imperiously under their designations. Breakfast Room. Laundry. Still Room. Nursery. No one came.

'Must be the maid's day off.' Troy was unable to sustain the jokey note. The remark came out as a sour sneer. He followed Barnaby round the side of the house, fighting angry memories. His mother had always had to remove her apron before answering the door. And her headscarf. He could see her now nervously patting her hair in the hall mirror, smoothing her collar. 'Mrs Willows to see you, my lady.'

They entered a cobbled yard at the back of the house and, as they did so, a small dog, very thin, with a grey muzzle and brindled chest, came hurrying towards them. He was an old Jack Russell and his eyes were not good. He was quite close to the two men before he realized his mistake. Troy bent down to pat the dog but it turned, inconsolably, away. Barnaby approached the back door. 'Perhaps we'll have more luck here.'

It stood wide open, revealing a vast kitchen. A man, facing the door, sat at a refectory table in an attitude of complete dejection, his forehead supported on one hand, his shoulders sagging. Close to him, perched on the table's edge with her back to Barnaby, was a young girl. As Barnaby watched she leaned forward and touched the man's shoulder. Immediately he seized her hand then, looking up, saw the two men in the doorway and leapt to his feet. The girl turned to face them more slowly.

Years after the case was closed Barnaby would still remember his first sight of Katherine Lacey. She was wearing a silk dress, ivory and apple-green stripes, and was the loveliest thing he had ever seen. And her beauty was more than simple perfection of face and form (and how often in any case did you come across that?); it had the remote perfection of a distant star. It smote the heart. She came towards them, her exquisite lips parted in a smile.

'I'm sorry – have you been ringing long? I don't always hear in the kitchen.' Barnaby explained the reason for their visit. 'Oh, of course – please come in. We were all so shocked to hear the police had been called in, weren't we, David?' The man, who had re-seated himself in one of the wheelback chairs, did not reply. 'She taught my father, you know, Miss

Simpson. Both my parents were very fond of her. I'm Katherine Lacey by the way. And this is David Whiteley, our farm manager.'

Barnaby nodded and queried her movements on the day in question whilst glancing at the man at the table. He was over six feet tall, with the bronzed, almost weathered complexion of someone who works continually in the open. He had vivid cobalt-blue eyes and hair the colour of flax, worn rather longer than might have been expected. He appeared to be somewhere in his late thirties and was now looking more resentful than dejected. Barnaby wondered what would have happened if he and Troy had not appeared on the doorstep. Was the girl's touch on his shoulder a gesture of comfort? A caress? Would his fervent handclasp have led to a rebuff? Or a kiss?

'. . . the afternoon's easy. Most of it was spent in the village hall getting ready for the gymkhana on the Saturday. You know . . . putting the trestles up . . . sorting things . . . I was helping on the WI stall.'

'I see . . .' Barnaby nodded, trying in vain to picture Miss Lacy in the Women's Institute. 'What time did you leave?'

'Oh around four I think. But it could've been earlier. I'm hopeless about time, as Henry will tell you.'

'And did you go straight home?'

'Yes. To pick up the Peugeot. Then I drove over to the barn at Huyton's End to collect Henry. He has an office –'

She broke off suddenly, then said, 'Look – wouldn't it be more sensible if you talked to us both together? We always have some coffee around now in the drawing room. You're welcome to join us.'

Barnaby declined the coffee but agreed that her suggestion was a helpful one.

'You come too, David.' She smiled again, this time at the man in the chair, and the three of them followed her back view, only marginally less heavenly than the front, across a hall and down a long carpeted corridor. One wall was lined with ornately framed oil paintings of Trace's past, the other with delicate watercolours to which Barnaby lent an expert and envious eye. At the end of the corridor double glass doors opened on to an orangery: a dazzling pattern of white iron loops and curls. Through the glass Barnaby caught a glimpse of formal lawns, elegant topiary and a glittering fountain. He wondered if there were peacocks. Katherine spoke over her shoulder.

'Apart from Henry the only other person living here at the moment is Phyllis Cadell – his sister-in-law. Her room is upstairs.' She turned sharply and opened the first door on her right.

They entered a very long drawing room. The walls were stippled apricot and cream and there were rich Persian rugs scattered over the high honey-gloss parquet. Rocailles of gold leaf decorated the ceiling. At the far end of the room a man sat in a wheelchair by a magnificent Adam fireplace. There was no fire but the space was filled with a starburst of white and silver flowers and leaves. The man's knees were covered by a travelling rug. He had a grave – almost stern – face with two deep grooves running from his nose to the corners of his mouth. His dark hair was streaked with grey and his shoulders were slightly bent. Barnaby was surprised to discover later that Henry Trace was only forty-two. He wondered if it was quite without thought that David Whiteley took the seat nearest to his employer. There could hardly have been a crueller contrast. Even in repose Whiteley had an air of aggressive vitality. His limbs, so straight and strong, seemed almost to be bursting the seams of his cords and check shirt. Marlboro man, jeered Troy to himself. Katherine explained why the police were there, then sat on a footstool close to the wheelchair and took Trace's hand.

'A terrible business,' he said, 'surely it's not true that there's been foul play?'

'We're just making a few inquiries at this stage, sir.'

'I just can't believe anyone would wish to harm her,' continued Trace, 'she was the kindest soul alive.'

He didn't add, noticed Troy, flipping open his pro-forma pad, that she taught his mum. Probably went to a private school. All right for some.

'I actually saw her on the day she died,' said Katherine, her voice quite untainted by the slightly salacious excitement that usually accompanies this sort of remark.

'When was this?' asked Barnaby, glancing at Troy who described an arc with his pencil to show awareness.

'In the morning. I don't remember the exact time I called at the cottage. She'd promised me some honey for the stall. She gave me some parsley wine as well. She was always very generous.'

'And that was the last time you saw her?' Katherine nodded. 'To return to the afternoon . . . you left the hall around four . . . took the Peugeot . . . ?'

'And drove over to Henry's office. I picked him up, we came back here, had supper and spent the evening wrangling over –'

'Discussing.'

'– discussing' – she screwed her head round and gave him a teasing look – 'a new rosarium. I left about half-past ten.'

'You don't live here then, Miss Lacey?'

'Not until next Saturday. We're to be married then.' She exchanged glances with the man in the wheelchair. Hers was simply fond but his was not only adoring but triumphant. The triumph of a collector who has spotted a rare and beautiful specimen and, against all the odds, captured it for himself. If you've got the money, thought Sergeant Troy, you can buy anything.

'I live in a cottage on the edge of the beechwoods. Holly Cottage. It's quite outside the village, really.' A shadow darkened her eyes. She added so quietly that Barnaby could hardly hear, 'With my brother Michael.' He asked the exact location of the cottage and she described it, adding, 'But you won't find him there at the moment. He's gone into Causton to buy some brushes.' Even volunteering this hardly disturbing piece of information seemed to distress her and she folded her lips together tightly and frowned. Trace patted her head gently as if soothing a fretful animal.

'Did you pass Miss Simpson's house on your way home?'

'Yes.'

'Did you see anyone? Or hear or notice anything?'

'I'm afraid not.'

'Was the light on? The curtains closed?'

'I'm sorry – I just don't remember.'

'Thank you.' Barnaby turned his attention to Henry Trace. He felt the questions here were a mere formality, yet not to have asked them would have appeared insensitive to say the least. Whilst Trace could perhaps have wheeled himself down to Miss Simpson's cottage and poisoned her (in which case his fiancée was lying about their evening together) he could hardly have been frolicking in the woods that afternoon, even assuming any man on the point of marrying Katharine Lacey would have been mad enough to want to. There had been no wheel or tyre marks anywhere near the place. Barnaby assumed the paralysis was genuine. It was surely only in films that strong, healthy people spent years concealed under a rug in a wheelchair simply so that they could leap out at the crucial moment and commit the perfect crime.

'Do you confirm Miss Lacey's account of your movements together, Mr Trace?' He heard the flick of paper from Troy's corner.

'Yes I do.'

'And were other people about when you were in your office?'

'Oh yes. Tractors are stored there. All the fertilizers. There's a hopper . . . out-buildings. It's a very busy part of the farm.'

'How large is the farm?'

'Five thousand acres.'

Sergeant Troy's pencil stabbed savagely at his page.

'And could you give me the name of your doctor?'

'My doctor?' Henry Trace gave Barnaby a bemused stare. Then the stare faded. He said, 'Oh – I see.' The grooves on his face deepened. He smiled, a smile totally without any mirth or pleasure. 'Trevor Lessiter's my GP. But you'd best have a word with Mr Hollingsworth, University College, London.' He added bitterly, 'He'll be able to confirm that my paralysis is genuine.'

There was a cry of indignation from the girl at his feet and she stared at Barnaby angrily. Trace said, 'It's all right, darling. They have to ask these things.' But she remained unmollified and continued to glare at the two policemen during the questioning of David Whiteley. Troy thought this made her look more beautiful than ever. The farm manager's replies were brief. He said he had been working on the afternoon in question.

'Where precisely was this?'

'Three miles down the Gessler Tye road. I was repairing some fencing. There was a nasty accident a couple of days before and a considerable amount got smashed.'

Barnaby nodded. 'And when you were through there?'

'I drove into Causton to order some more netting. And then went home.'

'I see. You didn't return to the farm office?'

'No. It was nearly six by then. I don't have to clock on and off, you know. I'm not a hired hand.' He strove to sound amused but there was a flick of temper in his voice.

'And home is . . . ?'

'Witchetts. The house with the green shutters opposite the pub. Goes with the job.'

'And in the evening?'

'I showered. Had a drink. Watched a little television. Then went to the Bear at Gessler for a meal and some company.'

'What time was that?'

'About half eight I suppose.'

'You're not married, Mr Whiteley?'

'Mind your own business!'

'David!' cried Henry Trace. 'There's no need –'

'I'm sorry but I really don't see how the hell whether I'm married or not is relevant to an inquiry into the death of an old woman I barely knew in the first place.' He closed his mouth stubbornly, folded his arms and crossed his legs. A moment later he uncrossed them. Then crossed them the other way again. Barnaby, looking completely incurious, sat placidly in his armchair. Henry and Katherine looked rather embarrassed. Troy eyed Whiteley's straining calves and biceps caustically. He knew the type. Fancied himself as a stud. Probably couldn't even get it up without half a dozen beers and a soft porn video. The silence lengthened. Then David Whiteley heaved an exaggerated sigh.

'Well yes, if you must know I am married, but we've been living apart for the past three years. Since shortly before I came to work here, in fact. She's a domestic science teacher and lives in Slough. And, just to save you ferreting out every little genealogical detail, we have a nine-year-old son. His name is James Laurence Whiteley and last time I saw him he was just over four feet tall and weighed in at around five stone. He was into Depeche Mode, BMX and computer games and played a mean game of basketball. Of course that was some considerable time ago. It's probably all different now.' Sarcasm and anger failed in the last remark. His voice, thick with emotion, broke off suddenly.

'Thank you, Mr Whiteley.' Barnaby waited a few moments then continued, 'To return to the evening of the seventeenth. Can you tell me when you left the Bear?'

Whiteley took a long deep breath before replying. 'Roughly half an hour before closing time. They might remember. I'm a regular there.'

'And you drove straight home?'

'Yes.'

'Could you give me the make and registration of your car?'

'It's a Citroën estate. ETX 373V.'

'Fine.' Barnaby rose. 'You've been very cooperative. I believe, Miss Lacey, you mentioned there was someone else living here?'

'Well yes,' Henry Trace said, 'there's Phyllis. But isn't she down at her new place?'

'No.' Katherine rose to her feet. 'I heard her come in half an hour ago. I'll show you the way.' She pointed her words in the general direction of Barnaby but without looking at him. As she took the first step away Henry caught her hand.

'Come straight back.'

'Of course I will.' She bent her head and kissed the corner of his mouth. It was a chaste kiss, but the look she got in return was far from chaste. They made a charming picture, thought Barnaby. Trace with his distinguished severe profile, the girl fresh and lovely bending over him, both posed against a fall of grey watered-silk curtains. Perhaps it was this final rather theatrical touch that gave Barnaby the feeling that the charming scene was in some way unnatural. It seemed so contrivedly perfect; brimming with false pathos like a sentimental Victorian greeting card or an illustration from

Dickens. He couldn't quite explain this perception. It was not that he believed either of them was playing a part. He shifted his gaze to include David Whiteley. Perhaps his presence had been father to the thought. Perhaps it was simply that the girl was with the wrong man. That youth should call to youth. Barnaby watched Whiteley watching the girl. His glance was far from chaste as well. Barnaby thought that Henry Trace would be a very unusual man if, when his fiancée and his farm manager were both out of his sight, he didn't occasionally wonder . . . A collector will naturally expect a covetous attitude on the part of other collectors. Especially with regard to his prize specimen.

Katherine led them up a tall curved staircase and down yet another corridor, this one sporting little highly polished half-moon tables holding vases of flowers, snuffboxes and miniatures.

'What is the lady's full name?'

'Phyllis Cadell.'

'Miss?'

'Very much so.' The squeeze of lemon in her voice intrigued and pleased Barnaby. Too much sweetness and light could cloy after a while, in his opinion. Rather a short while too. He liked what he called 'a bit of edge'. He wondered what Phyllis Cadell's exact position in the household was and if it would change after the marriage. Surely any new wife would want to take the reins into her own hands. And, with a disabled husband, she would need to be exceptionally capable. He looked at Miss Lacey's slightly sunburned hand as she knocked at the door. It looked stronger than her rather flower-like appearance would lead you to expect.

'Oh Phyllis – I'm sorry to disturb you . . .'

Barnaby followed her into the room. He saw a rather plump, middle-aged woman with a slab-like face, gooseberry-green eyes and dull brown hair done in a youthful style with a fronded fringe and hard tight little curls. Atop her long pale face it looked foolish, like a wig on a horse. She was sitting in front of a large flickering television set, a box of fudge on her knees.

'. . . it's the police.'

The woman jumped. Cubes of fudge went flying everywhere. She crouched, concealing her face, but not before Barnaby had seen fear leaping to life behind her eyes. Katherine bent down too. It was assorted fudge: three shades of brown (vanilla, mocha, chocolate), and some squares were studded with walnuts and cherries.

'You won't be able to eat these now, Phyllis –'

'I can pick up a few sweets, thank you. Leave me alone.' She was cramming fluffy cubes anyoldhow into the box. She still didn't look at the two men.

'You'll show Chief Inspector Barnaby out then, will you?' Receiving no reply Katherine turned to leave, saying just before she closed the door, 'It's about Miss Simpson.'

At this remark Barnaby noticed the colour rush back into the older woman's cheeks but unevenly, leaving the skin mottled, as if she had been roasting her face by the fire. She gushed at them, 'Of course, poor Emily. Why didn't I think? Sit down . . . sit down both of you.'

Barnaby selected a fawn fireside chair and looked around him. A very different atmosphere from the drawing room downstairs. Not uncomfortably furnished yet quite lacking in individuality. There were no ornaments or photographs and hardly any books. A few copies of *The Lady*, a couple of insipid prints and a dying plant on the windowsill. Apart from the television set it could have been any dentist's waiting room.

Phyllis Cadell switched off the box and sat facing them. Any anxiety she may have felt at their arrival was now firmly under control. She turned a bland but concerned gaze upon them both. If it had not been for the knees, far too firmly clamped together, and the cords standing out in the soft, flabby neck Barnaby might have thought her quite relaxed. She was affably forthcoming as to her movements on the seventeenth. In the afternoon she had been in the village hall setting up the tombola. And she had spent the evening 'quite blamelessly I assure you, Chief Inspector' watching television.

This did not surprise Barnaby. He found it hard to picture the matronly figure, flesh springing free from rigorously confining corsets, rolling and frolicking in the greenwood. He did not of course discount the possibility. The most unlikely characters have stirred others to romantic yearnings. How often had he heard his wife say 'I don't know what he sees in her'? Or, less frequently, the reverse. No, the count against Phyllis Cadell being the woman in the woods was not her unglamorous appearance but the fact that she had nothing to lose by discovery. She might even, taking into account society's attitude towards unattached middle-aged females, have a lot to gain. So, in that case, why had she been so frightened when they had first arrived?

'And what time did you leave the hall, Miss Cadell?'

'Let's see' – she tapped her top lip with a tallow-coloured finger – 'I was almost the last to go . . . it must have been half-past four . . . quarter to five.'

'Did you leave with Miss Lacey?'

'Katherine? Good gracious no. She left much earlier. Was hardly there at all, really.' She caught the glance that Sergeant Troy turned on to Barnaby's unresponsive profile. 'Oh dear' – she made an arch little moue of false regret – 'I hope I haven't said anything I shouldn't?'

'And did you go out at all after you'd returned home?'

'No. I came straight up here when we'd finished dinner. Wrote a couple of letters, then as I have already stated, watched some television.'

As I have already stated, echoed Troy to himself, transcribing carefully. People often said things like that when they were talking to the police. Formal jargony sorts of remarks they'd never dream of making any other time. He listened as Miss Cadell proceeded to give details of all the programmes she'd watched, then, as if this in itself might be thought suspicious, added, 'I only remember because it was Friday. The gardening programmes, you see?'

Barnaby did see. He watched them himself whenever he was home in time. He said, 'Do you have staff living in here?'

'No. We have a gardener and a boy. Between them they look after the grounds, clean the cars and do any maintenance. And there's Mrs Quine. She comes about ten o'clock. Does the general cleaning, prepares any vegetables for dinner, cooks a light lunch, then goes about three. I cook in the evening and she will clear away and wash up when she comes the next day. I do hope Katherine will keep her on. She brings her little girl and not everyone will accept children. Oddly enough we shared her with poor Miss Simpson. She went there for an hour each morning before she came to us . . .'

'And will you continue to live here after the wedding, Miss Cadell?'

'Good heavens, no.' A strangled yelp which might have been a laugh. 'A house cannot hold two mistresses. No, I'm being pensioned off. Henry has several cottages on the estate. Two have been . . . I believe the term is knocked together. There's a small garden. It's . . . very nice.'

Not as nice as being mistress of Tye House, thought Barnaby, picturing again the splendid vista previously seen through the orangery. Not nearly as nice.

'Has Mr Trace been a widower long?' There it was again. As clear and bright as a match struck in a darkened room. The flicker of fear. Phyllis Cadell looked away from him, studying the more nondescript of the two landscapes on the wall.

'I don't see how that can possibly have any relevance to Miss Simpson's death.'

'No. I beg your pardon.' Detective Chief Inspector Barnaby waited. In his experience people (hardened criminals apart) who had something to hide and people who had nothing to hide had one thing in common. Faced by a policeman asking questions they could never remain silent for long. After a few moments Phyllis Cadell began to speak. The words tumbled out as if she couldn't wait to be rid of them and done with the matter.

'Bella died about a year ago. In September. A shooting accident. It was a terrible tragedy. She was only thirty-two. There was a full report in the local paper at the time.'

All that on one breath, thought Barnaby. And through lips the colour of milk. He said, 'Is that when you came to run the house?'

'Not at all. I moved here just after the wedding. Bella wasn't really interested in the domestic side of things. Country pursuits were her forte. Riding, fishing. And looking after Henry, of course. They'd been married nearly five years when she died.'

'Miss Lacey seems to be very young to be taking on so much?' hinted Barnaby, but in vain. Her emotions were now as tenaciously confined as the swoop of her pouter-pigeon chest.

'Oh I don't know. I should think she'll make a charming lady of the manor. And now' – she got up – 'if that's all . . . ?'

She led them briskly down the staircase to the front hall, then stopped suddenly between two old, once-gilded wooden figures. For a moment they all stood on the black-and-white-tiled floor like chess pieces, useful but impotent until nudged into play. Phyllis shifted from one foot to another (beleaguered queen) then spoke.

'Umm . . . you must have thought I looked quite startled to see you . . . taken aback . . . when you first arrived?'

Barnaby looked politely interested. Troy established eye contact with the taller of the two figures; a king with a soaring crown and traces of lapis lazuli still on his pupils.

'The truth is . . . I . . . well it's my car tax. You know how it is . . .' A nervous smile twitched into being, showing strong stained teeth. 'One always means to make a note of these things . . .'

'Yes,' agreed the chief inspector, 'that is a sensible idea.'

As the door closed quickly behind them Troy said, 'Pathetic.' He could have meant the woman's appearance, her position in the household or the awkward and obvious lie about the road tax. Barnaby could only agree on all three counts.

Katherine Lacey wandered slowly across the cobbled yard, watching the two policemen walk away. In spite of the heat of the day she felt cold. Benjy whined sadly from the shelter of the first silo. She crossed over and picked him up. He started to struggle in her arms. His fur slipped over his ribs as if there were no flesh at all to separate them.

'Darling . . . ?' She heard the soft bump as Henry negotiated the kitchen step and wheeled himself towards her. She put the dog down. 'Is something the matter?'

She strove to compose herself before turning to him. She didn't reply, just shook her head, the bell of glossy dark hair swinging over her face.

'Is it Benjy? You must give way on that you know, Kate. We've both tried everything we can. He's simply not going to eat. Please . . . let me call the vet . . .'

'Oh – just another day!'

'He's an old dog. He misses her too much. We can't sit here and watch him starve.'

'It's not just that.' She turned then, crouching clumsily by the chair. 'It's . . . I can't explain . . . oh Henry . . .' She seized his hands: 'I've just got the most terrible feelings . . .'

'What d'you mean?' He smiled down at her, his tone indulgent. 'What sort of feelings?'

'I can't say exactly . . . just that things are going to go dreadfully wrong for us . . . the wedding won't happen . . .'

'I've never heard such nonsense.'

'I knew you'd say that. But you don't understand . . .' She broke off, studying his face. Kind, handsome, a shade complacent. And why shouldn't it be? The Traces went back to Norman times. Effigies of Sir Robert Trayce and his wyffe Ismelda and her cat rested eternally in the cool of the thirteenth-century church. Traces had shed a modest amount of their landowning blood in the two world wars and returned to their squirearchical duties garlanded with honour. The words security of tenure were meaningless to them. They had never known anything else.

'. . . You don't understand,' Katherine repeated. 'Because you've never wanted anything you couldn't have you can't see that life isn't always like that. I think these things that are happening . . . Miss Simpson dying . . . and now Benjy . . . and Michael refusing to come on Saturday . . . I think they're omens . . .'

Henry Trace laughed. 'Beware the Ides of March.'

'Don't laugh.'

'I'm sorry, darling, but there's no one squeaking and gibbering in the streets that I can see.'

'What?'

'And as for Michael . . . well . . . he's hardly an omen. You must've known for weeks that he'd probably refuse to give you away. You know what he's like.'

'But I thought . . . on my wedding day . . .'

'Do you want me to talk to him?'

'It won't make any difference. You'd think after all you'd done for us it would –'

'Hush. You mustn't talk like that. I've done nothing.' As she got up, leaning on the arms of his chair, he said, 'Poor little knees, all dented from the cobbles.' He lifted the hem of her dress and touched the dimpled flesh tenderly. 'Dear little knees . . . Henry make them better.'

At a window above their heads Phyllis Cadell turned abruptly away. She switched on the television set and slumped into the nearest armchair. Voices filled the room. On the screen a couple, mad with ecstatic greed, were struggling to embrace a mountain of consumer durables whilst an audience, hardly less ecstatic, screamed abuse and encouragement. Wearing a fixed insane grin, the woman slipped, dislodged a can and brought the whole pyramid crashing to the ground. Phyllis pressed her remote control and got a besotted duo in love with each other's breakfast cereal. Button three activated a bucolic scene showing an elderly couple saturated with contentment reading their golden wedding telegrams, surrounded by their loving family. Button four brought an old black and white movie. Two men were holding a third by the arms while Sterling Haydon battered him to bits. A left to the jaw, then a right. Smack. Crunch. Then two to the belly, breath sucked in, an agonizing whistle. Then a knee to the groin and a punch in the kidneys.

Phyllis settled back. She seized the box of fudge and started cramming the gritty, fluff-embellished cubes into her mouth. She packed them in fiercely and without a break as if making an assault on her jaws. Tears poured down her cheeks.

Chapter Four

'I expect the wedding'll be a posh do. Marquees and all that?' Troy looked to the horizon as he spoke, casting a green eye on Henry Trace's assets. Miles and miles and miles of waving money.

'No doubt.' Barnaby turned left as they walked away from Tye House, making for the terraced cottages. Troy, not wishing to receive another put-down, did not ask why his chief was going in for a bit of mundane door-to-door. But in the event Barnaby chose to enlighten him.

'That bungalow' – he nodded towards the end of the terrace – 'is what interests me. There's someone there keeping a very sharp eye on things. I'm interested to hear what the neighbours have to say.'

'I see, sir,' was all Troy could think of in reply, but he felt warm with satisfaction on receipt of this small confidence.

The first cottage was empty, the occupants, as a very old lady next door informed them, being outsiders from London who hadn't been down for at least a month. And the man in the last cottage was out till six every weekday teaching in Amersham. Troy took his name for the evening checkers. The old lady was taciturn about her own affairs, simply saying she hadn't been out at all on the day in question. Then she jerked her head over the neat box hedge at cottage number three.

'You want to ask her where she was on Friday. She'd

poison her grandmother for a haporth o' nuts.' Next door a window slammed.

'And the bungalow . . . ?'

'Don't know nothing about them.' She shut the door firmly.

'That's a bit odd, isn't it?' said Troy as they walked down the path. 'A tiny place like this and she doesn't know anything about the people two doors down.'

'It is indeed,' replied Barnaby, arriving at the next cottage, lifting a grimacing pixie by the legs and letting go smartly.

An even older lady appeared and gave them roughly the same spiel, the only difference being that here the blood money came out as two pennorth o' cheese. Then she laid a freckled bunch of weightless bones on the chief inspector's sleeve. 'Listen, young man,' she said, suddenly appearing to him much the nicer of the two old ladies, 'if you want to know what's going on – or what's coming off either' – she gave a dry chuckle, shockingly lewd through withered lips – 'you have a word with Mrs Rainbird next house down. She can tell you what's in your hankie after you've blown your nose in the pitch dark behind locked doors. Spends all her time up in the loft with a pair of binoculars. Says she's a ornyowzit. Camouflage.' She repeated the word, tapping him on the lapel. 'In my young day you hung over the gate and gossiped in the open. I don't know what the world's coming to and that's a fact.' She then confided that Mrs Rainbird had a son in the box and casket trade. 'And a slimy little wart he is an' all. They reckon he keeps his knickers in the fridge.'

Sergeant Troy snorted and turned it into a cough. Barnaby, having met Mr Rainbird, could only assume that they were right. He thanked the old lady and withdrew.

The bungalow was called Tranquillada. Barnaby thought this suggested a slightly relaxed version of the Spanish Inquisition. The name suspended from the neck of a large ceramic stork killing time on one leg by the front door. There was quite a large garden, beautifully kept and full of ornamental shrubs and roses. The silver Porsche was parked in the drive. Sergeant Troy chose the bell rather than the knocker and got a brief shrill earful of the dawn chorus. Dennis Rainbird appeared.

'Well hullo again.' He seemed delighted to see Barnaby. 'And you've brought a friend.' He gave Troy a radiant smile which bounced off the sergeant's stony countenance like a ping-pong ball off a concrete slab. 'Come in, come in. Mother,' he called over his shoulder, 'it's the constabulary.' He prounced it consta*bew*lery.

'Oh but I was expecting them.' A gentle fluting from some distance away.

The bungalow seemed much larger than the outside suggested and Dennis led them past several open doors before reaching the lounge. A kitchen that gleamed, a bedroom (all white and gold) that glittered and a second bedroom adorned with lots of red suede and shining brass.

'I'm in the lounge, Denny,' carolled the voice. It managed to sound every vowel the word possessed, then generously tossed in another O for good measure. As they entered Mrs Rainbird rose from her downy cushions as if from a nest.

She was very, very fat. She spread outwards and towered upwards. At least a quarter of her height seemed to be accounted for by her hair, which was a rigid pagoda-like structure: a landscape of peaks and waves, whorls and curls ending in a sharp point like an inverted ice-cream cone. It was the colour of butterscotch instant whip. She wore a great deal of makeup in excitable colours and a lilac caftan, rather short, revealing bolstery legs and tiny feet. The chief inspector fielded her welcoming glance, direct and sharp as a lancet, and introduced himself.

'I knew you were on your way. I saw a car drive by whilst

I was studying some swallows on the telephone wires. Such a charming arrangement. Quite like notes of music.'

'Ah . . . perhaps it was you I glimpsed the other morning when I was in Church Lane? In your loft I think. An excellent vantage point.'

'Hide is the term we ornithologists prefer, Mr Barnaby.' A nip in the air. Barnaby begged her pardon. She waved a sparkling hand. 'Won't you sit down?' Barnaby sank into an armchair thickly barnacled with bumps of crochet.

'And what about you, dear?' Dennis danced around Sergeant Troy. 'Don't you want to take the weight off those legs?'

Bristling with machismo, Troy selected the hardest chair, sat in it bolt upright and produced his pro-forma pad. A piercing whistle filled the air.

'Denny? Pot to kettle.' As he disappeared she said to Barnaby, 'You'll need to be fed and watered.' Then, overriding his protests, 'Now, now. Don't tell me you're not absolutely exhausted asking all those people all those questions. It's quite ready.'

And so it was. Moments later, a gentle rattling preceding him, Dennis entered wheeling an overwrought trolley built along the lines of the altarpiece at the Brompton Oratory. This was loaded with tiny sandwiches in the shapes of playing card symbols and rich creamy cakes. Mrs Rainbird filled a plate for Detective Chief Inspector Barnaby and handed it over.

'Now you mustn't refuse, Mr Barnaby.' (She addressed him as Mr Barnaby throughout their conversation, perhaps believing that policemen in the higher echelons were, like their medical counterparts, titularly civil.) 'The inner man, you know.'

Her son poured the tea, his bloodless white fingers flickering over the crockery. He popped an apostle spoon with a large purple stone embedded in the handle in a saucer and handed it, with the cup, to Barnaby. Feeling slightly repelled, the chief inspector took it and leaned back rather uncomfortably on his crunchy support.

Dennis dealt an anchovy club, a salmon-spread spade, a potted-meat diamond and a marmite heart on to a plate, added a meringue erupting with chestnut-coloured worms, and swayed over to Sergeant Troy. He put everything on an occasional table, brought over the tea then swayed back to his mother. They beamed at each other then he plumped up her cushions before sitting, appropriately enough, on a pouffe at her feet. Finally Barnaby spoke.

'We're making inquiries into an unexplained death –'

'Poor Miss Simpson of course,' interrupted Mrs Rainbird. 'I blame the parents.'

'– and would be glad if you and your son could give me some idea of your whereabouts on the afternoon and evening of last Friday?'

'Myself doing the flower arrangements and plants in the village hall. No doubt you've heard about the gymkhana?' Barnaby indicated that he had. 'I left around four-thirty with Miss Cadell of Tye House. One of the last as always. I'm afraid I'm one of those dreadful people who has to have everything just so.' A little preen. A smug smile. She had a mouth like a goldfish which, even in repose, had a pushed-forward pouty expression. '"Delegate, Iris, delegate!" is my constant cry, but do you think I ever can? Where was I?'

'One of the last to leave.'

'Ah yes. I believe only Miss Thornburn, our dear Akela, remained.'

'Did you happen to notice what time Miss Lacey left?'

'A few minutes before four o'clock.'

'Are you sure?' Foolish question. He already felt he was in the presence of something oracular rather than merely observant. Mrs Rainbird obviously had the eye of an eagle and, almost as important, an eagle's Olympian lack of interest in the welfare of its prey.

'Quite sure,' resumed Mrs Rainbird. 'She slipped away, in my opinion, *in a very furtive manner indeed*.' She deigned to glance at Sergeant Troy on the last few words to make sure he was noting them down. 'But I'm rather curious as to why we're being asked about the afternoon. I understood that Miss Simpson died much later.'

'We're not sure exactly when she died.'

'Well she was definitely alive around five o'clock because I saw her.'

'You saw her!'

'Certainly I did.' She basked for a moment in the warmth of his reaction. Dennis screwed his head round and gave her an approving smirk. 'I just happened to be in the hide at the time, charting the flight of a waxwing. Emily came hurrying along Church Lane from the direction of the woods. She stopped once, holding her side. I wondered if she were ill and had almost decided to run over when Denny arrived for his tea. Didn't you, pet?' Did her hand tighten on his shoulder? Certainly the sparklers were activated into instant life.

'Mm.' He laid his cheek briefly against her knees. 'I usually get home about five-thirty but that night –'

'If you wouldn't mind, Mr Rainbird. We'll take those details in a moment.'

'I can hardly wait.' Dennis bit his lower lip, pink with delight at being the recipient of such masterful instructions. He smiled at Sergeant Troy, a smile as sweet and sickly as the vanilla slice he was consuming. 'I don't think the sergeant likes his marron *Lyonnaise*, Mother.'

'Press him to a frangipane, then. Yes' – she turned her attention back to Barnaby – 'I was definitely concerned. In fact I'd almost decided to visit her after supper but then we got involved in a game of Monopoly and I felt it could wait till morning. She had a telephone after all and Miss Bell-ringer was close by. So we didn't go out at all, did we, pet?'

'No. Little home birds we.'

'And who won all of Park Lane?'

'Me, me! *And* a big chunk of Piccadilly.'

'I saw Katherine Lacey again, though. Around eight o'clock time.'

'Really? Wasn't that a little late to be pursuing your hobby, Mrs Rainbird? What on earth is on the wing at that hour?'

'Owls, Mr Barnaby.' A very sharp look.

'Ah.'

'Denizens of the night.'

'Quite so.'

'We had taken a little break from the game, Denny was making some coffee and I just happened to glance out of the window.'

'I see. Did you notice where Miss Lacey went?'

She leaned forward dramatically and, as she still had her hand on her son's shoulder, so did he. What a macabre double act they were, thought Barnaby. He was unaccount-ably reminded of the Joe Orton play his wife had been in last month. They would have fitted a treat into that.

'*She was turning into Church Lane.*'

'Do you think she was calling on someone?'

'I couldn't see. The road curves sharply to the right almost immediately. She'd got one of the beagles with her. And a letter in her hand.'

'So she may have been simply going to the post box?' Mrs Rainbird lifted an eyebrow like a crayoned new moon. It said that if he believed that he'd believe anything. 'And did you see her return?'

'I'm afraid not.' Her voice thickened with chagrin. 'Mrs

Pauncefoot rang. Wanted some more *Lilium regale* for the judges' platform. If only I'd known' – she punched her palm with her fist – 'I would have kept watch.'

Her expression was far more than just peevish. She seemed to seethe with frustration at this reminder of an opportunity missed. She obviously couldn't bear not to know what was going on between everyone, everywhere, all the time. Charting the flayt of a waxwing my backside, thought Barnaby, and turned to question her son.

'At work all afternoon, which my partner will confirm, left around quarter to five, drove straight home and stayed there.'

'I didn't realize you were a partner in the business, Mr Rainbird.'

'Mother bought me in on my twenty-first. I'd been there three years by then and just knew I wasn't ever going to want to do anything else.' He hugged his knees boyishly. 'I absolutely adore it. You understand?'

Barnaby tried to look as if he understood. In fact he was not overly concerned with the Rainbirds' alibis. What he was after at Tranquillada was something much more useful. Background information on the village inhabitants. And gossip. If he had summed up Iris Rainbird correctly both should be forthcoming once the correct opening gambits had been played.

He said, 'I'm sure you'll appreciate, Mrs Rainbird, in a case like this how grateful we are to have someone as alert . . . as observant as yourself to call on. To fill the gaps as it were.' The pagoda inclined graciously. 'Tell me . . . Miss Lacey and her brother . . . have they lived in the village long?'

'All their lives. Although not always in Holly Cottage. Their parents had a large farmhouse just a little way out on the Gessler Tye road. No land to speak of, just an acre of garden. Oh very upper class they were then. Old family nanny, the children at Bedales, ponies and cars and off to France every five minutes. And shooting and hunting in the holidays. Thought themselves real gentry. They weren't, of course. No breeding at all.' Sergeant Troy, his pencil at rest, recognized the concealed resentment in this remark immediately, without knowing why. 'People liked Madelaine but he was an appalling man. Drank a lot and drove like a maniac. Violent too. They say he used to ill treat her. Quite heartless –'

'Just like his son.' Dennis spoke impulsively, his sallow cheeks flushed. This time there was no mistaking the warning grip on his shoulder. He added, stammering, 'Well . . . so I've heard.'

'Then, when the children were about thirteen all the money went. He'd been speculating, raised a second mortgage, raised more against that and lost the lot. It killed Madelaine.'

'Do you mean literally?'

'I certainly do. Drove her car into the Thames at Flackwell Heath. She hadn't been dead more than a couple of months before he married some chit of a girl he met in London and off they went to live in Canada.'

'And the children.'

'Well . . . that was the end of the private schools of course. They had to come and attend at Gessler Tye with the rest of the hoi polloi.' Satisfaction rang in her voice. Troy gave an unconscious nod of approval.

'And where did they live?'

'Now of course the Traces come into the picture. Henry was one of the first people that Gerald Lacey turned to for money. And he loaned him a considerable amount. I think he felt afterwards that it would have been better if he hadn't. If he'd tried to help Gerald sort his affairs out instead. At least that's the impression I got from Mrs Trace – Bella, that is . . .'

Chief Inspector Barnaby tried to imagine the late Mrs Trace discussing her husband's financial affairs with Mrs Rainbird, and failed. He wondered where she had really picked up the information.

'Hence Holly Cottage.'

'Oh?'

'A gamekeeper lived in it originally. Henry offered it to the children and the nanny stayed to look after them. They gave her a terrible time, poor old soul. Thick as thieves when they were little, always leading her a dance. Then, when they were older, endless rows. Well you know what adolescents are. Not that my Denny ever gave me any trouble.' Denny simpered into his vanilla slice. A fringe of cream, hardly in colour any different from his skin, graced his upper lip. 'She used to come over here, Nanny Sharpe, just for a cup of tea and a bit of peace and quiet. Cat and dog wasn't in it. Have you seen that mark on Michael's face?'

'We haven't yet interviewed Mr Lacey.'

'She gave him that . . . his sister. Threw an iron at him, apparently.' She noticed his change of expression and sniffed. 'Oh you can look, Mr Barnaby. Those pansy faces take everyone in but they don't fool yours truly.'

Mrs Rainbird's detachment, which he had so admired at the start of their interview, seemed to have temporarily deserted her. The fact that the son she obviously if somewhat unhealthily adored had been slighted in some way seemed still to rankle.

'Did Mr Trace support the Laceys financially?'

'Oh yes. The father didn't leave a penny piece behind. And, as far as I know, Henry still is supporting Michael. Not that he'd get a word of thanks.'

'Doesn't Mr Lacey work, then?'

'If you can call painting work.'

'And is he successful? Does he sell much?'

'No he doesn't. And I'm not surprised. Ugly violent things. Lays the paint on with a shovel. Mind you there's no shortage of models.'

'No,' chipped in Dennis. 'That Lessiter girl's always hanging round. Not that it'll get her anywhere – frumpy old thing. Michael painted me once, you know.' He bridled, all pallid petulance, in Troy's direction.

'And a hideous thing it was too.'

'Oh I was pussycat of the month all right while he was doing the portrait,' continued Dennis, 'all a-taunto I was. Then – when he'd got what he wanted – he told me to sod off.'

'Denny! Another iced sombrero, Mr Barnaby?'

'Thank you, no. And is the nanny, Miss Sharpe, still here?'

'Mrs Sharpe. No. She went to live in Saint Leonards as soon as they could look after themselves. Glad to get out of it. They were about seventeen then, I think. She didn't even drop in to say goodbye. I must say I was a bit hurt. I got her address off the Traces and wrote a couple of times but she didn't reply. I sent a card at Christmas, then gave up.' Frustration surfaced again. It was plain she would have preferred an extended farewell drama full of awful revelations. As she launched into a vivid description of one of the more spectacular domestic confrontations at Holly Cottage, Barnaby, nodding attentively from time to time, stretched his legs by strolling to the patio doors at the end of the room.

Outside the lawn was clear and sharp as glass. More flowering trees and shrubs and a pretty gazebo at the far end. He wondered how Mr Rainbird had made his pile. There must have been plenty of it, what with the bungalow, and Denny's partnership and silver Dinky toy. Not to mention the tea trolley.

He turned back to the conversation. He was beginning to feel very uncomfortable. Although it was a warm day the radiators were full on. He looked at Dennis, batting his almost colourless eyelashes at Sergeant Troy, and wondered if he felt the cold. He certainly didn't have any flesh to spare for insulation.

The room really was unbearably oppressive. It was crammed full of voluptuous showy furniture. And there were cabinets of china, mostly Capo di Monte, and shelves of dolls dressed in differing national costumes, plus several original deeply awful paintings. The one nearest to Barnaby showed a cocker spaniel in – he peered disbelievingly closer – floods of tears. The whole shebang was what his daughter would have called twentieth-century grotesque.

'Thank you so much, Mrs Rainbird.' He stemmed the tide, courteous but firm.

'Not at all, Mr Barnaby.' She flung a dazzling arc in his direction. He could not avoid shaking hands. It was like seizing a lump of dough. 'What are we here for if not to help each other?'

As the two policemen walked down the drive Sergeant Troy said, 'Men like that ought to be castrated.' When Barnaby did not reply he tacked an ameliatory 'sir' on the end, adding, 'as for his mother . . . nothing but a spiteful old gasbag.'

'Mrs Rainbird and folks like her are a godsend in any investigation, Troy. Just don't mistake gossip for facts. And when they give you what they say are facts, always check them thoroughly. And don't come to early conclusions. An open mind, Sergeant, an open mind.'

'Yes, sir.'

They made their way to Burnham Crescent and council house number seven, the home of Mrs Quine.

As Barnaby and Troy passed through the space in the sour and dusty hedge flanked with rotten gate posts, Mrs Rainbird and her son closed the door of Tranquillada and turned to each other, alight with excitement.

'Did you get it?'

'Mummy – I did.'

'Ohhh . . . where . . . where?'

'Wait a minute. You haven't said . . .'

'You're a good boy. Now – show me.'

'No.' His face, an unpleasant orange colour beneath the hall lantern, became closed and stubborn. 'That wasn't properly. You've got to do it properly.'

'You're a goodboy,' she crooned, kissing him full on the mouth. Her breath was very sweet, a soft explosion of violet cachous and cream and rich vanilla. 'Mummysbestboy.' Her fingers slipped into his shirt, caressing the bony wings of his shoulder blades. 'Bestestonlyboy.'

He licked her ear with its dropping cluster of rhinestones. 'Mmmm.' His breathing quickened. 'Clever Denny.'

'Now' – she took his hand, leading him down the corridor towards the french windows and the garden – 'show me . . .'

'I want to play some more.'

'Later we'll play.'

'All sorts of things?'

'Everything. Come on . . . where is it?'

They stepped out on to the lawn. Behind the gazebo was a large dark pile of something dripping wet, the water seeping out on to the bright green grass in concentric rings. Dennis led his mother up to it proudly. Hand in hand they gazed down. Mrs Rainbird's eyes shone.

'Where did you find it?'

'In the pond behind the beechwoods. I saw them throw it in tied round some stones.'

She made no reply; just breathed out, a long slow contented hiss.

'My mo-mo's all wet. I had to put it in the boot, you see.'

'We'll buy you another one.'

'Oh Mummy . . .' Ecstatically excited, he squeezed her arm. 'Do you think it's worth a lot, then?'

'Oh yes, my dear.' She took a step forward and poked the sodden mass with the toe of her shoe. 'A very great deal. A very great deal indeed.'

Chapter Five

The garden of number seven was a tip. Literally. There was a small pyramid of junk teetering up against the side of the house. Bed frames, broken prams, old boxes, rusty iron chains and a large splintering rabbit hutch. The curtains downstairs were tightly closed. Barnaby rattled the letter box. Somewhere in the house a child was crying. He heard a woman scream, 'Shut it, Lisa Dawn.' Then, 'Wait a minute can't you?' Thinking this might apply to him he waited.

Eventually Mrs Quine appeared. She was a thin woman with a concave chest and a cluster of red spots around her mouth. She was smoking and had an air of constant movement even when standing still, as if she had just been wound up and was raring to go.

'Come in.' She stepped back as they entered. 'My neighbour said you were going round everybody.'

The room they entered was thick with smoke and dimly lit with a centre light, a wooden chandelier with parchment galleon shades. The television was blaring loudly. Mrs Quine made no move to turn it down. The room was untidy and not very clean. A little girl was sitting at a plastic table, sniffling and snuffling.

'Now look who's come, Lisa Dawn.' The child looked across at Barnaby. 'Told you I'd get a policeman if you warn't a good girl.' More tears. 'Look what she's done, Mr Policeman.' Mrs Quine seized a dark wet object from the table. 'Her *Baby Jesus Pop-Up Book*. Only had it Christmas. Blackcurrant everywhere.' She opened the book. Jesus, Mary, Joseph and a clutch of assorted beasts rose up from the page, richly and symbolically empurpled. 'Nothing's new for five minutes in this house.'

'Oh I'm sure it was an accident.' Barnaby smiled at Lisa Dawn, who knuckled her eyes sadly and sniffed again. He turned to Mrs Quine who was now pacing briskly around the room sucking violently on her cigarette and flicking the ash about. 'I have to be on the go,' she explained.

'I understand that you worked for Miss Simpson?'

'That's right. There and Tye House. I worked for old Clanger an' all. Only for a week though. She said I could do what I liked as long as I never moved anything. Well how can you clean without moving anything? You tell me.'

'That would be Miss Bellringer?'

'Right.'

'Did you turn up as usual the morning Miss Simpson died?'

'Course I did. No reason not to was there? Miss B. was keeping an eye through the window. She came out and told me. You can sit down if you want.'

'Pardon? Oh – thank you.' Barnaby sat on the edge of a black vinyl settee. One of the cushions was disgorging multi-coloured foam chips through a razored slit.

'She gave me a cup of tea in case I felt bad. Then I went on to Tye House.'

'It must have been a shock?'

'It was an' all. The doctor'd only been a few days before. She'd had a bit of bronchial trouble but he reckoned if she took good care she was all right for another ten years.' Mrs Quine lit a new cigarette from the stub of the old. 'Course we know why she went now, don't we? Bloody rapists. There was one on the telly the other night in full view. I know what

112

I'd do to them.' She settled briefly on the fireguard, throwing her stub into the empty grate. Her foot drummed furiously on the carpet. She inhaled with such force that the flesh beneath her cheekbones fell away into great hollows. 'Poor old gel. At her age an' all.'

Forbearing to comment on this wild bit of embroidery, Barnaby asked if Miss Simpson had been all right to work for.

'Oh yes . . . she liked everything just so but I knew her ways. We got on OK.'

'And Tye House?'

She gave a gratified smile, showing glacially perfect false teeth. 'Been round there, have you?' When Barnaby nodded she continued, 'Laugh a minute there, 'ent it? Old Phyllis Cadell hanging on for grim death. You could see the way the wind was blowing there all right. Grooming herself for the situation vacant, warn't she? Worked her drawers off even when Mrs Trace were alive. Making herself indispensable – so she thought. You should've seen her after the accident. Trying to look sorry when anyone was about. Sorry! She was tickled to death. You could see what she thought would happen. Then Miss Great Britain from Holly Cottage starts popping in and out and swaps the jackpot. I thought Miss Cadell was going to chuck herself under the nearest bus the morning the engagement was announced. It made my day, I can tell you.'

'To return to last Friday, Mrs Quine . . . were you in the village hall during the afternoon?'

'Me? Mucking in with that lot? You've got to be joking. Women's Institute? Load of cowing snobs. They can stuff their flower arrangements. And their bloody walnut pickle.'

'You were at home, then?'

'Yes. Watching the telly. Weren't we, Lisa Dawn? All afternoon. Except she ran up the shop for some crisps.' Barnaby looked at Lisa Dawn, whose thin legs dangled at least eighteen inches from the floor. Reading the look, Mrs Quine continued, 'She's ever so good crossing the road. And she always comes straight back. She's a big girl, 'ent you, Lisa Dawn? Tell the nice policeman how old you are.'

'Nearly four,' whispered the little girl.

'You *are* four. She's a good four,' insisted Mrs Quine, as if the child were a pair of shoes. 'And who bought you some sweeties in the shop?'

'Judy.'

'*Auntie* Judy. That's Doctor Lessiter's daughter. She often treats her. Bought her an egg at Easter, full of rabbits.' Lisa Dawn started to cry. 'Oh God – shut up can't you? What'll the gentlemen think? I shouldn't have said that . . . about the egg. The dog next door got off his chain and had her rabbit.'

'Poor Smokey.'

'All right, all right. We'll get you another.'

'What time was it when your daughter went to the shop?'

'Dunno exactly. We was watching *Sons and Daughters* so it must've been gone three.'

'And this was definitely the afternoon of the seventeenth?'

'Told you, haven't I?' She lit a third cigarette.

'And you were in all that evening?'

'Can't go anywhere with her.'

'Thank you.' Whilst Troy read the pro-forma back and Mrs Quine inhaled and tapped her feet and sighed, Barnaby tried to talk to Lisa Dawn but she shrank back in her chair and would not look at him. Bluish black marks, pretty as pansies, flowered along her inner arms. Before they had passed again between the rotten gate posts Barnaby heard her start to cry.

Barnaby switched on the fan in his office and asked for some coffee and a sandwich from the canteen. Before leaving to fetch them Policewoman Brierley said, 'I've put a message underneath your clip, sir. A Miss Bazely. She left her office number and asked if you'd ring.'

Barnaby lifted up the phone and dialled. The blue propellers of the fan, whilst making an efficient whirring sound, did no more than shift the warm air in a sluggish stream past his perspiring face. 'Miss Bazely? Detective Chief Inspector Barnaby here.'

'Oh yes . . . hullo . . . you know when we talked the other day and I thought there was something I hadn't told you?'

'Yes.'

'Well I've remembered what it was. I'll tell you now shall I?'

'Yes please.'

'I was in High Wycombe yesterday with my sister. I'm going to be her bridesmaid next month, you see, and we went to try on my dress. The shop's quite near the station actually, which means you can sometimes squeeze the car in – not for long of course – and it's called Anna Belinda. And that's what Miss Simpson said. Well, nearly.'

'Do you remember exactly?'

'Yes I do. She said, "Just like poor Annabella."'

'You're sure?'

'Positive.'

'Not simply Bella?'

'No. It was definitely Annabella.'

Barnaby replaced the phone and sat staring at it thoughtfully. His sandwich (chicken and watercress) arrived, and some delicious coffee from the office hotplate. Barnaby took it saying, 'Give the Social Services a ring, would you? I think someone should call at seven Burnham Crescent, Badger's Drift.'

'What shall I say, sir?'

'Ohh . . . possible child abuse. The woman's name is

Quine. She needs help too. On the verge of a breakdown, I would say. And if you could get on to Slough. I need the address and number of a Mrs Norah Whiteley. She's a domestic science teacher. One son aged nine.' He took a ravenous bite of his sandwich, reducing it by half, picked up the receiver and dialled again.

'Miss Bellringer? Do you happen to know if your friend knew anyone called Annabella?' There was a longish pause then a negative reply. 'It wouldn't perhaps be Mrs Trace?'

'Oh no . . . her name was Beatrice. She called herself Bella because she thought it was more glamorous.'

'But did Miss Simpson know this?'

'She did indeed. I remember her saying to me what a mistake it was. She thought Beatrice a beautiful name. And Bella rather common.' She paused for breath. 'There was an Isabella in my music class years ago. An immaculate child. I believe she's now a deaconess. Is that any help?'

Barnaby thanked her and said goodbye. He had forgotten for the moment that Miss Simpson had been a teacher for over forty years. The chances were that, even given the comparative rarity of the name, one or two Annabellas may have passed through her hands, swanking brightly amongst the mousey Jeans and Joans and Junes and Janes. But then Miss Simpson's recollection of the name had been triggered by the sight of a fornicating couple. How young had they started having it away twenty, thirty, forty years ago? Probably, he reflected, about as young as they did now. Some things never changed.

And why poor Annabella? He took another swig of his coffee and watched, out of the corner of his eye, an abseilling spider swing back and forth. Had she been destitute? Depraved? Dead? Barnaby thought of all the characters an eighty-year-old woman could have met with in a long and fairly well-travelled life. And heard about. And read about.

He sighed, took another bite of his sandwich and faced the facts. Annabella could be practically anybody.

'Something I can do, sir?' asked Troy.

'Yes.' Barnaby emptied his mug. 'You can run me over to the *Echo*. I want to read the account of Bella Trace's death.'

'You don't think there's any connection?'

'I don't think anything at this stage. But it's an unnatural death in the same small area involving a circle of people whom we must now regard as suspect. It can't be overlooked. So finish your tea and look sharp about it.'

In a basement beneath the offices of the *Causton Weekly Echo* Barnaby spoke to an old man who seemed as much a fixture of the place as the ancient green filing cabinets and rusty water pipes writhing over the back wall. There was a huge boiler too, now unlit and quiet.

Barnaby asked to see the editions for September and October the previous year. The old man shuffled off to the files and shuffled back. He didn't speak or even remove the loosely wrapped unlit cigarette from his mouth. A few shreds of ginger tobacco fell on the newspapers as he handed them over. Barnaby took them to a reading stand by the window. The light was poor, the panes being of thick cobbled glass the colour of milk laced with whisky. To the accompaniment of a variety of overhead footsteps he flicked through the first two copies. The inquest on the death of Mrs Bella Trace was in the third. It was reported extensively and took up over half a page.

The shooting party had been a small one as these things go. Henry Trace, David Whiteley (who was described in a delicately worded if unnecessary addendum as assisting Mr Trace), Doctor T. Lessiter, friend of Mr Trace and also his personal physician, Mrs Trace, Miss Phyllis Cadell and two neighbouring landowners George Smollett and Frederick

Lawley. Plus two beaters: Jim Burnet, a farm boy, and Michael Lacey, a young friend of the family.

Mrs Trace was apparently a few yards away from the main party when the accident occurred. As always on these occasions the accounts were confused and sometimes contradictory. Doctor Lessiter thought she had stumbled and was actually falling when the shot ran out, implying that she had tripped and fallen over her gun. She had already stumbled once over a tree root. The doctor admitted that this earlier incident might have contributed to his view of Mrs Trace's death. Michael Lacey said the shot came first but, after being questioned closely by the coroner, seemed less sure. The rest of the group noticed nothing until Mrs Trace was seen to be lying on the ground. Mr Trace, desperate to get to his wife, wrenched his wheelchair round too quickly and tipped it over. The dogs were rushing everywhere; all was confusion. Michael Lacey, nearest to Mrs Trace at the time, ran to the spot but was instructed by the doctor not to touch the injured woman but to run and phone for an ambulance.

Giving evidence, Doctor Lessiter said that Mrs Trace was dying even as he reached her. There was nothing anyone could have done. She did not speak but lost consciousness almost immediately and died a few moments later. There were some technical post-mortem details describing the angle at which the shot had entered the heart and left the body, splintering one of the vertebrae. The point was made both by Doctor Lessiter and Mr Trace that, at the time of the accident, all the other members of the party with the exception of Jim Burnet had been either behind or to the left of Mrs Trace and therefore could not have fired the fatal shot. Jim, although ahead, had been a good thirty yards to her right. Although both beaters had returned later, on Mr Trace's instructions, to search for the shot it had, not unnaturally given the dense surrounding woodland, remained unfound. The coroner expressed his condolences to the bereaved man and issued a verdict of Accidental Death.

Barnaby read the report again. It was very clearly written, everything seemed quite straightforward, yet there was something bothering him. Something buried in there that didn't seem quite right.

He returned three of the papers to the desiccated old man – who seemed even less interested to have them back than he was to part with them in the first place – and showed his warrant card. 'I'd like a photostat of this report,' he said, drawing a rapid circle around the details of the inquest.

''Ere!' The remains sparked inadvertently to life. 'You can't do that. That's from the files!'

'Is it?' Barnaby looked at the circle severely and shook his head. 'I don't know what the world's coming to and that's a fact. By four o'clock if that's all right with you.'

Chapter Six

The chief inspector noticed as Troy drove down Church Lane that Beehive Cottage already had a faintly neglected air, like that of a recently abandoned shell. The edging plants were straggling over the path, the curtains hung straight and still. On the wall outside Miss Bellringer's house Wellington lay, swiping at and occasionally consuming passing butterflies.

Opposite the layby where the houses ended a wooden sign said: Gessler Tye: One Mile. The track was quite wide and tyre marks were clearly visible. Barnaby indicated that they should drive down and Troy eased the car carefully between the edges.

'Good job we're not in the Rover, sir.'

'If we were in the Rover,' snapped Barnaby, 'I'd hardly be asking you to attempt it, would I?' His chicken and watercress sandwich had met with and was being vanquished by Mrs Rainbird's monstrously calorific spread. And he had left his tablets in the office.

'Suppose you wouldn't, sir.' Sergeant Troy thought Barnaby was a good name for someone who was always behaving like a bear with a sore head, and pictured himself in some years' time cutting his own sergeant down to size. He drove through a gap in the hedge which opened out into a large piece of roughly levelled ground and parked. Both men got out.

Creepy, thought Troy at his first sight of Holly Cottage. It was grey and austere, squatting on the very edge of the wood like a humped toad. In spite of the warmth of the day he shivered. You could imagine a witch crawling out of there all right and gobbling up Hansel and Gretel. Really Grimm. He smirked a little at his cleverness, wondered whether to relay this witticism to Barnaby, and decided against it. Things were fraught enough today as it was.

Then, as they approached the porch, the sun came out, striking the south-facing wall. The flints caught fire, glowing with the most subtle colours. Barnaby touched one. It was like a huge boiled sweet, all toffee-brown and cream striations. He knocked on the door. No reply.

He noticed a honeysuckle then, almost at his feet, small and struggling in a rank clump of nettles. Perhaps the girl had planted it, weeding the ground, watering, no doubt hoping that it would eventually climb all over the porch. Two flowers had opened against all the odds. It looked like a Serotina.

'Let's try the back.'

Behind the house was a small concrete yard, many more nettles, a water butt greenly stagnant with a thick crust of slime and three black plastic bags suppurating with rubbish. There were also two small windows, the panes filmed with dust. Barnaby rubbed at one and peered through.

A man wearing a blue shirt and corduroy jeans stained with paint was standing at an easel. He had his back to the window. He seemed to be working feverishly, the brush shifting from palette to canvas and back again in sharp, almost stabbing movements.

'He must have heard us, sir.'

'Oh I don't know. People in the throes of creation . . . he's probably miles away.'

Sergeant Troy sniffed. The idea that painting made you deaf was not one that he was prepared to countenance. He had no time for what he called the arty-farty element who contributed nothing whatever of value to society and then expected to be paid good money for it. Barnaby rapped on the window.

Immediately the man swung round. There was a blur of movement, a white face quickly turned away, and he almost ran from the room, slamming the door behind him. Barnaby heard a key turn then walked quickly back to the front of the house. He and Troy arrived in the porch just as Michael Lacey opened the door.

He was only slightly taller than his sister and enough like her to make the relationship unmistakable. The same deep violet eyes, the same dark hair cut very short and curling tightly all over his well-shaped head. He had neat small ears set rather far back which, coupled with the wide-set eyes, gave him a slightly dangerous look, like that of a wicked horse.

Remembering Mrs Rainbird's remark about the iron, Barnaby was expecting to see some dramatic and livid mutilation but, at first glance, Michael Lacey's face seemed completely unmarked. Then Barnaby noticed that from the top of the left cheekbone down to the corner of his mouth the skin was unnaturally tight; glassy sugar-pig pink skin. It must have been some burn to have needed a graft that size. As well as good looks (which the strangely shining strip of skin hardly seemed to mar) he exuded crackling sardonic masculinity. Not warmth, though. Michael Lacey would organize the world and its inhabitants to suit himself. Barnaby felt sorry for Judy Lessiter. And even, come to that, for the repellent Mr Rainbird.

He said, 'May we come in for a moment?'

'What do you want?'

'We're police officers –'

'So you're police officers. What am I supposed to do? Run up a flag?'

'We're visiting everyone in the village –'

'I don't live in the village. I'm amazed that your deductive powers have led you to believe that I do.'

'– and the surrounding area. This is quite usual, Mr Lacey, during a general –'

'Look. I'm sorry about Miss Simpson. I liked her. But I take no part in village affairs, as any of the local gossips will confirm. And now you'll have to excuse me –'

'We won't keep you a moment, sir.' Barnaby moved forward very slightly and Michael Lacey stepped back very slightly, just enough to let the two men enter the cottage. Uncarpeted stairs were directly to the left of him and he sat on them, leaving the other two standing.

'Did you know Miss Simpson well?'

'I don't know anyone well. She let me do a series of paintings of her garden . . . different times of the year . . . but that was ages ago. I hadn't seen her for . . . ohh . . . a couple of months at least.' He gazed at the chief inspector, alert, detached, a little amused, deciding to treat this enforced interruption as an entertainment.

'Could you tell me where you were on the afternoon and evening of last Friday?'

'Here.'

'Well that's certainly a prompt reply, Mr Lacey. Don't you need to reflect at all?'

'No. I'm always here. Working. Sometimes I take a break to walk in the woods.'

'And did you walk in the woods that day?' inquired Barnaby.

'I may have done. I really don't remember. As all my days are the same I don't need to keep a diary.'

'It seems rather a dull life for a young man.'

Michael Lacey looked at his bare feet. They were beautiful feet: long, narrow, elegant, with papery skin and fine bones.

Byzantine feet. Then he looked directly at Barnaby and said, 'My work is my life.' He spoke quietly but with such a charge of passionate conviction that Barnaby, dabbler in water-colours, casual member of the Causton Arts Circle, felt a stab of envy. He then told himself that conviction didn't mean talent, as many an exposure to Joyce's drama group had confirmed. Armed with this rather churlish perception, he said, 'There are one or two more questions, Mr Lacey, if you wouldn't mind –'

'But I do mind. I hate being interrupted.'

'I understand,' continued Barnaby smoothly, 'that you were present when the late Mrs Trace was killed.'

'Bella?' He looked puzzled. 'Yes I was but I can't see . . .' He paused. 'You don't think there's any connection . . . ?' His previous animosity seemed forgotten. He looked genuinely interested. 'No . . . how could there be?'

'I gather from the newspaper report that you were the first person to reach Mrs Trace.'

'That's right. Lessiter said not to touch her but to run and ring for an ambulance, which I did.'

'Was there anyone at Tye House at the time?'

'Only Katherine. Toadying away like mad.'

'I beg your pardon?'

'In the kitchen making sandwiches, stuffing vol au vents, chopping up hunter's pie.'

'Whilst you were helping with the beating.'

'That's different. I was being paid!' Barnaby's dig stung the anger back into his voice. He confirmed that no one in the party had been in a position to shoot Mrs Trace, then said, 'I don't know why you're asking me. I didn't even have a gun.'

'I understand that you and the other beater searched for the cartridge afterwards?'

'I wouldn't put it quite as strongly as that. We had a

cursory poke round but it seemed so pointless that we soon gave up.'

'Thank you, Mr Lacey.'

As the two policemen climbed into the car Troy, remembering his earlier gaffe about the Rover, strove to think of something perceptive and intelligent to say. 'Did you notice that he locked the door of the room where he was painting? I thought that was a bit strange.'

'Oh, I don't know. Creative people often have an intensely protective attitude about work in progress. Look at Jane Austen's creaking door.'

Sergeant Troy reversed, using a large, double-sided mirror which had been fixed in the hedge, giving a view of the approaching path and the front of the cottage. 'That's a point, sir,' he replied. There was no way he was going to let on he knew nothing of Jane Austen's creaking door. As for Michael Lacey being love's young dream, well . . . He glanced in the mirror and briefly smoothed his carrot-coloured hair. Surely it was only in romantic novels that girls preferred dark men.

Michael Lacey watched from the porch while the car drove away then returned to his studio. He picked up his palette and brush, stared at the easel for a moment, then put them down again. The light was dying. In spite of the recent interruption he had had a good day. Sometimes he worked in a fury of resentment; tearing up sketches, painting over scenes that would not come right in a frenzy, occasionally weeping with rage. But days like that paid for days like this. From the striving came, sometimes, a marvellous and felicitous ease. He studied the figure in the painting. There was still a lot to do. He had put on the dead colour, that was all. But he was excited by it. He had the absolute conviction that it was going to be successful. It was tremendous when that happened. The belief that, no matter what he did, how he approached it, whatever the technique, it was going to work. His conviction was so strong that he felt he couldn't spoil it even if he tried.

He went to the kitchen and opened a can of baked beans and sausages and, spooning them into his mouth, returned to his workroom. The fading light appeared to alter the shape of the place, made the walls shifting and amorphous. Four vast abstracts covered with thick white paint loomed at him from a few feet away. In the corner of each was a dark, imploding star, now no more than a smudge in the crepuscular light.

On top of the corner cupboard was an old-fashioned pewter student's lamp. He lit the candle and wandered round the room looking at the many canvases stacked against the walls. Although there was a strong fluorescent strip light on the ceiling Michael Lacey loved the effect of candles. Colours on the paintings became richer, many-layered; eyes seemed to flicker and mouths twitch with the illusion of light. Solid flesh was transformed into something rare and delicate. The effect was stimulating and seemed to fill his mind with wonderful and subtle ideas.

In the corner cupboard was a pile of paperbacks and art catalogues, all well thumbed, the spines cracked and, in some cases, broken. He pulled one out at random and sat contemplating a plate by Botticelli. How seductive, he thought, the tender vivacious faces adorned with fresh spring flowers. He finished the beans and sat for a moment longer utterly content, imagining himself walking round the Uffizi, standing in homage in front of the original. Then he opened the window, threw up the tin and kicked it, a shining arc, through the window and into the night.

Chapter Seven

Late that evening Barnaby sat toying with a salad. He had deliberately stayed on at the station, looking through the proformas as they appeared in his tray, until he felt dinner would be beyond redemption and a tin opened with no hard feelings. He had forgotten there were such things as tomatoes and cucumber and beetroot . . .

One would have thought that not even Joyce could have maltreated a salad to the point where it became inedible, but one would have been wrong. Abustle with wild life, it was also soaked in a vinegary dressing. Barnaby lifted a soggy lettuce leaf. A small insect emerged, valiantly swimming against the tide.

'It's Bakewell Surprise for afters,' she called from the kitchen, doubly percipient. He was hungry too. This last phenomenon always surprised him. It was rather touching, really: no matter how much stick he gave his stomach there it was, a few hours later, hopeful if apprehensive, wondering if this time its luck would change.

'And Cully's coming next weekend.' She gave him the tart, a cup of tea and a fond kiss. 'All right?'

'Lovely. How long for?'

'Just till Sunday teatime.'

Barnaby and Joyce looked at each other. They both loved and were immensely proud of their only child. And they both thought it much nicer when she was not at home. Neither of them ever said so. Even when quite small Cully had had a sharp eye and an unkind tongue. Both had become more finely honed with the passing years. Outstanding at school, she was now reading English at New Hall and confidently expected to get a good second in spite of the fact that she seemed to Barnaby to spend all her time rehearsing some play or other.

'Will you be able to pick her up on Saturday?'

'Not sure.' Barnaby put his Bakewell Surprise to the sword, which was more than it deserved, and wondered what his daughter would be next seen wearing. She had always dressed in a provoking manner but he and Joyce had assumed, seeing her off on the Cambridge train, that the days of dishcloth and safety-pin skirts and tie and dye makeup were over (indeed they half expected her to be sent smartly home again) but each brief and infrequent visit since had presented them with ever more exotic and alarming transformations. The nice thing about these occasions was that having left home, as she put it, whilst she still had her health and strength, Cully protected these twin assets by always arriving with a goodly supply of gorgeous food from Marks and Spencers and Joshua Taylor's deli.

'You won't forget to ring your father?'

Barnaby took his tea and sat by the fireplace. As he had been ringing his parents once a week for a quarter of a century he'd hardly be likely to. They were both in their eighties and had retired to just outside Eastbourne twenty years before. There they inhaled the ozone, played bowls and gardened, as spry as tinkers.

'No, I won't.'

'Do it now before you settle down.'

'I have settled down.'

'Then you can enjoy your tea.'

Barnaby dutifully hauled himself out of his chair. His

mother answered the phone and, after a token inquiry about his own health and that of his family, launched into an account of her week which included a splendid row at the Arts Circle when a nonagenarian had suggested a life class. She ended, as she always did, by saying, 'I'll just call Daddy.'

Barnaby senior then described his week which had included a splendid row at a meeting of the preservation society over a Victorian bandstand. What a bellicose lot they were down there, thought Barnaby who, when his parents had moved, had pictured them passing their hours dozing peacefully in their conservatory. A rather unsound piece of image-making, he now admitted. They had never been the dozing kind. His father finished describing how he had finally scuppered an unscrupulous opponent on the bowling green.

Barnaby listened patiently then said, almost as an afterthought, 'Never mind. We're in the middle of the cricket season. I expect you're glued to the set most days.'

'Certainly am. Rented one of those video gadgets. Play back the best bits. Terrible about Friday, wasn't it?'

Barnaby smiled indulgently. His father must know that he was never around in the daytime to watch cricket, yet always assumed he knew exactly what was being discussed.

'What happened?'

'Why, no match, dear boy. Not enough light. The umpire offered Allenby the option and he decided to stop play. Eleven ack-emma. Everything was ready this end. Cucumber sandwiches, jug of mint tea. Settled in for the duration. We were totally distraught. Well, to be honest, your mother wasn't too bothered but it did for my day, I can tell you.'

After due commiserations Barnaby returned to his armchair and a fresh cup of tea. 'People have started lying to me, Joyce.'

'Oh yes, dear . . .' The pale silky knitting grew. 'In this business at Badger's Drift, you mean?'

'Mm. Katherine Lacey was seen in the village during the evening she said she didn't go out. Judy Lessiter said she was at work all afternoon and was seen in the village shop at half-past three. Trevor Lessiter said he was at home watching cricket . . . "superb bowling" . . . and the match was cancelled. And Phyllis Cadell went rigid with fright when she saw us, then tried to cover it by some silly story about her road tax.'

'Goodness . . . that seems plenty to be going on with.' The names meant nothing to Joyce Barnaby and she knew Tom was really only thinking aloud, getting his thoughts into some sort of order. She listened intently all the same.

'And Barbara Lessiter, the esteemed doctor's wife, had something in this morning's mail that turned her white as a sheet.'

'How do you know?' Barnaby told her. 'Oh – it's probably a final demand. I expect she's been buying clothes and run up a terrible bill somewhere.'

'No.' Barnaby shook his head. 'It was something more than that. And where was she the night Emily Simpson died? Driving round. Very vague.'

'But innocent people are vague. They don't always have alibis. Or know precisely what they were doing and when. You've always said that. What was she doing in the afternoon?'

'Shopping in Causton.'

'There you are, then,' said Joyce, irrefutably. 'She's been overspending.'

Barnaby smiled across at her, drained his cup and replaced it in the saucer. Something told him that it was not that simple. That none of it was going to be that simple.

Chapter Eight

Next morning, the day before the inquest was due to be reconvened, Barnaby got to his office early and settled down for a rapid read-through of pro-formas, statements and reports. The gist of these would later be transferred to a rotating card system (they were still waiting for a computer). He called for some coffee and began.

He read fast and skilfully, seizing on tiny details, passing quickly over the mundane and merely repetitious. The result was pretty much as he had expected. The only males in the village not at work on the afternoon of the seventeenth or at home with their wives were two unemployed men who spent the time on their respective allotments in full view of each other. The vicar had been in his study working on next week's sermon. A fact confirmed by his housekeeper who had been making jam in the kitchen and was highly indignant that the vicar, a frail old party of seventy-three, should have been questioned at all. In the evening the men were either at home with their families or in the Black Boy. Policewoman Brierley brought in the coffee and Barnaby took it gratefully.

The women of Badger's Drift also seemed to be accounted for. Some were out at work. The old ones at home. The rest (with the exception of Mrs Quine) in the village hall preparing for the morrow. The young women who had left the hall in plenty of time for a quick frolic in the bracken had all met their children off the school bus and gone home to a blameless tea. In the evening three carloads had gone to Causton for a keep-fit class and the rest had stayed at home. Assuming that the couple in the woods were inhabitants of the village, which Barnaby was still inclined to do, the circle of suspects was very small indeed.

He finished his coffee, noting with some surprise, as the liquid went down, the gradual emergence of a green frog wearing a friendly smile and a straw boater, and playing a banjo. He turned to the scene-of-crime reports.

There were not many surprises. The larder window had been forced and traces of white paint were on the inside shelf. There was not, alas, the weather being dry, a lump of mud with the pattern of a shoe sole clearly visible. No fingerprints on the piecrust table, the hemlock-filled jar, garden trowel, door handles and all the other places one would expect to find fingerprints. And none on the telephone – which was strange, as the last person to handle that should have been Doctor Lessiter. And what reason would he have for wiping it clean? The pencil mark on the copy of *Julius Caesar* was a 6B. Not perhaps as common as some but hardly a vanishing species. The pencil had not been found. Elimination tests showed that any prints belonged either to the deceased or to Miss Lucy Bellringer.

He skimmed the second report again briefly but he had missed very little the first time. A search for the rug was in progress but Barnaby was not optimistic. Anyone who was so punctilious over fingerprints would hardly leave the thing lying around in the back of a car or flung over a sofa. Of course it was hardly common knowledge that the fibres of a rug had been found and not everyone knew that semen stains were as conclusive as fingerprints. The police might just be lucky. Troy opened the door.

'Car ready when you are, Chief.'

* * *

'Of course, sir,' said Sergeant Troy, turning off the Gessler Tye road towards Badger's Drift, 'that could've been arse bandits in the woods. You know . . . gay.' There could not have been more venom in the last word if the couple had been seen devouring children.

This was the fifth suggestion he had made in the last ten minutes, all scrupulously punctuated with 'sirs'. He was very free with his 'sirs', was Troy. You couldn't fault him on etiquette. Nor on discipline. Sergeant Troy played it by the book. He passed his exams with room to spare, his reports were models of concise yet comprehensive information. He was without the silly romanticism that lured so many men and women into the force and also without the rather watery compassion that usually evaporated when confronted by their first one hundred per cent amoral, ruthlessly proficient, frequently armed villain. Especially he was without the compassion. He was about to chirp up again. Really, thought the chief inspector, with a more likable personality you could have called him irrepressible.

Before Troy could speak Barnaby said, 'That had occurred to me as well but, as far as we know, only Dennis Rainbird fits that description. I checked with his partner and he definitely didn't leave work until quarter to five on the Friday. Also there seems to be no reason why he should conceal any such relationship. It's no longer against the law.'

'More's the pity,' said Troy, adding, with unusual percipience, 'I bet his mother would be jealous, though.' Then, 'Shan't we be a bit early for the Lessiter girl?'

'It's her half day.'

'*Oh my God!*' Sergeant Troy slammed on the brakes. The car screamed to a stop. Barnaby pitched forward, saved from a collision with the windscreen by his belt. A figure had leapt out from behind the village post box almost directly in their path. Barnaby wound the window down and spoke through blanched lips.

'It's really not a good idea, Miss Bellringer—'

'How fortuitous.' She beamed at them. A faint scent of carnations and orris root pervaded the interior of the car. Before Barnaby could stop her she had opened the door, climbed in and disposed herself on the back seat. 'Now,' she said, 'first and before I forget, the funeral's tomorrow. Eleven-thirty. I don't know if you wish to come?'

Barnaby murmured something noncommittal. Sergeant Troy dug out a packet of Chesterfields with trembling fingers.

'And don't do that in here, young man. You'll put us all at risk.' He dropped the cigarettes on his lap, leaned back and closed his eyes. 'Now,' she smiled sweetly at Barnaby, 'tell me how you're getting on with your disquisition. Are you any further forrard?'

'We're continuing our investigations.'

'There's no need to be so hoity-toity, Chief Inspector. After all if it weren't for me you wouldn't have a case at all. And you did say I could help.' She accompanied this outrageous lie with a shining glance, as clear and candid as a child's. Before Barnaby could get his breath she added, 'Have you spoken to that dreadful Mrs Rainbird?'

'We have.'

'What's she say? Did she see anything?'

The chief inspector saw no need to conceal Mrs Rainbird's revelations. No doubt they were all over the village by now. 'She did see Miss Lacey that evening. Going out to post a letter.'

'Hmmn.' Miss Bellringer snorted. 'That girl is far too beautiful for other people's good. Look here – there's no point in dancing around the mulberry bush. It's pretty obvious to an old hand like myself why we're all being questioned about the afternoon as well as the evening. Emily saw something in the woods and it's my belief that what we're talking about here is illicit passion.' Her voice rang out, investing the words with positively Brontëan splendour. 'To wit Katherine Lacey and her *inamorato*. It's as plain as a horse's tail. Can you imagine what discovery would have meant? No marriage, for a start. Henry might be besotted but he's not that much of a fool. It would have been goodbye to Tye House and all that money and, incidentally, to an easily cuckolded spouse. Madly in love and confined to a wheel-chair? Talk about a combination devoutly to be wished. She'd be able to do more or less as she liked. And there's bad blood in that family. The father was no good. Drove his poor wife into her grave.'

'So I understand.'

'Old sins cast long shadows.' Barnaby was silent. 'Did Mrs R see the girl coming back?'

'Apparently not. She started playing Monopoly with her son.'

'The slithy tove?' Barnaby smiled appreciatively.

'She did say Miss Lacey had one of the beagles with her.'

'*One of the beagles.*' Miss Bellringer seized his arm. 'Are you sure?'

'Mrs Rainbird's sure.'

She crumpled back into her seat. Even her buoyant draperies, today trimmed with what looked like shredded beetroot, seemed to wilt. 'Then our case collapses.'

'Why is that?' asked the chief inspector, letting the 'our' pass for the time being.

'There was no noise from Benjy. He was good if a person he knew came to the door . . . good as gold . . . but let another dog as much as set foot in the garden and he went berserk. And I would certainly have heard him. Living so close.'

'Perhaps Miss Lacey could have tied him up,' suggested

Troy, stimulated in spite of himself by the vitality of the narrative. 'The beagle I mean.'

'Hooo.' A sound like a ship's hooter. 'You don't know beagles. They won't sit meekly down and wait while you go about your business. They're a highly vociferous lot. If she'd tied him up the whole village would have known about it. No – not a dog barked, I'm sure. Ah well' – she opened the right-hand door, knocking ten years off the life of a passing cyclist, and stepped smartly out – 'we'll have to think again. I'm loathe to part with the Laceys, mind you. What about the brother?'

'The brother has no motive, Miss Bellringer. And now I'm afraid you'll have to excuse me.'

'If someone had wrung her neck I could understand it.' Troy drew a deep, juddering breath as he drove off. 'They just don't care, do they? Your genuine eccentrics? They don't care what you think.'

'A genuine eccentric,' replied Barnaby, 'doesn't even notice what you think.' He added, 'Keep an eye out for that dog,' as Troy entered the cobbled yard of Tye House and parked, almost chastely and quite without his usual pizzaz, near the kitchen door. But the warning was unnecessary. Benjy did not come to meet them but lay on the step, very thin, his grey muzzle resting on his paws. His tail heaved off the ground and thumped up and down once or twice as he peered anxiously towards them. Like Ulysses' hound he waited, faithful to the last.

'Poor old boy,' said the sergeant. 'Good boy.' He was about to stroke the dog but as he bent down Benjy turned his head and something in his eyes stayed Troy's hand. 'They should've had this dog seen to by now.'

Barnaby pointed to the far end of the lawn. 'In the garden,' he said. As the two men descended the steps between the stone urns brimming with flowers he felt a welcome breeze against his temples. It pressed the lemon voile of Katharine Lacey's dress close against the slender curves of her body. She was standing behind Henry's chair, her arms across his chest, her head close to his. As Barnaby approached she pointed to a nearby grove of poplars. Henry shook his head and they both laughed. Then she started to push the chair in Barnaby's direction.

'We're going to have a hundred people here on Saturday, Inspector,' called Trace. 'Where do you think we should put the marquee?'

Spoilt for choice, really, thought Troy, in a garden that size. Still all the money in the world wouldn't make his legs more lively. Imagine going down the aisle to a gorgeous piece of skirt like that in a wheelchair. He smiled confidently and said, 'Good afternoon, Miss Lacey.'

'Wherever we put it,' she smiled at the two policemen, 'it's going to make a terrible mess.'

'Oh grass soon recovers,' replid Henry. 'Are you a gardening man, Inspector Barnaby?'

Barnaby indicated that he was and asked if they'd come to any decision yet about the rosarium. This led to a lot of pleasant horticultural chat and to Henry describing his wedding gift for Katherine, which was nineteen old-fashioned moss and climbing roses: 'A flower for each year of her life.'

'Then we shall plant one on all our wedding anniversaries until we're old and grey,' said Katherine. 'And that will be our rosarium.'

Barnaby let this amiable pool of conversation fill up for a while then dropped his stone. 'Oh – a small point, Miss Lacey. When I spoke to you a few days ago I understood you to say that you spent the evening of the seventeenth here with Mr Trace.'

'That's right, I did.'

'And you didn't go out at all?'

'No. We were here all the time.'

'You were seen walking in the village.'

'Me?' She looked genuinely puzzled. 'But I couldn't have – Oh! Of course. I ran out to post a letter. D'you remember, darling? We said we'd order a Notcutt's catalogue and I thought I'd do it straight away.'

'Wouldn't it be quicker to do that by telephone?'

'They're not free. You have to send a cheque.'

'That would be their main branch at Woodbridge?' She nodded. 'Do you remember how long you were out?'

'Not exactly. I just ran Peel to the end of Church Lane and home again. Surely,' she added crisply, 'whoever saw me going out saw me coming back?'

'Apparently not.'

'Dear me. Sleeping at their post were they?'

'You didn't see anyone whilst you were out?'

'Not a soul.'

'You would support what Miss Lacey says, sir?'

'Well . . . I didn't see Katherine leave—'

'No, you dropped off after dinner. That's the only reason I went just then, really.'

'Yes. I often do these days,' he smiled at Barnaby. 'She was certainly here when I woke.' As he was speaking two black and gold vans – 'Lazenby et cie' – crunched over the gravel and through the main gate.

'It's the caterers,' cried Katherine. 'I'd better go—'

'Actually, Miss Lacey, I did want a further word . . .'

'Oh.' She looked at her fiancé uncertainly.

'Don't worry – I'll go.' Henry Trace pushed himself away, making for the wooden ramp by the terrace steps. Katherine followed him slowly, Barnaby by her side, Troy bringing up a salivatory rear.

'I wonder,' said Barnaby, 'if you remember the day Mrs Trace died?'

'Bella? Of course I do.' She looked at him curiously. 'It's not the kind of thing one forgets in a hurry. It was terrible.'

'I understand that you were not a member of the party?'

'No. I stayed here, preparing the tea. Usually Phyllis helped but on that day she went out with the shoot.'

'That was unusual, was it?'

'Very.'

'So the first you knew about the tragedy . . . ?'

'Was when Michael came racing in, grabbed the phone and shouted down it for an ambulance.'

'I see. Would you say . . .' – he hesitated, picking the words over carefully in his mind – 'that Mr and Mrs Trace were happy?'

'Well . . . yes . . . they always seemed so to me. Although of course outsiders never really know, do they? They were both very kind to Michael and myself. And Henry was absolutely distraught when she died.'

Barnaby turned and looked back over the line of poplars and wooded ground beyond. 'Was it over there the accident happened?'

Katherine followed his gaze. 'Oh no . . . in the beechwoods that lie behind Holly Cottage.'

'I see. Well, thank you again.'

They had reached the terraced steps by now and walked up them together. As they crossed the yard Benjy made a sound from the doorstep and staggered to his feet. Katherine turned away from the sight.

'Oh, why won't he eat!' she burst out passionately to the two men. 'I bought him everything – lovely meat, biscuits. He's got his own basket and blanket and dish – everything he had over there . . .'

'They pine, I'm afraid,' said Barnaby.

'But you'd think they'd want to stay alive, however sad they are.'

'He's a pretty old dog, miss,' said Troy sympathetically. 'I think he's just tired. He's had enough.'

'Are you through with Katherine, Chief Inspector? I really need her over here.'

'Well – that's that,' sighed Barnaby a few moments later as they drove away. 'I suppose it was too much to hope that Katherine Lacey and the Lessiter girl would have been wandering up and down Church Lane at the same time last Friday night.'

'But . . . you do believe her, sir?' asked Troy, still a little dazed by the rainbow lustre of the Lacey smile. 'About the letter?'

'Oh yes. I'll get it followed up of course but I've no doubt that she posted it when and where she says. If she's innocent there'd be no point in making up such a story. And if she's guilty she'd make doubly sure anything we could check on was genuine.'

'*Guilty*.' Troy unwisely took his eyes off the road to give Barnaby an incredulous glance and missed the opening to the Lessiters' drive.

'You really must give up this physiognomy, Troy. It can only hinder your career. She's got more to lose than any of them.'

'But the dog, sir. The dog didn't bark.'

'Yes, the dog's a problem, I admit.'

Or perhaps the dog wasn't a problem, he thought as Troy reversed and drove up to the Lessiters' front door. Perhaps the dog meant he could score a line through Katherine Lacey once and for all. One down, six to go. Or seven if he kept a really open mind and included the seemingly impossible Henry Trace. What about if he had fallen hopelessly in love with Katherine when his wife was still alive and had hired someone to lurk in the undergrowth and pop Bella off? Barnaby dragged his attention back to the present and reminded himself yet again that he had no reason to suppose that Mrs Trace's death was anything but an accident. And that he was in fact now engaged in investigating something quite different.

The doctor's surgery still had fifteen minutes to run, which suited the chief inspector very well. Judy Lessiter opened the main door, looking even less attractive than she had the previous day. She had a frowsty air, like that of a small animal emerging after a long period of hibernation.

'Yes.'

'We'd like a word with your father—'

'Surgery round the side.' She started to close the door. Barnaby moved forward. 'And with you also, please.'

She stared at him sullenly for a moment then shrugged and led them into the kitchen. She turned to face them, leaning against the sink.

'Miss Lessiter, you told me earlier that you were in the library during the afternoon of the seventeenth.'

'No I didn't.'

'I'm sorry but I checked your statement before coming here.'

'I said I was at work. I don't stand behind a counter stamping books. Part of my job is to visit schools, technical colleges . . . liaise with administrators, check if there are any projects that may mean ordering special books. On Friday afternoon I was at Gessler Tye primary school.'

'I must say I feel that you have deliberately attempted to mislead us in this matter.'

'That's your problem,' she said rudely.

'So if you would go through your movements again?'

'I take sandwiches for lunch. I ate them then—'

'This is in the library at Pinner?'

'Yes. Made some coffee. Drove to the school, arriving

about two, and stayed till they finished around three forty-five.'

'And you then returned to the library?'

'No. It hardly seemed worth it. I drove straight here . . . stopping off at the village shop for some cigarettes.'

Jammy, thought Sergeant Troy, always convinced that everyone but himself, jobwise, was getting away with murder.

'Your father will vouch for your time of arrival?'

'My father?' She looked puzzled, then wary.

'He was here all afternoon, I understand.'

There was a pause while she looked from Barnaby to Sergeant Troy and back again. 'Is it a trick?'

'What?'

'I mean . . . are you trying to catch me out?'

'I don't understand you, Miss Lessiter. Your father has stated that he was at home all afternoon. I'm merely asking if he can corroborate your time of arrival.'

'Well . . . I went straight upstairs . . . so . . . I wouldn't have seen him.'

'I see. And the evening?'

'Oh I've nothing to change there. I just went for a walk, as I've already said.'

'Down the lane, past the fields for about half a mile, then back?'

'That's right.'

'And you didn't stop anywhere or call on anyone?' He added quickly before she could speak, 'Please think very carefully before you answer.'

She stared at him. He looked serious, encouraging and, somehow, faintly knowledgeable. He could see she was wondering about the close re-questioning. 'Well . . . I'm not sure I remember . . . exactly . . .' She swallowed and chewed her bottom lip.

'I know how difficult it must be to change a story, but if

you need to now's the time to do it. I must remind you that withholding information that may assist a police inquiry is a very serious matter.'

'Oh but I'm not! Nothing that would help, that is . . .'

'I think you should let me be the judge of that.'

'Yes.' She took a deep breath. She stopped leaning on the sink and stood upright looking taut and fearful, like someone preparing for a high dive. 'I have . . . that is I'm friendly with Michael Lacey. At Holly Cottage. I hadn't heard from him for a few days and . . . well, he said he wanted to paint me so I thought I'd . . . drop in . . . you know, to see when he wanted to start.' Barnaby listened sympathetically. In trying to sound casual she had simply underlined her desperation. 'So I walked up to the house but when I got there . . . I could see through the window that he was working—'

'Which window was that?'

'The front window by the porch.'

'He doesn't usually use that room, surely?'

'Sometimes – in the evening. To get the last of the light.'

'Ah, I see. Carry on.'

'He gets very angry if he's disturbed when he's painting. He says it's very hard to get back into the feel of it again. So I thought I'd better not . . . well . . . I just crept away.'

'You think he didn't know you were there?'

'Oh I'm sure he didn't. I was very quiet.' She paused a moment then, looking at Barnaby for the first time, burst out, 'You mustn't believe what people say about Michael. They hate him here because he doesn't care about things they all care about . . . petty, boring things. He's a free spirit! As long as he can paint and walk in the woods and look at the sky . . . and he's been so unhappy. Katherine's so bourgeois – she only cares about material things – and now once the wedding's over he'll be all alone . . .' There was a clarion note of hope in the last few words. For a moment her eyes shone so brilliantly that her rather stodgy face was transformed. Barnaby saw for the first time why Michael Lacey might have asked her to sit for him. He glanced at the clock over the kitchen door. Judy, as if already regretting her passionate declamation, presented her back to them and turned on both the taps. She stood watching the water bouncing off the gleaming metal, hearing the two sets of footsteps move to the door and cross the hall. She reduced the water to a thin colourless stream. The front door closed. She switched the taps off.

Her hands trembled and she gripped the edge of the sink to still them. Talking about Michael always had this effect on her. Describing her abortive visit, her lack of courage and her humiliating retreat on tiptoe, had made her feel quite sick. But it had put the record straight, that was the main thing. She was glad about that. Especially after her silly attempt to be clever about her movements in the afternoon. Then she realized that her recent confession had brought about a secondary benefit. If Miss Simpson's death had been due to foul play (and why else would there be all this questioning?) she had given Michael an alibi. He may well not care about this one way or the other but the fact could not be denied. She hugged this small service to her heart. Perhaps he would never know but it was something she could keep in reserve to be offered up if the right moment ever came.

She heard the click of the phone. It must be Barbara. Judy had been standing so very still and quiet for the past few minutes that her stepmother might have assumed she was in her room. Or in the garden. Because there was something so soft, almost furtive about that click. Judy crept on slippered feet across the vinyl tiles, step by careful step. Barnaby had left the door a little ajar and Judy stood looking through the crack.

Barbara had her back to the kitchen and was shielding the

mouthpiece with her hand. Nevertheless her hoarse whisper made every word clearly audible.

'Darling, I'm sorry but I had to ring. Didn't you get my note? . . . What d'you mean there's nothing you can do? You've got to help me. *You've got to* . . . You must have some money . . . I've done that. I've sold everything that I thought he wouldn't notice, even my coat . . . No, it was being stored for the winter . . . How the hell do I know what I'll say? . . . Three thousand and it cost him ten so I'm still nearly a thousand short. For God's sake – I'm only in this mess because of you . . . You bastard, it wasn't me who said I was counting the hours – I'm sorry, I didn't mean that. Darling? I'm sorry – don't hang up! Please – you *must* help. It'll be the end of everything here if he finds out. You don't know what my life was like before. I'll never go back to that. I'll – hullo, hullo . . . ?'

Feverishly she clicked at the receiver rest. She stood for a moment, her shoulders drooping in despair, then she slammed down the phone and ran back upstairs.

Judy stepped back from her narrow secret observation post and smiled.

The surgery was empty. As they entered, a woman, her skin the colour of clay, came out of the consulting room and stood looking around in dazed disbelief. The receptionist hurried out from her cubicle but the woman pushed past her and the two men, almost running from the room. Doctor Lessiter's buzzer sounded and a moment later they were shown in. He was replacing a file in a big wooden cupboard. 'Horrible part of the job,' he said, sounding brisk and unconcerned, 'there's no way to break bad news is there?'

'Indeed there isn't, Doctor Lessiter.' Barnaby could not have wished for a neater opening. 'I favour the straightforward approach myself. Could you tell me what you were doing on the afternoon of Friday the seventeenth of this month?'

'I've already told you.' He sat behind his desk and got on with a bit of knuckle cracking. 'What an inefficient lot you are, to be sure. Don't tell me you've forgotten already.'

'You stated that you were watching the Test match on television.'

'That's right.'

'All afternoon?'

'Absolutely.' He pulled a final finger. The crack sounded very loud in the quiet room. Suddenly the silence seemed to thicken; change character. The doctor was staring at his fingers with some surprise as if he had never seen them before. He looked at Barnaby's grave features, at Troy and back to Barnaby again. 'Yes. Absolutely . . . that's right.' But the certainty had gone. It was no longer a statement of fact. He had the air of a man who knows he's been rumbled but doesn't yet know how.

'The light stopped play at eleven that morning. For the day.'

'Oh . . . well . . . maybe it was Thursday I watched. Yes, actually it was. I remember now—'

'You have your rounds on Thursday. Or so you declared in your previous statement.'

'Oh yes – of course I do. How silly of me . . .' Sweat beaded his forehead and started to roll, like transparent little glass beads, down his nose. His eyes flickered around the room seeking inspiration from the instrument cabinet, the chrome, rubber-covered examination trolley, the big wooden cupboard. 'I don't see the point of this, you know. I mean we all know the old lady died in the evening.'

'I can assure you our inquiries are very relevant. We don't waste our own and the public's time unnecessarily.'

Trevor Lessiter still did not reply. Barnaby was anxious

not to give him too much leeway. Already he could see the doctor rolling with the punch of his broken alibi, trying to dredge up a suitable alternative. Time for the frighteners.

'You would not deny that you have the knowledge and equipment here to prepare an infusion of hemlock?'

'What! But that's ludicrous . . . you don't need special equipment. Anyone could—'

'Not anyone could sign a death certificate.'

'I've never heard such an outrageous . . . I was here all evening.'

'We only have your word for that, sir.'

'My wife and daughter—'

'Went out, if you recall.'

'I swear to you—'

'You swore to us about your whereabouts that afternoon, Doctor Lessiter. You were lying then. Why should you not be lying now?'

'How dare you.' He swallowed, and his Adam's apple rode furiously up and down as if seeking an escape from his throat. 'I've never heard such—'

'Can you explain why, when you were the last person to use Miss Simpson's telephone, no prints were found on it?'

'Of course not.'

'What reason did you have for wiping that receiver clean?'

'Me! I didn't touch it . . . I didn't.' Some more nervous gulping. 'Look . . . all right . . . I wasn't here in the afternoon. Now, Barnaby . . . will what I'm going to tell you now remain absolutely confidential?'

'I can't guarantee that, I'm afraid. Of course if it doesn't relate to the case there's no reason why it should ever be made public.'

'But it will go on record, won't it?'

'We shall take a further statement, certainly.' Right on cue Troy produced his notebook.

'I'd have to give up the practice if this became public. Leave the area.' Trevor Lessiter slumped in his smart leather chair. His chipmunk cheeks, now quite deflated, were tuckered grey bags. Then the grey flushed red with panic. 'You won't tell my wife?'

'We don't "tell" anyone anything, sir. That's not how we work. Alibis are checked to eliminate the innocent as much as to discover the guilty.'

'Oh,' he cried, 'I haven't done anything wrong.'

The range of people who thought lying to the police wasn't doing anything wrong, reflected Barnaby, was widening all the time. He waited.

'You've ... er ... met my wife, Chief Inspector. I'm envied, I know, by many people ... men that is ...' Here, in spite of his intense anxiety, a shimmer of satisfaction flitted across his features. Barnaby was reminded briefly of Henry Trace. '... but Barbara is ... oh dear, I don't know how to put this without sounding disloyal. She's a wonderful companion ... great fun to be with but not very ...' His face looked smaller, shrunk with embarrassment. He forced a laugh. 'I'd better be John Blunt here, I can see. She's not too interested in the physical side of marriage.'

So much for the fancy wrapping, thought Barnaby, recalling the painted eyes and heavy scent and the twin peaks that might have caused stout Cortez himself a stagger of disbelief.

'So,' continued the doctor, 'obviously wanting her to be happy, I don't press my attentions.' He dropped his gaze, but not before Barnaby had seen a flash of spite and sour resentment in his eyes. The look of a man who has kept his side of the bargain and been sold down the river. 'However' – a light-hearted shrug – 'I have needs ...' Here his left lid trembled on the edge of a collusive wink, '. . . as we all do, and I . . . er . . . occasionally, *very* occasionally, visit an establishment that . . . um . . . caters for them.'

'You mean a brothel?'

'Ohhh!' No longer John Blunt, he looked almost disgusted at Barnaby's lack of finesse. 'I wouldn't say that. Not at all. It's very . . . refined, really. There's a little shop which sells all sorts of jolly things. And they put on a little show. And a get-together with one of the young ladies afterwards if one is so inclined. And one usually is inclined. The performances are quite stimulating. Tasteful but stimulating.'

'And that is where you were on the afternoon of the seventeenth?' The doctor nodded. 'And the name and address of this establishment?'

Lessiter rootled about in his wallet and produced a card. 'Perhaps you know of the . . . er . . . club . . . ?'

Barnaby glanced at the card. 'I believe I do, yes.' He then asked for a photograph.

'*A photograph!*' The doctor gave a horrified squeak.

'Purely for identification purposes. It will be returned, I assure you. Or perhaps you would like to accompany me . . . ?'

'Good God no.' He paused for a moment. 'I've just had some passport pictures done. They're in the study.' He left the room, returning a few minutes later with four neat black and white squares. He handed over two of them. 'I think this one . . . look . . . where I'm smiling is the most—'

'I just need the one, thank you.' As Barnaby turned away the doctor added, 'You must ask for Krystal. She's my special friend.'

Chapter Nine

The Casa Nova was not easily visible to the casual eye. It lurked in a grubby, unpoetic alley, Tennyson Mews, flanked by a stationery warehouse and a handbag factory. The windows of the latter were wide open, inviting the hot July sun into the already stifling workrooms. The smell of baking leather wafted out together with the jungle drumming of machinery. Troy parked near a peeling magenta door half garlanded with sickly lightbulbs offering '10 BEAUTIFUL GIRLS 10' and, eyes alight with anticipation, undid his seat belt.

'Casanova eh?' he sniggered. 'Naughty.'

'New house to you,' replied Barnaby. 'Although I've no doubt the tricks'll be as old as the hills.'

'Looks promising though. Ten beautiful girls.'

'A vulture's egg is promising, son,' replied Barnaby, getting out of the car. 'You can wait here.' He smiled as he pressed the buzzer, feeling the lance of Troy's resentment between his shoulder blades. Barnaby said, 'Krystal please,' to a squawking voice box.

'Mind how you go on the steps, dear.'

The flight of stairs was dimly lit. At the bottom one of the ten beautiful girls – ten – stepped forward. She could have been any age between thirty and sixty. The only certain thing was she hadn't been a girl since he'd been a boy scout. Her hair had the colour and dusty bloom of black grapes. She wore lipstick like vermilion Vaseline and thick makeup journeyed over the eruptions and into the craters of her complexion. You could join all those dots up till the cows came home, thought Barnaby, and never reach the hidden treasure. She wore leopard-patterned shorts, a matching open-ended bra and heels so high that she seemed to be balancing on patent-leather stilts. She teetered forward, held his arm with an expert touch and smiled, showing teeth like pearls from a polluted oyster.

'I expect you want to be a naughty boy, don't you, dear?'

'Not really,' said Barnaby, disengaging himself and producing his warrant card.

'Jeezuseffchrist. What the hell do you want? We're all legal here, you know.'

'I'm sure.' He produced the passport snap. 'Do you know this man?'

A quick glance. 'Course I do. That's Mr Lovejoy.'

'Was he here last Friday afternoon? The seventeenth?'

'He bloody lives here, mate.'

'I need to know precisely.'

'You'd better talk to Krystal then.'

'Would you ask her to come here, please.'

'She'll come anywhere will that one – for a price.' She gave him a nudge. 'You look a well-set-up bloke. Why don't you pop back when you're off duty? Loosen up a bit. Treat yourself.' She gave his blank stare a minute to change its mind and then said, 'Oh well – be miserable then. Krystal's doing the art class. She'll be ten minutes yet. Second door on the right.'

Barnaby lifted a velvet curtain and found himself in a cold stone corridor. There were doors on both sides. He opened the second on the right and found himself facing another very musty curtain. He pushed this aside and passed through with unnecessary caution. Not a head turned. They were all watching the stage.

On a brightly lit dais a well-developed girl stood registering alarm in the commedia dell'arte manner: eyes wide, hands splayed out to ward off danger, half turning to flee. She wore a schoolgirl's pleated skirt, white shirt and blazer. A felt hat with a striped band perched insecurely on her head. She had waist-length blond hair. A young man in tight trousers, velvet jacket and matching beret was painting the air in front of an easel. A harsh male voice, underpinned by a lot of martial bump and grind music, blasted out of two wall speakers.

'And so the lovely Bridgeat, desperate to purchase medicines for her dying father, was tricked by the notorious artist Fouquet into leaving the convent and posing in his attic studio. Despite his fervid assurances to the contrary the lecherous Fouquet revealed, once she was securely in his lair, that the money would be paid only for a nude study!'

Here the young man mimed rather graphically what he wanted the lovely Brigitte to do. She wept and wailed and wrung her hands, then, tremblingly, affectingly, started to undress. First the blazer, then the little white schoolgirl blouse that she was bursting out of, then the tiny pleated skirt. She cowered realistically, folding slender arms across an extravagantly ample bosom. The voice crackled on.

'"If you wish to save your beloved father's life you know what you must do," cried the evil Fouquet.'

Weeping, the girl removed her lace-up shoes, knee socks and bra. The evil Fouquet, not to be outdone, slipped out of his velvet smock, revealing a hairless dark brown chest. Brigitte was now left in the sort of briefs any self-respecting Mother Superior would have consigned to the flames with tongs.

'But as the lascivious artiste attempted to position the lovely virgin he was swept away on a tide of desire.'

Surprise, surprise, thought Barnaby, yawning. He slipped

back through the curtain and waited in the Colditz corridor. The dreary posturings in the art class gave him a sudden sharp perspective on his home life and the clean sweet embraces he shared with Joyce. So her Bakewell Surprise could double as a manhole cover. So his daughter looked like the wreck of the *Hesperus* and had a Swiftian line in put-downs. He compared her with Doctor Lessiter's special friend and counted his blessings.

Released at last by a fake orgasmic cry, the punters shuffled out. Young, middle-aged, elderly. No one, it seemed, had come with a mate. They emerged solitarily, blinking in the hard light, like melancholy moles. He gave it a few moments then re-entered the room.

'Brigitte' was perched on the artist's stool, smoking and wearing a wrapper. Her flesh shimmered through the gauzy stuff. The pearly flesh, long silver-white curls and butter-milky complexion gave her an appearance of wholesomeness totally at variance with her surroundings. She looked as if she would be more at home on a farm milking something. She spoke.

'Give us a bleeding chance, lover. Next show's half an hour. Pay outside.' He produced his wallet. 'Fuckin 'ell.' She stubbed out her cigarette but not before he had recognized the smell. 'I don't take the hard stuff, you know. You'd be on something, believe you me, if you had this bloody job.'

'I'm making one or two inquiries—'

'I'm not talking to you without witnesses.' She disappeared through a door behind the stage. It opened directly on to a tiny dressing room. Barnaby just managed to squeeze in. The room stank of cheap scent, hair lacquer, sweat and cigarette smoke. It was occupied by two girls, their rear ends shoe-horned on to a couple of plastic chairs. They wore bright bedraggled feathers and nipple stars. They sussed him straight away, giving him hard aggrieved stares.

'What you done then, Kris?'

'Bugger all. And he can't say I have.'

Barnaby showed her the photograph of Trevor Lessiter. 'Do you know this man?'

'Yeah – that's poor old Loveless. Or Lovejoy as he calls himself. Dunno what 'is real name is.'

'Was he here last Friday afternoon?'

'He's here every Friday afternoon. And Monday and Wednesday. He's no trouble. A bit of bondage. The daffodil routine. But mostly straight. His wife won't let him 'ave any, you know.'

'Yeah.' This interjection from the red feathers had the force of a bunched fist. ''E gave her a mink coat for Christmas an' all.'

'I worked it out,' said Krystal, 'and I told him. I'd have to do it five hundred times to buy a mink. A decent one, I mean – not one that scarpered back to the zoo the minute the whistle went.'

'You'd be too shagged out to wear it, Kris.'

'You bloody reckon?' She gave a mirthless shriek.

'They stink an' all if you're out in the rain,' said the red nipple stars. 'Them that fall off the back of the bunny wagon.' More mirthless shrieks. Barnaby cut in firmly.

'Can you tell me what time Mr Lovejoy left last Friday?'

'Half-past five. I remember 'cause that's when I knock off for an hour. He asked me to go and have some tea with him. He was always asking me out. You have to pretend . . . you know . . . that you like them, and then, some of them – the simple ones – they really believe you. Try to get you to meet them outside. It's pathetic, really.'

She raised both hands and lifted the heavy mass of silver curls. Underneath lay dirty red hair chopped savagely and clumsily short. She grinned at the chief inspector's involuntary start of surprise.

'He thought it was real – didn't you, sunshine?'

'I love the innocent ones, don't you?' said the girl with the strong vocal attack. 'They really make you want to piss yourself.'

'I was innocent once,' said Krystal. 'I thought a dildo was a prehistoric bird before I discovered this place.'

Caws of laughter; the tattered feathers shook. They gazed at him with hard bright eyes. They looked both predatory and harmless, like debeaked birds of prey. He made an excuse and left.

Chapter Ten

The little country church was packed. Barnaby slipped in unnoticed and stood behind a rear pillar. It was a brilliant day; sun poured through the clerestory windows. Behind the chancel rail all was white: the white-haired, white-robed vicar; two lovely arrangements of white flowers flanking the altar; a simple sheaf of lilies on the small coffin.

Most of the mourners were in ordinary clothes but there was an inky spattering of black. Several men wore arm bands, some of the women dark scarves. Barnaby was surprised to see that almost a quarter of the gathering were what he thought of as young: i.e. under thirty.

Miss Bellringer, clad in rusty, jet-encrusted black, sat in the front right-hand pew, her eagle profile expressionless under a plumed cavalier hat, her eyes dry. In the opposite pew (kept for the squire and his relations?) Henry Trace sat, sombre-suited, with Katherine. She wore a coffee-coloured silk dress and a black chiffon scarf with little gold coins sewn into the edge. The Lessiters sat, together but separately, staring straight ahead. You would never have thought they were a family.

Dennis in his role as usher had gone right over the top, tying a huge black bow to his arm, the ends shyly resting on his hip. His mother lay, becalmed, a mountain of bullet-coloured taffeta and grey net veiling in the second pew. Mrs Quine was there showily wiping away a non-existent tear, with Lisa Dawn still sighing and snuffling. Phyllis Cadell was in navy, David Whiteley in jeans and a dark striped shirt. In the back row the old man Jake wept openly, mopping up his tears with a red-spotted handkerchief. Then, when everyone knelt and Henry Trace bowed his head, Barnaby saw Michael Lacey, who remained upright in his seat glancing round at the respectful congregation with a mixture of impatience and scorn. He had made no concession to propriety and was wearing a paint-stained boiler suit and a peaked denim cap.

'For man that is born of woman hath but a short time to live . . .'

Emily Simpson had lived, by comparison with a large proportion of the world's population, quite a long time, but she had still not been allowed her allotted span. No one, thought Barnaby, should be sent out on to that long journey a day, an hour or even a second before their natural time. He loosened his collar against the heat, closed his eyes and rested his forehead for a moment on the cool stone.

Figures moved behind his lowered lids: Laceys and Lessiters, Phyllis Cadell, David Whiteley, the Rainbirds, Henry Trace. They approached each other, met, mingled, broke apart in a passionless pavane. Who belonged with whom? If he knew that he would know everything.

Barnaby had started dreaming about the couple in the woods: two shapes twisting and turning, loops and knots of white limbs now fixed like sculpture, now softly melting together. Last night they had spun very slowly, a mobile of lust on an invisible thread, and he had waited in his sleep, breath seemingly held, for his first sight of their faces. But as the figures finished their slow circumfluence all he saw were two blank white hairless ovals.

A beam of dust-filled sunlight ambered the sheaf of lilies. Everyone rose to sing 'The Day Thou Gavest Lord is Ended'. Behind Barnaby a dark branch of yew, activated by a sudden flurry of wind, knocked on the glass.

PART THREE

REPETITION

Chapter One

On the afternoon the inquest was reconvened the coroner's court was packed. Every light-oak-stained folding seat was taken. Badger's Drift seemed to have turned out in its entirety. It appeared (Barnaby scanned the rows of faces) that only David Whiteley and Michael Lacey had not turned up. The jury – striving to look serious, disinterested and worthy of the trust placed – were in position.

Barbara Lessiter was incongruously dressed in a black and white spotted frilled dress more suitable for a garden party, a little black hat with a frou-frou of spotted veiling concealing her face. Judy wore a fair-isle jumper and tweed trousers, Katherine Lacey a culotte suit in white linen. Her hair was held back by two scarves, brilliant turquoise and acid yellow, twisted around each other in a tight circlet. Mrs Rainbird had gone the whole hog and was wrapped, like some gargantuan Christmas gift, in shiny crimson satin topped off with a green hat covered in little berries. The coroner took his seat and the inquest began.

The statement of Doctor Trevor Lessiter was read out. In it he made the point most strongly that, on examining the deceased, he certainly had noticed congestion of the lungs, but as he was treating Miss Simpson at the time for bronchitis he thought the fact hardly surprising. Naturally he had not checked for symptoms of coniine poisoning. What physician in those circumstances would? The coroner said there was no blame to be apportioned in this matter and the doctor stared hard at the reporter from the *Causton Echo* to make sure he'd got that down. He then signed his statement and walked importantly back to his seat, his round head and pudgy shoulders looking pompous even from behind.

The pathologist's report was read. There was a buzz of interest at the word hemlock and the Rainbirds held hands excitedly. Next a scientist from the Police Forensic Laboratory gave evidence relating to the analysis of fibres found in an area of beechwood near the village Badger's Drift, and the identification of dirt and leaf mould adhering to tennis shoes belonging to the deceased as coming from the same area.

Two scene-of-crime officers described the large flattened space near which a deep impression of the same shoes indicated that Emily Simpson had been standing for some time. Here Barnaby noticed Miss Bellringer flush with anger and glare at the man giving evidence. He continued to describe an impression that could have been made by someone of Emily Simpson's height and weight having fallen a few feet away. The coroner asked for a pause whilst he checked back on Doctor Lessiter's statement. He then asked the doctor if the bruises on Miss Simpson's shin could have been caused by the earlier fall. The doctor sighed mightily and, in a voice indicating that they had already wasted enough of his valuable time, said that he supposed so.

Scene-of-crime continued. Fingerprint details. The marked passage in the volume of Shakespeare, a 6B pencil which had not been found. The afternoon wore on. The postman was called, as was Miss Lucy Bellringer. She assured the court that on the morning of her friend's death the larder window was undamaged and the hemlock not in the house. And that, as regards the 6B pencil, Miss Simpson would never have defaced her beloved Shakespeare. 'She never put a mark in any of her books. They were far too precious to her.'

Detective Chief Inspector Barnaby described Miss Bellringer's first visit and his meeting with Terry Bazely at which there was an even stronger buzz of interest. He glanced around the court as he mentioned Annabella but saw only a few puzzled looks. No flicker of recognition. As he sat down he glanced at the jury. Their seriousness now was not assumed. They were totally engrossed, looking intently at the coroner. One woman had gone very white. An usher crossed to her and murmured something but she shook her head, edging further forward in her seat.

The coroner started his summing up, concluding with directions to the jury which were unmistakable. They conferred together only for a moment before giving their verdict, which was that Emily Simpson had been murdered by a person or persons unknown.

Immediately the reporter from the *Echo*, perhaps influenced by too much *film noir*, flung on his brand-new white trench coat, pushed back an invisible eye shield and raced from the courtroom. Everyone else left more slowly – talking, questioning, looking at each other with a mixture of excitement and dismay like a bunch of critics at a prestigious first night whose worst hopes have just been confirmed.

Barnaby watched Barbara Lessiter leave on the arm of her husband. She had sat, apparently placid, through the whole proceedings, but he had noticed her hands moving. He walked now to the end of the row which held her seat and looked along the floor. Just in front of her chair was a little pyramid of shredded tissues. He remembered the letter which she had so quickly thrust out of sight the other morning, and regretted the veil. He would have liked to have seen the expression on her face when the verdict had been announced.

Almost everyone had now gone. But on a bench, some

distance away, a solitary figure sat bowed, head low. He crossed the space and sat down.

'Miss Bellringer . . . ?' She looked at him. Her skin was ashen, her fine eyes dull. 'Are you all right?' When she did not reply he said quietly, 'Surely you understood where our investigations were leading?'

'Of course . . . that is . . . I suppose I did.' Her ebullience was quite gone. She looked very old. 'But I hadn't put it into words to myself. Why is it so much worse now that it's been put into words?' She looked at him inquiringly as if he would know. There was a long pause.

Barnaby said, 'I'm sorry.'

'Such wickedness.' A flash of anger raked her face and left a spark in her eyes. 'After a lifetime of caring for other people. She was a wonderful teacher, you know. Better than I've ever been. And of course she knew them, whoever it was. That's the terrible thing. She must have welcomed them in.' Silently Barnaby agreed. 'Well, they must be caught,' she continued, her voice strengthening by the minute. 'Right – what are your instructions, Chief Inspector? What shall I do next?'

'Nothing, I'm afraid. We—'

'Oh but I must do something. I can talk to people, can't I? Find out if anyone noticed anything, anything at all on the day she died. And what about this mysterious Annabella? Perhaps I can discover who she is.'

'I'm sorry, Miss Bellringer—'

'But I've got to help. Surely, Chief Inspector, you can see why?'

'Of course I understand your—'

'Poirot,' she interrupted wistfully, 'had his Hastings, you know.'

'And I, Miss Bellringer, have all the resources of a modern police force at my disposal. It's a different world.'

'They can't be everywhere at once. And in any case I'm sure' – she laid a gloved hand on his arm – 'they can't all be as intelligent as you.'

'Please be sensible,' said Barnaby, resisting as well as he could such blatant flattery. 'I'm sure your friend would not wish to put your life at risk.'

She removed her hand. 'What on earth do you mean?'

'In a community as small as Badger's Drift everyone will know what you're about. Someone who has killed once and who thinks he can protect himself by killing a second time will not hesitate to do so. And don't forget' – he turned and they walked together towards the exit – 'that if Miss Simpson knew the murderer very well, so do you.'

Chapter Two

It was nine o'clock that same evening. Phyllis Cadell stood by
the chiffonier in the larger of the two sitting rooms at Tye
House. She stood stock still, listening. She had gobbled her
pudding so quickly she thought the other two might notice
but, as was sickeningly usual, they paid close and affectionate
attention only to each other.

She stared at the half-open door. Katherine was safely in
the kitchen stacking the plates in the dishwasher. Henry
would inevitably be nearby, gazing with fatuous admiration
at this difficult accomplishment. Quickly Phyllis unstoppered
the heavy cut-glass decanter. She picked up a chunky tumbler
and half filled it with brandy. There was a clear chink as glass
and decanter collided. She glanced at the door again, replaced
the stopper and started to drink.

It was wonderful. Fiery and strong. It lagged her misery
with warmth like a cosy coat. There had been wine at dinner
but what were two bottles of wine between three people?
And in any case wine no longer seemed to have any effect.
She emptied her glass, eased out the stopper and poured
another, splashing a little in her haste.

'A small one for me too, Phyllis, if you would?'

'Oh!' She swung round. Henry was propelling himself
across the carpet. 'Of course ... I'm sorry ... I didn't hear
you.' She turned her back on him, concealing the nearly full
tumbler in her hand. She pushed it behind a plant and took a

drink over to her brother-in-law. 'And one for Katherine?' she asked, proud of the balance in her voice.

'I shouldn't think so. She hardly drinks at all, as you know.'

She doesn't need to, does she, thought Phyllis savagely. Do you think I'd drink if I had her life? Her looks? Her future? Concealing the glass in her hand she walked over to the window and placed herself behind a tall jardinière. She took another long, deep swallow.

She began to feel better. Then, as the unhappiness receded, her sense of her surroundings became strangely distorted. The velvet pile of the carpet seemed to be alive, rubbing around her feet like a cat; stripes on the curtain raised themselves and went zinging up and down like railway lines. A tumbling spray of stephanotis in the jardinière poured out a rich, sensuous smell, filling her nostrils cruelly. Reminding her of the coming nuptials. If you prick us do we not bleed she thought chaotically.

Perhaps it wouldn't be too bad at the cottage. At least she'd be out of their way. The place was a good ten minutes' walk from the main house and they'd hardly be dropping in all the time. They might visit a bit at first, feeling vaguely uncomfortable at her solitude, but that would soon wear off.

The kitchen was quiet now. Katherine would be joining them any minute. Phyllis took a deep breath and tried to pull herself together. She blinked very hard, willing herself to see the room as it really was and not as a crudely drawn, unnaturally lively stage set. Then she saw the bride-to-be walking across the yard carrying the wilting flowers from the dining table. Phyllis stared at her through the glass. Perhaps, she thought, there will be no wedding after all. Perhaps Katherine would have an accident – fall into the lake, smash up the Peugeot, walk into the combine harvester. The images in her mind frightened her. No. Katherine was young and strong and would live a long, long time. Probably for ever.

And there might be children. Somewhere deep under the cosy coat a knife turned. She would be useful then. Poor old Aunty Phyllis. Funny Aunty Phyllis. A tear plopped into her empty glass. God, she could do with another drink. She became vaguely aware that Henry was saying something.

'. . . and we're both very worried about you.'

'. . .'Bout what, Henry?'

'Haven't you been listening?' She stared at him with intense drunken concentration. 'About you, of course.'

'Nothing matter with me.'

He put down his glass and propelled himself over to where she stood. 'Look – you don't have to go to the cottage, you know, Phyllis. It was you who suggested it. Kate and I would be happy for you to stay here.' She made a peculiar sound which could have been a sob or a laugh. 'In any case we both hope you'll still spend a lot of time with us. Katherine isn't used to running a big house, you know. She'll be grateful for all the help you can give her. As I have always been.'

'Is that what I'm reduced to then? An unpaid domestic?'

'Of course not. I simply—'

'Is that the price I have to pay for my tied cottage? Scrubbing floors.'

'Now you're being ridiculous.' She watched his face crease into irritation. Henry hated rows. Bella had always been wonderful at defusing them before they really got a hold. She would have stopped right now. 'You don't know what it's like. What I've had to put up with since she came. All the sneering remarks, the little humiliations. She never does it when you're around.'

'You're imagining things—'

'Am I? Oh, she's clever. You were blind but I saw what she was up to. Bella was hardly in her grave before she was up here . . . helping with this . . . helping with that . . . simpering shyly . . . pushing in where she wasn't wanted.' Oh stop, Phyllis, stop! You'll make him hate you. 'I wouldn't be surprised if it was going on while Bella was still alive.'

'That's enough. You know that isn't true. I won't have you speaking of Katherine in that way.'

'She's only marrying you for your money. Do you think she'd look twice at you if you were paralysed and poor?' She drove on and on. Henry Trace watched her, more amazed and distressed than angry. So much venom. He almost expected to see bile, black and thick as treacle, bubbling between her lips. When she had finished he said quietly, 'I'd no idea you felt like this. I thought you would be pleased at my happiness. I thought you were fond of me.'

'*Fond* . . .' She cried out then, hard ugly sounds. Her cheeks remained dry and red with anger. When Katherine appeared in the doorway Phyllis Cadell ran from the room, pushing the girl's slim figure aside, unable to look at her face, which she was sure would be filled with sly laughter – or worse, with pity.

'Oh Pookie.' Barbara Lessiter curled her tongue into her husband's ear like a pliant little snail. 'I'm sorry I've been so . . .' She took a deep breath, putting an impossible strain on the thin lace and crêpe-de-chine nightdress. Her headache was better at last.

'There, there. You mustn't worry,' replied Pookie, romping happily between satin sheets. Like a very hungry man after a vast banquet he felt that what he had just received (twice) would last him forever. Which was fortunate because, as things turned out, it was going to have to from that particular source at any rate. 'Change of life, I expect.'

At this reference to her age he felt Barbara withdraw slightly. Well, a little dig from time to time wouldn't come amiss. Keep her on her toes. Show her she wasn't dealing with the lovesick swain of five years ago. He'd be damned if he was going to be grateful for something that was his by rights. If her headache had gone on much longer it could have featured in the *Guinness Book of Records*. His hand moved again.

'Darling . . . Pooks?'

'Mm?' Ah, there was nothing like silk and lace. Unless it was warm bare flesh.

'Don't, sweetheart . . . listen to Barbie . . .'

Growl, growl. And a pretend doggy panting.

'It's just that . . . I've been so terribly worried . . . I know I've got to confess . . . but I don't know how to tell you . . .'

Apprehension sluiced the passion from his loins, leaving him cold as ice. He seized her arms, glaring at her in the light from the ivory figurine. How could he not have guessed the reason for her neglect and distant behaviour? 'You've been with someone else!'

'Oh Pookums!' she cried, and covered her face with her hands. 'How could you even think such a thing of your poor Barbie?'

Relief repaired some of the sexual damage. Down in the forest something stirred. 'Well . . . what can it be, then? Can't be too dwedful. Whisper it in Pookie's ear.'

The lace expanded again in heartfelt preparation. 'Well . . . when I got my mink coat out of store for the Traces' wedding the other day I left it on the back seat of the car . . . just while I went shopping and . . . Oh sweetheart . . . someone stole it . . .' She burst into a flood of tears, then, as he did not speak, peeped coyly out between her fingers. This action, which he had once thought charming, now struck him as suitable only for a child of three. A nauseatingly winsome child at that.

'What the hell do you want to wear a mink coat for in July?'

'I wanted you to be proud of me.'

'Have you been to the police?'

'No . . . I was in such a state . . . I just drove around worrying . . . and then I came home.'

'You must do that tomorrow. Give them all the details. Fortunately it's insured.'

'Yes, darling . . . I don't suppose?' – a serpentine arm twisted over his shoulder and around his neck – 'Pookie will ever buy his naughty Barbie anovver one?'

Pookie's stare gave nothing away. He was trying to recall Krystal's remark; little Krystal who was always so pleased to see him; whose welcome was never anything but warm and friendly. What was it she had said? 'I'd have to do it five hundred times to get a coat like that.' He smiled calmly, almost forgivingly, at his wife and patted her smooth brown shoulder.

'We'll have to wait and see, won't we?'

171

Chapter Three

Barnaby sat in the incident room. He was in his shirt sleeves before an open window. The soft thud of tennis balls and an occasional reproachful cry floated in from the nearby recreation ground. He twirled his rotating cards for the hundredth time and called for some coffee.

'And not in that mug with the blasted frog squatting in it.'

'Oh. I thought he was rather sweet,' said Policewoman Brierley, her lips twitching.

'Well I didn't.'

'No, sir.'

Barnaby spun one more time, realizing that he knew all the information by heart, hoping that a fresh reading might show a piece of the puzzle in a different light, juxtapose seemingly disparate facts, reveal with a whisk of the conjuror's cloth something which had hitherto been darkly concealed. At least with poor old Loveless/Lovejoy/Lessiter accounted for all afternoon there was one suspect fewer.

Barnaby toyed with the idea that the murderer might be fancy free, killing to protect the reputation of his or her partner. It sounded a bit far fetched but if the partner's legal spouse held the purse strings it might be a possibility. Money had been behind many a killing. Money and sex. Interlocked. An eternal ampersand. And a motive for murder since murder began.

Two days had passed since the funeral and Barnaby had

spent one of them discussing the death of Mrs Trace with all the members of the shooting party with the exception of the farm boy and neighbouring landowners whom he had left to Troy. The only new bit of information to arise from this was that, at the time of the shooting, Phyllis Cadell was on her way back to Tye House, having got bored by the whole proceedings. Henry had expressed surprise that she had decided to accompany them in the first place. Phyllis in her turn had assured Barnaby that Bella had been urging her for some time to come out with them. Phyllis had done a certain amount of shooting when she was younger and knew how to handle a gun but had simply lost the taste for it. 'I regretted joining them almost as soon as things really got going. I stayed for a bit then decided to give up. I didn't want to draw attention to myself so I just slipped back to the house.'

Another example of unusual behaviour. Barnaby's mind turned back to his cards and Miss Simpson. On the day of her death she too had behaved 'out of character'. Were the two deaths connected? There was no sensible logical reason for believing this. Yet he still couldn't leave the idea alone. Barnaby read the photostat of the inquest report again although by now he knew it backwards. He remembered his first quick conviction that there was something odd, some fact buried in there that didn't make sense, but by now the whole piece was so stale he wondered where that original impulse had sprung from. Certainly repeated readings had done nothing to support or elucidate this instinctive belief.

On the morning of the second day he had interviewed Norah Whiteley in the tactfully vacated office of the headmaster at the school where she worked. She was a thin woman with a bitter mouth, mistakenly wearing very youthful clothes. What she had to tell him was disturbing.

'I left David because I was afraid. I could just about cope with his women. At least that meant he left me alone. But he was very violent. You never knew what would start him off. The dinner wasn't right, the car wouldn't start. I could put up with it for myself but when he started on Jamie . . . I told him to go and when he wouldn't I packed all his stuff, put it outside and had the locks changed. But even then I had to get a court order to stop him molesting us.'

'Does he have access to the boy?'

'No.' There was a hard, unhappy, yet satisfied set to her lips. 'He applied but I blocked it. I fought. I wouldn't trust him to keep his fists to himself.'

'And do you know if he has a . . . liaison with someone at the moment?'

'Bound to. David's never without a woman for long. He's sex mad.'

As she said this Barnaby had a vivid recollection of his first sight of the man sitting close to Katherine Lacey in the kitchen of Tye House. He had mistrusted his own quick assumption at that time. Shades of D.H. Lawrence. And those wonderful torrid grainy films of his childhood: *Double Indemnity. The Postman always Rings Twice*. It was all there: the beautiful bride, the inadequate husband, the lusty stud. So obvious, such a cliché. And yet, and yet . . . How often the obvious turned out to be the truth.

But Barnaby saw no point in pretending that he had recognized any signs of guilt as the couple had become aware of his presence and broken apart. Whiteley had looked depressed and irritable, Katherine merely interested and concerned. And there was something so cool about the girl: an almost asexual purity in her beauty. He could imagine her body being offered up to its legal possessor when all the knots were properly tied, not without love necessarily, but perhaps with a moderate degree of fond attachment. It was harder to imagine her being swept away by a passion so strong it was worth risking a gilded future for.

David Whiteley was something else: amoral, self-interested and now known to be violent. Barnaby did not find it too difficult to visualize him in the role of murderer. But the death of Miss Simpson had been curiously nonviolent, almost subtle. Barnaby could not see the farm manager annotating *Julius Caesar* and he could never, with those brawny arms and legs, have climbed through the larder window. Nor could Barnaby see him committing murder to save any neck but his own.

Mechanically he gave the wheel another spin. He could not escape the comparison with Russian roulette. Five spins got you nowhere. The sixth could blow your mind. He drained the coffee, pleased to see nothing nearer to animate life in the bottom of the mug than a sweet dark primeval sludge. And then the phone rang.

Policewoman Brierley said, 'I've got a Mrs Sweeney on the line, sir. She asked to speak to whoever was in charge of the inquiry about Miss Simpson.'

'Put her on.'

'It's Mrs Sweeney here of the Black Boy. To whom am I speaking?'

'Detective Chief Inspector Barnaby.'

'Are you the gentleman what came in for a half and a ploughman's the other day?'

'That's right.'

'Well I think you ought to come over. There's something funny happening at the Rainbirds'.'

'What sort of thing?' The voice, which he recalled as flatly lugubrious, now positively rippled with excitement.

'I don't rightly know . . . it's almost like someone singing only it's not like any singing I ever heard . . . more like wailing, really. It's been going on for ages.'

Afterwards Barnaby remembered that moment very clearly. As he replaced the receiver he had the strongest sense that the machinery of the case, which had seemingly ground almost to a halt with alibis, unproven and unprovable statements and, on the part of at least two people, the deliberate wish to deceive, was now moving again. Although he could not know with what speed the machinery would gather force or that a hand, as yet unknown to him, would hurl a spanner into the works with such terrible repercussions.

There must have been fifty people standing at the gate of Tranquillada. As soon as Troy cut the engine he and Barnaby could hear the sounds. A terrible keening. Mrs Sweeney left the gathering and hurried to meet them.

'Since I talked to you I rung the bell but nobody came. I felt I had to do something.'

The two men walked up the path. No one attempted to follow. That in itself underlined the feeling of dread that permeated the hot still air. Normally, reflected Barnaby, you had to hold them back. He and Troy stood on the step. The threnody continued. Barnaby wondered how anything so apparently emotionless could produce such an effect on the heart of the listener. It stopped and started with inhuman regularity, like a needle stuck on a record. After using the knocker with no result Barnaby crouched down and shouted through the letter box: 'Mr Rainbird . . . open this door.'

The lament escalated a notch or two, became almost a screech, then suddenly stopped. Immediately the crowd fell silent. Barnaby rapped the knocker hard again. The sounds were like pistol shots in the quiet street.

'Shall I have a go at the door, sir?' Troy was excited. He kept looking at the people by the gate, at Barnaby and at the house, underlining the importance of his position.

'Window's quicker. Try to find one open first.' As Troy ran down the side of the house Barnaby looked again at the group. Instinctively they had drawn closer together. Their shadows fell, short and squat, on the warm pavement. One woman had a toddler in her arms. As Barnaby watched she turned the child's face away from the bungalow and into her breast. The ceramic stork stared indifferently at them all.

Barnaby turned back and noticed, for the first time, a neat pile of mushrooms on the step. What the hell was keeping Troy? He'd been gone long enough to climb in and out of half a dozen windows. Barnaby was about to raise his fist again when he heard the click of the latch and the door swung open. Troy stared blankly at the chief inspector. He didn't speak, just stood aside for Barnaby to enter. As the older man did so he felt his skin prickle as if someone had laid a frost-covered web against his face.

He walked through the hall past a red telephone dangling on its flex, past the scarlet-stippled wall and doors, glancing into each room as he went, finding them empty. He looked for the source of a silence more terrible than the sounds had ever been and found it in the lounge.

He stood for a moment on the threshold sick with horror. There was blood everywhere. On the floor, on the walls, on the furniture, on the curtains. But most of all on Dennis Rainbird. He looked as if he had been bathed in blood. His face, like that of a warrior brave, glistened with fingers of red. Red matted his hair and gloved his hands. He wore a red soaking wet tie and a red-flowered shirt. His knees and his shoes were red. Red tears rolled down his cheeks.

Barnaby turned back into the hall. 'Don't just prop the wall up. Get on the phone and get things moving.' Then as Troy moved somnambulistically across the hall, 'Don't touch that, you bloody fool! Use the set in the car. And don't open that door again without something on your hands. Anyone'd think you'd been in the force five minutes instead of five years.'

'I'm sorry . . .' Troy produced a handkerchief.

Barnaby returned to the lounge. He made his way towards the two figures in the centre of the room, placing his feet carefully on whatever unstained patches of carpet he could find.

How could one person have shed so much blood? Wasn't there something vaguely theatrical about the scene? Surely an over-enthusiastic stage manager had been at work hurling buckets of the stuff about, preparing for a performance of *Grand Guignol*. And the strange thing was that over and above the sweep of disbelief and horror Barnaby felt his memory give a powerful kick. *Déjà vu*. But how could that be? Surely if he had experienced anything even faintly like this spectacularly nightmarish scene in the past he could hardly have forgotten?

'Mr Rainbird . . . ?' He bent down and saw, with a fresh wave of nausea, that it was only Dennis Rainbird's encircling arm that was keeping his mother's head on her shoulders. Her throat had been cut so deeply that Barnaby could see the bluish white gristle of the slashed windpipe. There were cuts all over her face and neck and arms and her dress was slashed open.

The room was in a hell of a mess. Photographs and pictures were thrown about, there were cushions and ornaments on the floor, two tables were overturned, the television set was smashed. Grey shards of glass were ground into the carpet.

Barnaby said, 'Mr Rainbird' again and touched him gently. As if this movement activated some hidden mechanism the man started to croon gently. He was smiling; a radiant wide mad smile. The cruel simulacrum of bliss seen on the faces of earthquake survivors or parents outside a burning house. A rictus of grief and despair.

Almost twenty minutes passed, then: 'Good God . . .' Barnaby got up. George Bullard stood in the doorway. He carried a small black case and looked around him, aghast. 'What the hell's going on?'

'Careful where you step.'

The doctor stared at the two figures for a moment, his expression a mixture of pity and disgust, then picked his way gingerly across the floor. He knelt down and opened his bag. Barnaby watched as he cut into the stiff crimson cuff of Dennis Rainbird's shirt and held his delicate wrist.

'How long has he been like this?'

'We got here around half an hour ago. I should think for at least half an hour prior to that. Did you sort out an ambulance before you came?'

'Mm.' The doctor shone a light into Dennis' pupils. He didn't even blink. 'Should be here in a minute.'

'It's vital I talk to him—'

'For heaven's sake, Tom, use your sense. The man's catatonic.'

'I can see that. Can't you give him something?'

'No.' George Bullard rose to his feet. 'He's made a good job of this and no mistake.'

'How long do these states last?'

'A day. A month. Six months. There's no way of knowing.'

'That's all I need.'

'Sorry.'

Through the net curtains Barnaby saw the ambulance drive up followed almost immediately by three police cars. There was a murmur of excitement from the crowd. The ambulance attendants, perhaps inured to scenes of carnage by years of scraping people off the motorway, seemed much less shocked by what had happened in the lounge at Tranquillada than either Barnaby or Doctor Bullard. Whilst one of them talked to the doctor the other attempted to separate Dennis from his mother. He tugged gently at Dennis' wrist but the fingers were clamped on to her right shoulder and left upper arm as tightly as if he were hanging for his very life on a cliff edge. Patiently the man prised the fingers away one at a time and unhooked the thumb. Mrs Rainbird's head rolled back, attached to the neck only by a thin flap of skin. The torso tipped over and slid on to the carpet. Dennis' crooning ran down, then stopped.

'Can he walk d'you think?'

'Let's try him. Up you come, my lovely.'

Dennis rose to his feet, rubber limbed, still smiling. His face, always pale, was now almost albino-ish in its lack of colour.

'Shall we clean him up a bit?'

'Sorry,' interjected Barnaby, 'nothing must be touched.'

'Right. On our way then.' The three of them left the room, Dennis clinging trustingly like a child. Barnaby followed them out. The crowd, their wildest expectations more than fulfilled, played their part to the hilt, gasping aloud and crying out. One woman said, 'And to think I nearly stopped in to watch the six o'clock news.'

'Can you get everything he's wearing bagged up?' asked Barnaby. 'I'll send someone to collect it.'

'Will do.'

Barnaby re-entered the lounge to find the doctor pulling down the corpse's dress and shaking a thermometer.

'What d'you think?'

'Ohh . . . I'd say an hour . . . hour and a half at the most.' He drew the slashed opening of her dress together. 'He must've had some sort of brainstorm.'

'I have to get a man over to the hospital. I don't want Dennis Rainbird left alone.'

'Well, Tom, you know your own business best. But I can assure you he won't be going anywhere. Or doing himself a mischief.'

'I'm not worried about him doing himself a mischief.' He

could hear the scene-of-crime men entering the hall. 'But he might say something that could help us. He may even have seen something. He must have got home pretty soon after this happened.'

'You mean . . . ? Oh. I seem to have been jumping to the wrong conclusions. Anyway – Dennis or no Dennis – whoever did this must have been clean off his rocker.'

'His?'

'Well,' the doctor frowned, 'it always is, isn't it? An attack like this.'

'Don't you think a woman would be physically capable?'

'Physically yes . . . I suppose so . . . if the rage is there. Psychologically and emotionally . . . that's something else. It'd be a very peculiar sort of woman who could do something like this.'

Barnaby grinned. 'You are an old chauvinist, George.'

'So my daughter's always telling me. Anyway' – he stood aside to make room for the photographer – 'I suppose murderers are peculiar.'

'Not always. I only wish they were. It'd make catching them a lot simpler.'

'Is this where the body was found, sir?' asked the photographer.

'I should imagine so,' said Bullard.

Barnaby agreed. 'I think he just lifted her up and held her. I don't think he dragged her about at all. There's more blood here than anywhere else.'

Doctor Bullard looked around the room again and shook his head. 'Who'd believe we only had nine pints? And she's still got plenty left.'

Barnaby looked at Mrs Rainbird's bolstery legs which looked as plump and lifelike as they had a couple of days previously when he had talked with her. Her feet were bare. One tiny gold mule trimmed with white ostrich feathers lay, miraculously unstained, in the fireplace. The other was nowhere to be seen.

The room was filling up. Barnaby went into the hall, glad to escape from the rich metallic smell, and spoke to the principal scene-of-crime officer. 'Are we going to have a pod out here?'

'All lined up. Should be here within the hour. And I've got on to Technical Services . . . do a video for you.'

Barnaby nodded and looked around for Troy. On the pavement two officers were placing a cordon and the crowd, now monstrously enlarged, was being forced some distance from the gate. In spite of the emergence of Dennis Rainbird, a sight surely gruesome enough to satisfy the most ghoulish expectations, murmurs of dissatisfaction at this realignment could be heard. Troy, his colour back to normal, came down the path which ran along the side of the house.

'Where the hell have you been?'

'I was just checking round the back, sir. I found something a bit unusual.'

'You should know better than to go trampling about at the scene of a murder, Sergeant.'

'I didn't trample . . . kept to the concrete path. But look.' He led Barnaby to a small cedar shed a few feet from the gazebo. All around the path and the step adjacent was damp. Barnaby looked for a dripping tap or faulty hose and saw neither. 'I mean . . . it hasn't rained for days, has it, sir?'

'No.' The chief inspector glanced through the window. On the floor next to the lawnmower was a huge puddle of water. He couldn't see any containers that might be leaking. Well, all the outbuildings would be checked. No point in wasting time at this stage in fruitless surmise. Troy was looking both smug and hopeful of praise, like a dog who has successfully returned a stick. It was very irritating.

'Are you feeling all right now?' asked Barnaby unkindly.

'Me?' His sergeant looked first blank then intensely puzzled. 'I'm fine.'

The end of the back garden was marked by a double hawthorn hedge with a green gate in the middle. Behind the hedge was a narrow path bordered by a dense tangle of wild dog roses, hazels and cow parsley. The path and the last few feet of the garden were overlooked by the upstairs windows of number seven Burnham Crescent, glass eyes with cataracts of grubby lace. Mrs Rainbird wouldn't have liked that. Barnaby heard footsteps approaching, and stepped through the gates.

'Good afternoon, Mr Lacey.'

'Whoops.' Michael Lacey stopped in his tracks and stared at them. 'It's our friendly neighbourhood sleuths. Leaping out of the hedgerow to startle innocent passers-by.'

'Would you mind telling me where you're going?'

'I'm taking a short cut to the Black Boy. Still, as far as I'm aware, not a criminal offence.'

'A little early, isn't it?'

'She opens the jug and bottle if you knock on the shutters.' And before Barnaby could reply he had walked quickly away.

'I don't believe this,' murmured Troy. 'Not a single question as to what we're doing here. Why, half the village is gawping outside the house. How uncurious can you get?'

'Incurious. And he wouldn't know about the crowd if he'd come straight from Holly Cottage through the woods and up Church Lane.'

'Still, why dash off like that?' Troy pursed his lips shrewdly before adding, 'The murderer returns to the scene of the crime.'

'Hardly ever, Sergeant,' replied the chief inspector, 'at least in non-domestic matters. As your experience should have taught you by now.'

'But they are connected aren't they, sir?' continued Troy. 'The two deaths?'

'Oh yes.' The two men stepped back on to the concrete path. Barnaby could see through the french windows into the lounge. It seemed to be crammed with people milling aimlessly about. In fact, as Barnaby knew, the most precise cataloguing and analysis were taking place. And today the scent was warm. Discoveries would be made. No one killed without taking something (usually unintentionally) from the scene. Or leaving something behind.

He made his way to the kitchen door, stopping when he got there, glancing back the way he had come. He thought how impossible it was for a gardener to attempt to conceal his personality. Telling one's dreams could hardly be more revelatory. Unsophisticated harmony for Miss Simpson; tangled exuberance for Miss Bellringer; whilst here . . . He looked at the showy shrubs, the billiard-table-baize lawn, the pond with a concrete cherub peeing mechanically on a plastic lily. Here was ostentatious vulgarity, literally in full bloom.

He entered the hall. A pair of black Oxfords appeared just above his head and made their way down the pine steps from the loft, followed by tweed trousers, a short-sleeved shirt and a bearded, hot-looking face.

'Finished up there?' asked Barnaby.

'We have. Lots of prints. Looks as if they're all from the same person, though. Soon see.'

Barnaby climbed the stairs. There were about a dozen of them, broad and solidly based, quite unlike the capricious aluminium approach usually leading to a conversion. The opening had been enlarged, no doubt to accommodate Mrs Rainbird, and there was a rail on two sides of the entrance about three feet from the floor. Barnaby heaved himself up and Troy followed.

The loft was very large. The beams were unpainted, the

walls white, the floor covered with a porridge-coloured tweed carpet. At either end of the loft was a round window. Directly beneath each stood a plain wooden chair. They also each had a narrow sill holding a notebook and ballpoint. On the seat of one of the chairs was a magnificent pair of Zeiss binoculars. There were two large grey filing cabinets and that was all. Barnaby, who had been expecting either the usual piles of lumber or a wildly baroque spare room, looked about him in some surprise. He picked up the binoculars and looked out at the Street.

A face in the crowd sprang at him in the most astonishing detail. Open pores, nostril hairs, pink plastic rollers, petals on a flowered scarf. He adjusted the focusing ring and got a broader sweep. The forecourt of the Black Boy was now packed. More cars were pulling up by the minute. All human life seemed to be out there. And it was not a pretty sight.

'Empty those cabinets, Sergeant. Start taking the stuff downstairs.' He put down the glasses and flicked through one of the notebooks, picking a day at random. The entries read:

10.30 a.m.	Mr and Mrs W crossed over by the post box to avoid Miss G. The vegetable marrow award obviously still rankling.
11.14	A called on Mrs S. Stayed fifty minutes. Shopping bag, empty on arrival, bulging when she left. Returned home via the post office.
12.00 p.m.	Mrs W, Mrs G and Miss K gossiping for twenty minutes behind letter box. Miss K left first. Foolish woman.
12.42	Mr and Mrs D visiting church with roses.
1.00	Seven cars in the Black Boy forecourt. Several not local. (Here five numbers were listed.)
3.20	Mr Y calling at D's cottage. Carrying a bottle of wine.

4.50   Mrs L drove into the W garage. (Then a red
             star.)

5.03   Mr Y leaves the cottage. Posts two letters.
             Returns home.

Barnaby closed the book. Mrs Rainbird's daily occupation did not surprise him. He never underestimated the tremendous satisfaction that knowing all a neighbour's business gave to some people. A passionate interest in everyone else's affairs seemed to him a very human characteristic hardly reprehensible enough to be called a failing, let alone a sin. If he himself wasn't endlessly concerned with other people's behaviour he wouldn't be doing the job he was. He watched Troy lowering himself down through the loft opening, pulling a stack of envelope files after him.

No. What interested Barnaby was not the revelation that Mrs Rainbird watched human beings rather than waxwings but what she did with the knowledge she so obtained. There was something very pared down, almost ruthlessly functional about the room he thought as he collected the rest of the files and the other notebook and prepared to follow Troy. Downstairs all was voluptuous indulgence but this place was something else. This place, thought Barnaby, taking a last look round, meant business.

Chapter Four

The portable pod had just arrived, giving rise to great excitement. The delivery lorry was backing away. Hydraulic machinery wheezed, four legs dropped to the ground, the shell settled into position. A man in the crowd shouted, 'Glad – the libry's here. You brought your books?' Loud laughter. A woman said, 'Robbie – run home and tell your mam the Martians have landed.' A generator and cables were set up and a GPO line connected.

As soon as Barnaby reached the pavement he was nobbled by the white trench coat, now topped by a Fred MacMurray trilby, from the *Echo*.

'Chief Inspector – do you have a statement for the press?'

'Not at the moment.'

'The public has a right to know.' Dear God. Dialogue by RKO out of Universal Pictures. 'Is it true that the most terrible murder has been committed?'

'A suspicious death has been reported, yes.'

'Oh come off it, Inspector Barnaby. What's in the files?'

'Please . . . *oh please* . . .' A young girl lugging a Uher tape recorder stepped directly in his path. 'Are you in charge of the case?' She sounded breathless and exhilarated as if on her way to a party. 'Local radio,' she added, thrusting a bulbous windsocked mike under his nose. 'If you give me something now it will make the seven o'clock news.'

'Big deal,' muttered Troy.

'Has a communication relations officer been appointed yet?' cried the reporter, showing off in front of the girl.

'No. Give us a chance to breathe,' said Barnaby, pushing by.

'But Inspector—'

As Barnaby walked away he heard one of the villagers (the one who had made the remark about the library) seize his moment of fame. 'Oh it was horrible! Horrible!' he cried into the microphone. 'The son did it . . . he came out covered in blood. They've took him away in an ambulance. They reckon he had a brainstorm. He's queer, you see . . . it takes them like that . . .'

'But who's been killed?' asked the girl.

'Well . . . it'd be his mother, wouldn't it?' He gazed brightly round. 'Am I on camera?'

Barnaby stowed the files safely in the car boot and locked it.

'It didn't take long for them to start sniffing round,' said Troy.

'Oh there's always a village correspondent for the local rag. Does WI reports and flower shows. I expect they got in touch.' He started walking briskly down Church Lane, Troy hurrying alongside.

As they reached the wooden footpath sign to Gessler Tye Troy asked, 'Are you going after the suspects straight away, sir?'

Barnaby did not reply. He was breathing quickly, his face was flushed, his lips tight. For him the murder of Mrs Rainbird had shocked the case, yesterday so arid and at a standstill, into new pulsating life rich with fresh insights and possibilities. And although the killer still remained faceless his scent became strong and somewhere, not very far ahead, Barnaby could sense his quarry no longer running swift and gleeful, laughing over his shoulder but back-tracking, threshing about, sensible that the distance between them was shrinking.

Many years before, becoming gradually and sometimes sharply aware of the pleasurable exhilaration he felt at this moment in a case, Barnaby had become extremely depressed and unhappy. He had felt his role, a hunter of men, to be a base one. He had struggled for some time to work in a more disinterested manner. To pretend that this sweep of excitement as he drew the net tighter was not happening. Or that if it was happening it was nothing to be ashamed of. When that failed he went through a phase, lasting several years, when he had played the hard man, ignoring or angrily stamping on these earlier perceptions. The quarry was scum. There was only one thing they understood. Give them an inch and they'd cut your throat. It takes one to know one.

Promotion had been steady. He had done well. Three men he had caught during this period had been hanged. He had been offered a lot of respect, frequently from people he despised. But as this carapace of contemptuous hatred for the criminal hardened around him so, inexplicably, self-hatred grew until the day came when he felt he would almost rather die than be the man he was slowly turning into.

He had gone to see George Bullard, speaking in only the vaguest terms of stress and headaches, and was granted a month's leave with hardly a question asked. He had spent the time gardening, painting watercolours, talking things over with Joyce. At the end of the month he knew there was no other job he would ever wish to do and that the shell had been broken beyond repair. And so he went back and continued: at first insecure (although never less than competent), realizing that lack of instant and extreme opinions on matters of the day made him appear insipid to some of his former colleagues who usually had a surplus of both. He was also at that time over-reacting against his former harshness, loathe to bawl out and discipline when necessary. That was mistaken for weakness. Gradually he repaired this misconception. And now he walked down a dusty country lane having come, in a way, full circle. A policeman neither proud nor ashamed of his job entering the last phase of his career and of a murder hunt, feeling excited by this and accepting that excitement as a fact of life. Part of how he was. Troy touched his arm.

They were halfway along the dirt track leading to Holly Cottage. Barnaby stopped and listened. Someone was yelling, the words thick with rage and unintelligible. The two men moved silently along, hidden behind the tall hedge, to where it opened out into the car space. Keeping in the shadow of the trees they approached the house. A window on the ground floor was wide open. And the words became clear.

'But you must come, Michael . . . *you must* . . .'

'No must about it. You needn't expect me to present myself with a carnation up my nose and a pair of matching bloody candlesticks to watch you sell yourself to the highest bidder.'

'It's not like that. You're so unfair. I do care for him . . . I do. How can I help it? He's been looking after us for years.'

'I've never heard such sentimental crap. It makes me want to vomit. You've certainly pulled the wool over his eyes, poor bastard.'

'That's a lie! He knows exactly how it is . . . I haven't pretended to anything I don't feel. I shall be a good wife—'

'God! Tied to a bloody cripple at your age.'

'You just won't understand! It's different for you. All you care about is your work. It's all you've ever cared about. As long as you can paint, the rest of the world might as well not exist. But I'm not like that. I'm not especially good at anything. I'm not trained for anything. I have no money – I wouldn't even have a home if it wasn't for Henry. For

190

heaven's sake, Michael, what's so wrong with wanting security—'

'We've *got* security. He'd never turn us out. He's so besotted with you you could keep him dangling for years.'

'But I don't want to stay in this damp gloomy place. I hate it.'

'Well you certainly don't come cheap. Tye House and five thousand acres. I don't know why you don't just take to the streets and make a proper job of it.' There was the sound of flesh meeting flesh with some force. Michael Lacey shouted, 'Spiteful bitch!' Katherine cried out. Barnaby drew his sergeant behind a clump of larches. Moments later Katherine Lacey flew past them, her face contorted, making little strangled choking sounds, and disappeared down the path towards Church Lane. The cottage door slammed and Michael stood in the porch for a moment looking undecided. Then he turned and strode off into the woods behind the house, kicking a fallen branch furiously out of the way.

When he had disappeared Barnaby approached the house, opened the front door and slipped inside. Troy, concealing his surprise, followed. If I'd suggested this, he thought, I'd have got a right bollocking.

They stood in the hall, the dank chill seeping into their bones. It seemed perfectly natural that these walls should witness bitter words, tears and sorrow. Barnaby felt that any happiness accidentally immured in such surroundings would have no chance to develop and thrive but, like the honeysuckle by the porch, be slowly choked and strangled by the forces of despair. He led the way to the kitchen. It was not an attractive room. The units were cheap and showing signs of wear. A few rugs lay about on the original cold and bumpy brick floor. A half-empty can of spaghetti and a clumsily hacked wedge of bread were on the wooden table with a mug, teapot and half a bottle of cheesy-looking milk. There were flies everywhere.

The room adjacent to the kitchen facing the front of the house had rush matting, a table, four chairs, bookshelves, a two-seater settee and a telephone. The second room on the ground floor was locked.

'This is the place where he was painting when we came before, isn't it?'

'Yes.' Barnaby tried the door again, then left it. 'Well, there's nothing we can do about that without a warrant. We've bent the rules enough already.'

Too right, thought Troy, following his chief up the uncarpeted stairs. He couldn't see why they were roaming around the place at all. Surely the whole point of coming to the cottage was to check Lacey's alibi for that afternoon?

'The more you know about a suspect, Sergeant, the more cards you hold. And that includes his natural habitat.'

Troy blinked in some alarm at this spot of telepathy. A very worrying development. If a man couldn't call his thoughts his own a man could remain a sergeant for life.

There were three bedrooms. The smallest had a single bed, a wardrobe and a chest of drawers. The bed was rigidly and efficiently made, a hospital bed. A nightdress was folded neatly on the pillow. The wardrobe was nearly empty and the chest of drawers had a thin film of dust. A bunch of wild flowers in a jar gave the room a mild fragrance. Again Barnaby recalled the Serotina struggling in the nettle patch.

A much larger room was next door, empty but for a small old-fashioned bed, two wicker chairs and a garden table. 'I suppose this is where the nanny slept,' offered Troy.

The third room, biggest of the three, clearly belonged to Michael Lacey. The bed was unmade, the sheets tangled, one of the pillows on the floor. There was some grey scummy coffee on a scarred bedside table next to a copy of Vasari's

Lives of the Artists, and a packet of Gitanes. The acrid smell of the cigarettes hung in the air, mingled with the smell of stale sweat. The only chair was decorated with a shirt and a grubby pair of Y fronts. Sergeant Troy, 'clean from the skin out every day' as his wife was wont to boast in their local laundrette, turned up his nose and sniffed.

'A bit careless,' he said as they re-entered the hall, 'leaving the door unlocked.'

'Oh I don't know.' Barnaby opened it a fraction and checked the view, then stepped out. 'The only room where there might be anything worth pinching was secured.'

'Great works of art d'you mean?' jeered Troy as they walked back towards the hedge.

'I was thinking of canvases – they cost a hell of a lot. So do paints. Or of course he might be doing a Keating.'

'Come again, sir?'

'Tom Keating. A very successful forger.'

'Well whatever he's doing he's not successful. I've seen families on the Social living better. Didn't even have a telly.'

'And you can't sink much lower than that.'

Troy looked at his chief suspiciously as they walked on but Barnaby's expression remained bland. As they came to the junction of Church Lane and the Street several more police cars arrived. The crowd, now swelled by the return of the local work force, was being urged to move along or go home. Barnaby wondered how long it would be before the nationals got hold of the story. There was a rustle of speculation as the two men appeared, a rustle that became a loud hum as Barnaby and Troy turned into the Lessiters' driveway. The fact that everyone in the village would shortly be questioned was, even if it had been known, supremely irrelevant. It was the Lessiters whom the police were visiting. The Lessiters who were, in some way as yet unrevealed, connected with the crime.

As Barnaby stood once again beneath the Madame le Coultre and looked through the window he, once again, saw Barbara Lessiter. This time far from looking afraid and shaken she had taken a combative stance. He could not see her face but her shoulders had a martial set and her hands were clenched into angry fists. He heard Lessiter shout, 'You sang a different tune in bed last night.'

'That was last night.' She tossed her head as she yelled her rejoinder and Barnaby caught a glimpse of her tight angry profile. Troy raised sandy eyebrows, muttered, 'Naughty naughty.' He rang the bell.

Stepping into the sitting room was like stepping on to a battlefield. The whiff of the last two salvoes hung, still and trembling in the stifling air. Barnaby gave them a moment before ascertaining that they had both heard of Mrs Rainbird's death.

'Terrible business, terrible!' cried Lessiter. 'Head split open by an axe, I understand. I suppose he had some sort of fit . . . Dennis I mean. At least,' he added with a scornful curl of his lip, 'no one can accuse me this time of wrongly issuing a death certificate.'

Both the Lessiters looked at the policemen with interest, no doubt glad of a breather. However, the doctor did not wear his air of detached attention for long. Barnaby asked where he was between three and five that afternoon.

'Me?' He gasped at them, his rubicund complexion fading to a mere puce, 'What on earth has this to do with me?'

'Everyone is questioned in a murder case, darling.' Barnaby was glad no one had ever called him darling like that. 'What on earth's the matter?'

'Nothing.' He moved to his writing desk. 'Very well, Inspector. I . . . was visiting a private patient. I'll be glad to write the name and address down for you.' He scribbled something, tore off the sheet and was just crossing to

Barnaby when his wife ran forward and snatched it out of his hand. 'Barbara!'

She read the piece of paper then handed it to Barnaby. She seemed calm but her eyes glittered like diamond chippings.

'And you, Mrs Lessiter?'

'I was at my health club in Slough . . . the Abraxas if you want to check. I went for a salad lunch, a sauna and massage. I was there till around half three then I did some shopping. Got back here five-thirty.'

'Thank you. Is Miss Lessiter at home? I'd like a word with her.'

'No. We passed each other in the hall as I arrived. She was on her way out and looking very strange.'

'In what way?'

'Well . . . if it had been anyone but Judy I'd say she'd been with a lover.'

'That's remarkably catty even for you,' blurted out Lessiter, regretting it immediately as he caught the glimmer of satisfaction on Troy's face.

'She gave me an ecstatic smile – incidentally the first I've received from that direction since the day I moved in – and said she was driving into High Wycombe to buy a new dress before the shops shut. Which is also strange. I've never known her take the slightest interest in clothes. Quite understandable when you think that she's shaped like a couple of suet puddings.'

Whatever was on that piece of paper, thought Troy, had made her as bold as brass. She didn't look like a centrefold dream today. The facial lines under the bronzy powder seemed more deeply etched, her eyes were hard and her hair had an inelasticity that made it look completely artificial. Even her curves seemed rigid and unyielding.

'Someone will call later to talk to your daughter, sir,' murmured Barnaby, and bade them good evening. The door had hardly closed behind them before Trevor Lessiter turned to his wife.

'I hope you're not expecting—'

'You dirty sod!'

'Don't you speak to me like that. I shouldn't be driven to places like the Casa Nova if you were any sort of a wife.'

'I might be more of a wife if you had the slightest idea how to set about it. You're bloody pathetic.'

'At least they care about me there. Krystal's always—'

'*Care about you*? They must be laughing themselves sick.'

'How the hell do you know so much about it? I'm surprised you've even heard of the place.'

'They were talking about it in the Abraxas, if you must know. Some of the old slags come in for a spot of rejuvenation.'

'Doesn't work though, does it, Barbara?'

'What?'

'The rejuvenation. I mean you're really looking your age right now. That was one of the first lies you told me, wasn't it? About your age. God – today's opened my eyes all right. I feel as if I'm seeing you for the first time.'

Barbara walked over to the window, carefully selected a cigarette from the silver box and lighted it. She turned and faced him, blowing out a cool plume of smoke.

'Well that goes for both of us, husband mine,' she said, baring her teeth in an implacable smile. 'That goes for both of us.'

Chapter Five

David Whiteley opened the door of Witchetts wearing his working jeans and a sweat-stained shirt, with a tumbler of whisky in his hand. He showed them into the sitting room and turned off the blaring stereo. ('Bridge over Troubled Water.') He invited them to sit down and offered Barnaby 'a touch of Jameson'. The offer being declined he drained his own and poured another. His hand was as steady as a rock; his voice strong and clear and, although he consumed a third glassful during their brief visit, both hand and voice remained unchanged.

'You know what has happened, Mr Whiteley?'

'Yes. I stopped my car and asked one of the multitude outside the Black Boy. Load of ghouls.'

Barnaby asked about his movements during the afternoon. Whiteley was sitting in a bentwood rocker and tipped it very slowly back and forth as he surveyed them both. He looked incongruous in this traditional refuge of the old and resigned. There was something so potent about his masculinity; his blond good looks and rather crude sexual vigour. It seemed only fitting that, like the corn god, he should spend his days reaping and renewing the land. He said, 'I was supervising the hopper till about three . . . three-thirty . . . then I took a combine harvester down to Gessler Tye. We'll start cutting in a couple of days . . . well, probably not Saturday because of the wedding but Sunday I should think.'

197

'Sunday?'

'Oh yes. Once harvesting starts you can write off your weekends.'

'Did you know Mrs Rainbird at all?'

'By sight only. I don't socialize much in the village. Any . . . picking up I do is in the Bull over Gessler way. Or in Causton.'

'Nothing nearer home?' murmured Barnaby delicately.

'No. Oh I knew what you were thinking the other day, Inspector. In the kitchen at Tye House. But there's nothing doing there, believe me. At the moment that is. Mind you I don't think our Kate's nearly as cool as she makes out. I shall try again once she's safely married.'

No need for him to visit the Casa Nova, thought Troy, admitting for once to a male persona probably nearly as attractive to women as his own. Looking round the room Barnaby noticed, on the mantelpiece, the photograph of a child, the glass a cobweb of splinters and cracks.

He said, 'I got the impression when we met in the kitchen that you were depressed about something.'

'Me? You must be joking. I never get depressed.' He stared at Barnaby aggressively. 'Doctor Jameson cures all ills.' He lifted his glass then tipped it back. The sort of man, thought the chief inspector, who would use the loss of his son as a sympathy-producing counter in the game with women but who would never admit to fatherly affection in front of a member of his own sex.

Barnaby continued, 'And after you'd taken the harvester?'

'I drove back to Tye House in the Land-Rover, picked up that pathetic Jack Russell and took it to the vet. Katherine didn't want them to come to the house. It should've been done before now in my opinion but she kept trying to feed it. After that –'

'A moment, Mr Whiteley. Were Miss Lacey and Mr Trace at home when you picked up the dog?'

'Yes.'

'What time would you say this was?'

'Some time between half four and five, I suppose. I only caught a glimpse of Katherine. She ran upstairs when I came in – so as not to see me take him, I suppose. After I'd handed the dog over I drove back here, poured myself a drink and you turned up.'

'He's got the strength and build for it,' said Troy moments later as they crossed the road, making for Tye House. 'And with an estate the size of Trace's who's to know where he is half the time? I thought that actually, sir, when we questioned him about the first murder . . . you know, the couple in the woods.' Encouraged by Barnaby's silence he continued, 'I mean what's to stop him taking half an hour off for a quick screw when he's miles from anywhere? And take today . . . he could have left the hopper for a while. Or turned the combine into the nearest field instead of taking it to Gessler Tye, doubled back and done for Mrs Rainbird. Pity we've no idea of the motive.'

Barnaby, who had a very good idea of the murderer's motive, arrived again at the apricot-coloured farmhouse. Katherine Lacey opened the door. She looked very pale and, even if Barnaby had not witnessed the earlier scene at Holly Cottage, he would have known that she had recently been crying. Distress did not mar her remarkable beauty. Her violet eyes looked very large with tears as yet unshed. She was wearing a white dress of spotless linen and flat sandals. She gazed at them unsmiling and said, 'We're in the kitchen.'

Henry turned his chair around as the chief inspector entered, and wheeled it across the floor. 'What has really happened, Barnaby? Surely it can't be true that the Rainbird boy has attacked his mother?'

'Mrs Rainbird has certainly been killed, sir. In a very violent and unpleasant manner.'

Henry turned a stunned face to his fiancée. 'You see, darling.' She sounded gentle but firm. 'We can't . . . now . . .we'll just have to wait.'

'Katherine thinks we should cancel the wedding. It's ridiculous. A hundred invitations accepted. The catering organized. The marquee's being put up tomorrow. The house is bulging with presents –'

'I only meant for a week or two. Until all this awful business is sorted out. And perhaps by then Michael will have come round.'

'Since when has your brother –' He broke off. He was not the sort of man, Barnaby judged, to even admit to familial discord much less display it in front of complete strangers. He appeared older today. There were liver-coloured rings beneath his eyes and he looked distrait. 'I simply won't hear of it, Katherine. It's out of the question. After all, this is nothing to do with us.'

'Could I ask you both what you did this afternoon, Mr Trace?'

'Us? Well, we've been organizing for Saturday,' said Henry. 'I didn't go over to the office today. Katherine and I spent the morning arranging the wedding presents in the main dining room, then we had lunch, finally decided on the placing for the marquee, then Katherine went mushrooming –'

'Mushrooming?' Barnaby remembered the little pile on the doorstep of the bungalow.

'Yes. There are some flat open ones not far from Holly Cottage,' said the girl. 'And some *girolles*. They taste wonderful. Not like those awful things you buy in the shops. I wanted to do an omelette for supper.'

'There were some on Mrs Rainbird's step.'

'Yes – I was coming to that. The last time I saw her –'

'When was that?'

'Yesterday at the Parish Council meeting. She gave me a

recipe for mushroom and anchovy ketchup and I said next time I gathered some I'd let her have a few. So I went round and knocked but no one answered so I just left them on the step and came away. Now I can't stop thinking about it . . . he must have been in there . . . perhaps even . . . but it was so quiet . . . I thought she'd gone out, you see.' She repeated the words, her voice suddenly jangled and shrill. 'I thought she'd gone out.'

'Kate.' Henry held out his hand and she gripped it, crying, 'Everything's going wrong . . . just like I said the other day . . . it's all slipping away from us.'

'Now you must stop this, darling. All right? You're talking nonsense.'

Barnaby crossed to the table and the mushrooms. He picked one up and sniffed it. There was a large basket, only half full but still holding a lot of mushrooms. 'It must have taken you quite a while to pick all these?'

'Not really. About half an hour, I suppose.'

'When actually was this?'

'I left here . . . when was it, darling? About quarter past three and was back three quarters of an hour later . . .'

'You say the place where they grow is quite near Holly Cottage. Did you happen to call in at all?'

'Yes I did. I thought Michael might have –' She broke off, catching Henry's eye. 'Anyway it was a waste of time because he wasn't there.'

'Was this before or after you did the picking?'

'After.'

'Between four and half past in other words?'

'I suppose so.' She did not mention her later visit and the spectacular row and, as the timing made it irrelevant to his present inquiry, Barnaby saw no need to mention it either. He had no doubt that it would not meet with her fiancé's approval.

'And you were here when Miss Lacey returned, Mr Trace?'

'Yes. I was with Sam . . . he's the boy who does bits and pieces of maintenance and helps with the garden. I was unpacking Katherine's roses, he was mixing peat and bonemeal, preparing the ground. We made some tea. Kate rang the cottage to see if Phyllis would like to join us but she wanted to carry on doing her curtains and unpacking stuff.'

Barnaby asked, 'Has Miss Cadell moved out for good then, sir?'

'Not quite. She'll be sleeping here tonight. For the last time, I believe.' Barnaby was hard put to disentangle the mixture of emotions in Trace's voice. Relief, satisfaction and more than a little worry.

'Perhaps you'd be kind enough to direct us to the cottage?' asked the chief inspector.

'It's a bit difficult to describe,' said Katherine, 'I'll take you there.'

As they left the house Barnaby said, 'I'll leave Miss Cadell to you, Sergeant. You know what I'm looking for. And then you can try Holly Cottage again. I'll be in the pod when you're finished.' He watched them go off across the lawn towards the grove of poplars, the girl's shoulders bowed slightly, her dark hair stirred by the evening breeze. Troy walked a little closer to her than was necessary to deliver the animated stream of chatter that his lively profile suggested. Every now and again he pulled down his black leather *blouson* and smoothed his hair. Barnaby made his way back to the pod.

Here all was activity. A certain amount of simple forensic work had already been done. The exhibition officer had logged a fair bit of detail. All the blood came from Mrs Rainbird. There were filaments under her nails, not yet analysed, which suggested the murderer had worn a stocking or tights over the face. Soap in the bathroom was marbled with streaks of blood, indicating that a shower had been taken. Barnaby got on to the station and briefed Inspector Moffat to handle communications for the case. As he did so a TV pantechnicon drew up outside and a uniformed scene-of-crime officer entered the pod.

'Oh – you're back, sir. A message from a Mrs Quine. Said to tell you that she saw a Michael Lacey in the spinney approaching the bungalow and acting in a highly suspicious manner –'

'Actually we also saw Mr Lacey in the spinney acting in a fairly ordinary manner. But thank you. Has the body been taken away?'

'They're just bringing it out now, sir,' the man replied unnecessarily. You could have heard the gasps and murmurs half a mile away.

'Are you on to the outbuildings?'

'Not yet, sir. Just starting on the kitchen.'

'Right.'

Barnaby left the pod, set the newshounds (the two original plus five more and a television team) on to Inspector Moffat and returned to his car to wait for Troy. He took an armful of Mrs Rainbird's folders, sentimentally pink and blue, and one of the notebooks, locked himself in the back seat and started to read.

He flipped first through the notebook. Each page was pretty much like the one he had already read. People identified only by initials and, occasionally, sporting a red star. No one seemed to be doing anything out of the ordinary. Walking, talking, visiting, using the phone box. Every one skewered by the omniscient beam from Mrs Rainbird's powerful optics.

Barnaby put the notebook aside and started on the files. He realized immediately that his previous supposition when first checking out the loft had been the correct one. Mrs Rainbird appeared to have a fresh and not unreasonable approach to her profession. Barnaby hesitated to use the word Marxian to describe such an individualistic, anti-social business as blackmail, but there was no doubt that the woman's demands were nothing if not sensible. People paid what they could. From each according to his abilities.

One man had delivered over (Barnaby checked back) the last ten years eggs and vegetables twice weekly. Someone else regular loads of wood. A few months before these offerings had ceased and Mrs Rainbird had drawn a neat line underneath and written 'Deceased'. Poor old devil, thought the chief inspector, wondering what peccadillo the old man had been guilty of. Probably nothing too terrible. Ideas of right and wrong in a small village, particularly among the older inhabitants, often seemed archaic to more modern minds. He opened another file. Two pounds a week for three years, then nothing. Perhaps the victim had decamped. Driven out of the place as the only way to avoid payment. He read on. Fifty pounds a month. One pound a week. A regular servicing of Denny's Porsche. Ironing done, shrubs supplied. Who would have thought in a village of some three hundred souls there would have been so much 'sin' about?

But of course there was also Brown's. And Dennis with his slimy ways, driving round Causton visiting the bereaved and offering oleaginous comfort. People talked unrestrainedly in times of grief and gossiped at funerals. Rich pickings there. Between them he and his mother must have covered a pretty wide area.

Barnaby picked up the last pink folder, casually, with no sense of premonition. No idea that this would be the chamber with the bullet. Spin number six.

No need to wonder now, he thought, looking at the long column of figures, where the silver car came from or the partnership in the funeral parlour. Number 117C had paid out thousands. Even before he looked at the date of the first payment he knew what he would find. Not many crimes could command that sort of blood money. In fact perhaps only one. He felt a surge of emotion too strong to be called satisfaction. He felt on top of the world. He had not been able to let the shooting of Bella Trace alone. Without the slightest shred of evidence, indeed with all those present insisting that only an accident could have occurred, Barnaby had carried the incident around with him for a week whilst it plucked at the edges of his mind like a child with a story to tell. And now here he was, vindicated. A gentle tapping on the window of the car broke into his reverie.

'Ah, Troy.' He got out and slammed the door. 'Did you see Miss Cadell?'

'Yes. She's been at this new place all day, she told me. Then I tried Holly Cottage again like you said but it's still empty.' He hurried alongside Barnaby. 'Seems to have an endless supply of cottages, Mr Trace. Takes some people all their lives to buy –'

'Show me where Phyllis Cadell's house is, would you?'

'Oh, she's not there now, Chief. She left when I did. Eating with the Traces.'

'Right.' Barnaby crossed the road. 'How did she seem?'

'Well, she didn't know of course, about the murder. After I told her she went a bit funny. She laughed a lot but it sounded . . . oh I don't know . . . I think she'd been drinking, actually.'

Phyllis Cadell was standing by the window in the room where they had first met. She turned as they entered and as soon as Barnaby saw her face he knew his suspicions were correct. He stepped forward.

'Phyllis Cadell. I arrest you on suspicion of the murder of –'

'Oh no!' She turned from him and ran to the far end of the room. 'Not now ... *not now!*' Then she covered her face with her hands and started to shriek.

Chapter Six

Barnaby crossed the room. As he approached Phyllis became quieter and stared at him. The intensity of her gaze, the utter, utter misery in her eyes, lifted her for a brief moment from the realms of bathos and made her appear an almost tragic figure. Barnaby completed the caution. Troy, trying to look as if all this was no more than he expected, produced his notebook and sat down by the door.

Phyllis Cadell gazed at them both, blinking convulsively, then said, 'How did you find out?'

'We have removed several files from Mrs Rainbird's bungalow. Yours was amongst them.' She would never know that no details of the crime were stated in the file and that the blackmailer's victim was identified only by three figures and an initial. Or that, lacking any sort of proof, Barnaby had hoped to frighten her into an admission of guilt. She started to speak.

'I know you'll find this impossible to believe but when I first came here . . . of course I was much younger then . . .' Her glance at the floor was abject. It indicated how sad she found her age, her appearance, her general unlovableness. 'And Henry was . . . I did everything in the house, you know . . . and he was always so grateful. Then . . . gradually I felt his gratitude becoming something more. Bella was always so busy, you understand. Her position in the village meant she was expected to be on the Parish Council, do a certain amount of charity work. She was president of the WI, the local Conservative Association. Oh – she looked after Henry in a brisk sort of way but half the time she just wasn't here. He looked so wistful sometimes ... sitting by the window waiting for her car to turn in at the gate. Then one evening – I shall never forget it ...' Her puffy face became criss-crossed with tears and her voice thick with emotion. 'I was preparing some sandwiches – cream cheese with horseradish – and he took my hand and said, "Oh Phyllis. What would I do without you?" Not we' – she stared at Barnaby defiantly – 'I. "What would *I* do without you?" You see he was turning to me more and more as time went by. And I understood that. I loved him so much you see that it seemed only natural that he should start to love me a little. And then I thought' – her voice dropped to a whisper – 'how happy we could both be if it wasn't for Bella.'

She sat down then and was quiet for so long that Barnaby was afraid she had stopped for good. But, just as he was about to speak, she started again. 'There was no love lost between us, you know. Everyone thought how good it was of her to give me a home. But she would never have got a housekeeper to do all the things I did. And she enjoyed flaunting her happiness. She soon spotted that I cared for Henry. There were no flies on Bella.'

Barnaby moved and sat down without taking his eyes off her face. 'I'd learnt how to handle a gun when I was quite young. It's just something one does in the country. But I never liked killing things.' Her lips twisted on the paradox. 'I told Bella I fancied a change from domesticity and felt like joining them on a shoot. Henry seemed a bit surprised but quite pleased. I took a hip flask filled with vodka. I wasn't much of a drinker in those days. I hadn't any definite plan but I was sure there'd be an opportunity. People don't stay in a line or bunch you know, they fan out – break up a bit. But, as the time went by, it seemed to be getting more and more impossible. There was always someone between us or she moved too far away or too close. I started to get desperate. I didn't know what to do. I kept taking drinks from the flask. I knew I'd never get up the courage to go out with them again . . . all the dead birds, the blood . . . it was making me sick. Then I had a brilliant idea. I thought if I went round in front of them and I was hidden in the trees and . . . and did it from there no one would know. So I said I didn't feel too well or I'd got bored or something and left and worked my way round in a semi-circle till I was facing them. Guns were going off all the time. I suppose I could easily have been hit myself.' She buried her face in her hands, adding huskily, 'I wish to God I had been.

'Then . . . I shot her. It was terrible. I saw her pitch forwards and fall to the ground. And I panicked. I just got up and ran and ran. I threw the gun into some bushes. After a few minutes I stopped and drank the rest of the vodka and then of course I realized . . .'

'Yes?' So quiet Barnaby's voice. So still the room. Troy, pencil flying, felt they had forgotten he was there.

'. . . Why that everyone would know it wasn't an accident. All the others, except the farm boy were behind her, you see. And he was too far away. I thought what shall I do, what shall I do? I sat there and sat there. I thought of running away but then everyone would know it was me . . . so I made myself go back. By that time of course it was all over. The ambulance had been and gone and Trevor Lessiter told me that Bella had had an accident. Tripped and fallen on her gun. I just couldn't believe it. That anyone could be so lucky. I cried and cried with relief. I couldn't stop. Everyone was very touched. Such sisterly concern.

'When they'd all gone I made supper for myself and Henry. I didn't lay the table. We sat by the fire. I had to coax him to eat. I've never known such happiness. I expect you think that's wicked but it's the truth. All I could think of was, I've got away with it, and I've got Henry. Then about half-past seven the phone rang.' Her voice became dry, little more than a croak. 'Excuse me . . . I need a drink.'

'Sergeant.' Barnaby beckoned.

'It's all right.' She poured from a decanter and added a quick spurt of soda. 'Well, the call was from Iris. She said I was to go round. I told her what had happened to Bella and said I couldn't leave Henry. She just said, "You'll come now. Or would you like me to come to you?" She sounded very odd but even then I wasn't really alarmed. I got Henry some pudding and went off to the bungalow.

'She offered me some coffee, wouldn't take no for an answer, and Dennis went off to the kitchen. We sat facing each other in her revolting lounge. She wouldn't say what she wanted. She kept twinkling at me, saying how I'd be needed more than ever at Tye House. "Quite the chatelaine you'll be, dear." Then Dennis came in pushing the trolley. There was coffee and biscuits on the bottom tier and on the top . . . the gun. No one said anything. It was horrible. They just kept looking at each other then at me, and beaming. As if I'd accomplished something extraordinary. As I suppose I had.

'Then Dennis said he'd seen me shoot Bella and ditch the gun and run away and whilst they were both very anxious for my continuing happiness at Tye House they were sure I'd understand that poor people had to make their way in the world too and that they'd always known I was the sort of person to be generous to my friends. My plan had so obsessed me that I hadn't given anyone else a thought, least of all Dennis Rainbird. But he was mad about Michael Lacey then. Was always following him about. I should have remembered that. Anyway' – her shoulders sagged – 'there's not much else to tell, really. Since then they've cleaned me out. Henry gave me Bella's jewellery – they've had the money from that. Then there were my own few bits and pieces and fifty thousand my mother left . . . and you see' – a wave of sorrow washed over her features – 'it was all for nothing. He didn't love me at all. He was just being kind. And then Katherine came along.'

As the silence lengthened and she didn't speak again Barnaby said, 'Is that the end of your statement, Miss Cadell?'

'It is.'

'And Mrs Rainbird's death?' Even as he spoke the chief inspector knew what her answer would be. He could see her, buoyed up in the belief that Henry cared and primed with a flask of vodka, firing at Bella then, immediately overcome with shock and horror, running all over the place and hurling the gun away. What he couldn't see was that stout, foolish-faced woman wielding a knife again and again, wading through blood, steeped in blood. Coolly changing clothes, scrubbing the traces away. So it was without surprise that he heard her say, 'I had nothing to do with that.'

Yet he still felt it was in order to ask further questions. After all she had no alibi for that afternoon and she had everything to gain by Mrs Rainbird's death. He pointed out both these things.

'I don't see how I benefit by her death. I might've done eighteen months ago but they've both known for weeks that all the money was gone. And I told them that if I went down I'd make damn sure they went down with me. They knew I meant what I said all right.'

After she had listened to the statement being read back, and signed it, Troy positioned himself at the bedroom door whilst she packed. She came out carrying a small case and her handbag and wearing a shapeless raincoat. She looked much older. She had never been an attractive woman but a certain amount of vitality and a high colour had added some liveliness to her appearance. Now she looked drained, even her hair seemed greyer. As they reached the foot of the stairs a door opened and Barnaby felt his prisoner shrink closer to him.

'Phyllis.' Henry wheeled himself into the hall, with Katherine close behind. 'What on earth's wrong? What is happening?'

'You'll know soon enough.' She wouldn't look at him but hurried through the front door, Troy following. Barnaby closed the door and turned to the waiting pair.

'I'm sorry to have to tell you this, Mr Trace, but Miss Cadell has just confessed to the murder of your wife.'

'It's not possible!' Katherine looked absolutely astounded.

Henry seemed bereft of speech entirely. Finally he said, 'Are you sure? There must be some mistake. I can't believe it.'

'I'm afraid there's no doubt.' Barnaby re-opened the door. 'We have taken her into custody. You may wish to contact her solicitor.' Then he closed the door and walked after the others to the car.

Chapter Seven

Barnaby sat behind his desk in the incident room. He pushed the last of the Tranquillada's files aside and concentrated on his coffee. A few minutes before he had learned from the hospital that there was no change in Mr Rainbird's condition but that he continued comfortable. Barnaby doubted that. He doubted that very much indeed. Until the person who had killed his mother was caught Dennis Rainbird, once memory returned, would never feel comfortable again. Because Barnaby felt sure that whatever she knew he knew. And what now, unless madness had permanently addled his wits, was to stop him talking? Which was why there was a guard at the door of his hospital room as well as someone always by his bed.

Barnaby had in front of him the cutting on the Trace inquest. Now he knew the truth he read it again, remembering his earlier impression that there was something in there that hadn't seemed quite right. He assumed that whatever it was would now stick out a mile, but he was wrong. Ah well . . . it was no longer important.

All around him was activity. Muted, orderly but intense. Breathing space between telephone calls was slight. Fleet Street had picked up the news as had BBC television. Although no appeal had yet been made several members of the public, no doubt anxious to appear to be playing some part in such a dramatic event, had rung offering information and ideas.

Paper was piling up. Every little detail was put on an action form and those not already transcribed on to the rotary card system were circling round like homing pigeons. Forensic and other information was being recorded in the portable pod. A vast blown-up map of the village hung on the wall behind Barnaby's head. One of the monitors showed a local television reporter interviewing Mrs Sweeney, and Mr Fenton, senior partner at Brown's Funeral Emporium ('Every solace in your hour of need') had appeared for the opposition. The villagers were being questioned by the police as to their whereabouts between three and five p.m. All the normal procedures were being carried out. But whilst Barnaby was aware that everything that was being done must be done, his mind refused to expand to absorb all the minutiae of an official inquiry.

It held only five suspects (he had decided to jettison Henry Trace, and Lessiter had an alibi) and these five moved in a slow tantalizing pavane on a screen behind his eyes. Wherever he was, whoever he was with, whatever he was doing, the dance went on. He drained his coffee. Old green-eyes was back.

It was now almost nine o'clock. He wrote down an order for the Chinese takeaway – Black Bean and Ginger Soup. Sweet and Sour Prawns. Rice and Spring Rolls. Toffee Apples – and had just sent it off when the phone rang.

'It's a Mrs Quine asking for you, sir. She's in a call box. I've made a note of the number.'

'Right . . . Mrs Quine?'

'Hullo? What's going on . . . didn't that chap in the caravan tell you what I said? About that Lacey bloke?'

'Yes. The message was passed on.'

'Woss he doing still roaming round the village, then? We'll all be torn to bloody shreds before you lot get off your arses and do something. I saw him go up to that house bold as brass.'

'We also—' Barnaby stopped. Around him the phones continued to ring, a typewriter rattled, outside a car screeched to a halt. He heard none of those things. His concentration was yanked to a single fine point. There was just him, the telephone and Mrs Quine. His throat was bone dry as he asked, 'Did you say he went up to the house?'

'I *told* you. In the message. He went through the hedge, up the garden path to the back door. Got his old denims on and that cap. I'd know him anywhere.'

'What time was this?'

'Well . . . the *Young Doctors* had just finished and *Tickle on the Tum* hadn't started. I'd gone up to make the beds – which was how I came to spot him, y'see. Through the bedroom window. Lisa Dawn was making a cup of tea.'

'Yes,' said Barnaby, marvelling at the control in his voice, 'but what time would that be?'

'That'd be . . . um . . . five to four.'

He sat gripping the receiver for a moment longer. She continued speaking but her words were lost as a wave of exhilaration pounded through him. His brain felt as if it were being dragged all over the place by wild horses. Five to four. Dear God. *Five to four*. More words were getting through.

'Was it you sent that nosey bugger from the Social round? Upsetting Lisa Dawn.'

The pips admitted a merciful release. Barnaby went to find Inspector Moffat to get a search warrant. He yelled 'Troy!' as he went through the outer office – a shout that could have been heard as far as the cattle market and the Soft Shoe Café. His sergeant leapt up from a spot of hot-eyed dalliance with Policewoman Brierley and responded with a 'Sir!' automatically pitched at the same level.

'Car. Shift yourself.'

Leaving another 'sir' splintering the atmosphere Troy ran from the room. This was something like it, he thought, running across the car park and leaping into the Fiesta. Foot down. Siren blaring. Secret tip-off. Villain on the run. Troy and Barnaby closing in. Cuffs at the ready. But the Chief's getting on. Oh he was fast in his day but now . . . So it's Troy who makes the arrest. He was a tough bastard, too. One of the hard men. Afterwards Barnaby admitted as much. 'Without you, Sergeant, I couldn't have—'

'For God's sake don't just bloody sit there. Move!'

'Yes, sir.'

'Back to the village. And you can switch that thing off.' He didn't say slow down, though, and Troy touched eighty when they were clear of the town.

'What's up, sir?' Barnaby told him. Troy whistled and said, 'Wow. We've got him then.'

'Keep your eyes on the road.'

'But . . . that's pretty conclusive, wouldn't you say?'

'He's certainly got some explaining to do.'

'I hope he hasn't scarpered. He wasn't in the cottage when I went back to check.'

When they entered the village a mere handful of people was now hanging round the portable pod. The television van had gone on to the next drama. It was getting dark. As soon as Troy eased through the hedge space they saw a light in the cottage.

'He's back.'

'There's no need to whisper, Sergeant.' Barnaby got out. 'I should think our headlights alone have alerted him to the fact that we've arrived.'

The sun was setting. The house was softened by the glow. The dark mass of surrounding trees was rimmed with deepest gold. An upstairs window reflected the sun. Troy squinted against it as it hung in the very centre of the pane. He thought it looked like a lump of blood. Barnaby knocked.

'Heavens, not you again.' Michael Lacey regarded them

coolly from the doorway. He was eating a huge hunk of bread and cheese. 'You never stop, do you? Really it makes it a pleasure to pay my taxes. If I ever earned enough to pay taxes, that is.'

'We'd like to ask you a few questions.'

He gave a little moan but it sounded phoney. Part of a game. He opened the door. 'Come in then if you must. But I've already been asked a few questions. By one of your minions barely half an hour ago.'

'Then I expect you know that Mrs Rainbird has been done to death—'

'Done to death? How wonderfully archaic.'

'In a particularly brutal manner.'

'I hope you're not looking for insincere expressions of regret on my part. She was a very nasty woman. Almost as nasty as her golden-haired boy.'

'Indeed? I didn't realize you knew her well.'

'You didn't have to know her well.'

Supercilious sod, thought Troy, hugging Mrs Quine's revelation to his heart. Barnaby asked Michael Lacey where he was between three and five that afternoon.

'Working.'

'You wouldn't like to expound on that?'

'Not really. Thanks all the same.'

'So if someone said they saw you walking up the path of Mrs Rainbird's back garden at four p.m . . . ?'

'I'd say they wanted their eyes tested.'

Barnaby produced one of his two warrants. 'Mr Lacey, I have a warrant here to search these premises.' At this the man's expression changed. That's wiped the smile off his face, thought Troy, allowing the hint of one to appear on his own. 'I hope,' Barnaby continued, 'that you will cooperate in this matter.'

'You can't do that!'

'I'm afraid this bit of paper says we can. Sergeant . . .'
Barnaby nodded towards the stairs and Troy vanished.
'Would you accompany me to the kitchen, Mr Lacey?'

He searched the kitchen thoroughly while his companion
stood sullenly by the sink. Then the room with the settee and
bookshelves. He pulled out the paperbacks, lifted the
matting. Lacey perched on one of the uncomfortable dining
chairs and watched. Troy re-entered the room, giving
Barnaby what he fondly imagined to be an imperceptible
shake of the head. The chief inspector finished his task and
turned to the man at the table, who said, 'If that wild
semaphoring of absolute despair is anything to go by, your
clueless sergeant hasn't dug up anything either. So I suggest
you go on your merry way and leave me in peace.'

'Next door, Troy.' The sergeant nodded and walked out.
Lacey jumped up.

'That's my studio. I won't have my work disturbed.
There's nothing in there but paintings.'

Troy called, 'It's locked, sir.'

'Well, break it down then.'

Michael Lacey ran into the passage and hung on to Troy's
arm. Delighted, the sergeant immediately seized the man's
wrists, wrenching his arms behind his back.

'All right, Sergeant, all right.' Barnaby ambled up. 'He's
not going anywhere, are you, sir?'

Troy released Lacey, who glared at them both. But there
was more than anger in his expression. There was fear. 'Why
don't you just unlock the door and save us all a lot of hassle?'
asked the chief inspector.

Lacey ignored him. Troy put his shoulder to the wood. It
gave on the fourth heave. He moved the door into the hall
and stepped back, keeping an eye on Lacey who was leaning
against the stair rail, very still, his face expressionless.

Barnaby entered the studio, which seemed innocent

enough. And meticulously tidy in comparison with the rest of the house. Some canvases were stacked against the wall, one or two tied together with string. The easel was covered with a cloth peaked into a square by the canvas beneath. The floor was swept clean and there was the scent of turps and resin in the air. A trestle table held an orderly array of jars and brushes and there was an unlit Calorgas heater in one corner.

In the hall Troy stood, legs apart, ready for anything. Over his head the electric meter buzzed like a trapped bee. He glanced up. Slim grey cables snaked about. Funny to see a meter in a private house. Plenty of council tenants had them of course. Set too high as often as not so there'd be some cash to spare when they were emptied. A bloody irritating noise. He turned and looked up. It wasn't the meter buzzing. It was flies. Dozens of them; great filthy bluebottles with iridescent wings. They were clustered all over something. Something jammed behind the meter. He stood on his toes and stared harder.

'*Chief* . . .' Barnaby hurried out. 'Look – up there!'

'Get a chair – and something to hold it with.'

Troy climbed on to one of the dining chairs with a dirty tea towel in his hand and tugged at the knife. It bloomed with dark stains. The flies lifted sluggishly but didn't go far. As Troy held it out they hovered over his hand. Barnaby looked at Michael Lacey, who moved away from the banisters and came towards them, staring at the knife in astonishment.

'Can you explain what this is doing behind your meter, Mr Lacey?'

'Of course I can't.'

'Does the knife belong to you?'

When Lacey remained silent Troy gave him a none too gentle nudge. 'The chief inspector's talking to you.'

'I don't know . . .' He looked more closely, his mouth puckering with distaste. 'Yes . . . it's the knife we use for the vegetables.'

'And where have you hidden the clothes, Mr Lacey?'

'What?'

'The dungarees, the cap, the gloves. The tights.'

'*Tights*. What d'you take me for? A transvestite?'

'The clothes that you wore,' Barnaby continued implacably, 'when you killed Mrs Rainbird.'

'When I –' Lacey gazed at him open mouthed. 'You're raving mad. You're not hanging that on me. I've heard all about police corruption. You probably planted that yourself. Came round here earlier when I was out.'

Barnaby was turning back into the studio when Lacey ran for it. Pushing the chief inspector violently aside and hitting Troy in the chest, he flew through the doorway and raced across the open space in front of the cottage. Troy, picking himself up, ran after him and brought the man down by the car. When Barnaby reached them Lacey was handcuffed and Troy pink faced with exertion and pride.

'In the car, Lacey.'

Barnaby's prisoner stared at him. The look held everything he expected to see, fright and despair, but there was something else behind his eyes. A disturbing expression that the chief inspector could not put a name to. Troy bundled the man into the back seat. Barnaby put the knife into the boot, then said, 'Do you have a key to secure the house?'

'It's never locked.'

They drove off. As Troy slowed down to approach the junction of Church Lane and the Street Katherine Lacey came round the corner with two of the dogs. There was just enough light for her to recognize Barnaby, and she half smiled. Then she saw her brother and her face changed. She called out, 'Michael?' and started to cross the road towards them. He lifted his handcuffed wrists and made a square around his face, shouting, 'I've been framed!' Then the car gathered speed and drove off.

Chapter Eight

It was dark when they reached the station. Michael Lacey
received an intimation and was asked if he wished to make
any telephone calls. He declined and started looking round
him with some interest. He seemed to be recovering his
savoir-faire fairly quickly. By the time Barnaby handed him
over to the custody officer he was even exhibiting a certain
amount of bravado. Barnaby heard him place a facetious
order for toast, tea, a mixed grill, apple pie and ice cream.
The chief inspector asked how the other prisoner was faring.

'Sleeping like a baby, sir. And snoring her head off.'

Barnaby returned to the incident room where Troy was
completing a house-search form. It was too dark to start
looking for the murderer's clothes, but at first light they'd get
started. More action forms had come to roost on his desk
next to his cold gluey Chinese takeaway. No need to read
them all now. He'd got the murderer downstairs under lock
and key. He stood by the window looking up at the indigo
sky thickly patterned with bright stars, and wondered at his
feelings of unease.

'Sir?' Troy was holding out a telephone. 'Miss Lacey.' He
took the receiver.

'Detective Chief Inspector Barnaby.'

'What's happened? What were you doing with Michael?'
Barnaby told her. There was a terrible pause then Katherine
started shouting. Barnaby heard 'No... no... he

couldn't . . . it isn't true . . .' and Henry Trace's voice. Then Trace took the telephone.

'Tell me the exact situation, Barnaby. I can't get any sense out of Katherine. Darling . . . please . . . it'll be all right. Try to calm down . . . we can't do anything till we know just what's going on.'

Barnaby went through it again. He heard Katherine crying, 'I want to see him . . . Henry – I've *got* to see him.'

'May we see him, Chief Inspector?'

'I suggest you ring in the morning, Mr Trace. We've settled him down for the night now.' He could hear Katherine still sobbing hysterically as he replaced the telephone.

Barnaby leaned back and closed his eyes. He was feeling tired but not healthily so. He felt what his mother called 'worn to a frazzle'. Wound up, worn out and nothing to show for it. But what was he saying? Of course he had something to show for it. Downstairs, sealed securely away in a cell, he had the murderer of Iris Rainbird. And tomorrow they would find the clothes. Lacey can't have got far with them. Probably dumped in the pond in the woods. He remembered the little puddle of water in the Rainbirds' shed. He had water on the brain. And an unpleasant tightness under his belt. His stomach was never satisfied. When he fed it it complained. And it complained when he didn't. But everything was fine. Tired phrases that he would never normally use lumbered into his mind. An open and shut case. Caught red handed. No problem.

He threw the takeaway into the grey metal waste bin and heaved himself out of his seat. 'I've had it,' he said to the room at large. 'See you in the morning.' Troy, thriving on his twelve-hour shift, sprang up and accompanied Barnaby to the main door, holding it open for him.

'Quite a session wasn't it, sir?' he asked, his face burnished with satisfaction.

'You can say that again.'

'I mean' – Troy kept pace with Barnaby across the car park – 'how often in your career have you arrested two murderers in one day? This has to be a one-off wouldn't you say, Chief?' Barnaby unlocked the door of his Orion. 'God – I've seen some liars in my time but that Lacey . . .'

'Goodnight, Sergeant.'

Troy winged a final bright-eyed glance through the window. 'An open and shut case wouldn't you say?'

He watched the blue car drive away. Surly old sod. Troy thought that if he'd pulled off a double coup like that it'd be drinks all round for the lads and Policewoman Brierley's knickers in his glove compartment before the night was out.

Arbury Crescent was quiet as Barnaby eased into his garage. Dreaming suburbia. A few television sets still flickering but the guiltless inhabitants were mostly asleep, renewing their energies for the daily commuter slog to the city.

'Is that you, Tom?' called Joyce, as she always did.

He stood for a moment on the patio looking down the garden at the heavy mass of dark arboreal shapes. The leaves rustled in the night air and were touched with silver by the moon. He was glad he couldn't see his herbaceous borders. He hadn't touched them for a fortnight. He would get Joyce to do some deadheading at the weekend. This unfortunate phrase reminded him of work and the sighing of the trees ceased to be a comfort. He went indoors.

'I've kept you some soup hot.' Joyce was in her housecoat and slippers, her face cleaned of makeup.

'Oohh . . .' Barnaby slipped an arm around her waist. 'You shouldn't have bothered.'

'How did it all go today?'

'So so.' Barnaby took the mug.

'I'm afraid it's not home-made.'

Barnaby took the soup gratefully and drank deep. It was wonderful. Monosodium glutamate. Permitted stabilizers. HC and FCF. All the angst-producing E's. Bliss.

'You hadn't forgotten Cully's here for the weekend?'

'I had, actually.' Barnaby drained his mug.

'Would you like some more?'

'I wouldn't mind.'

She ladled some out but before he could drink put her arms around him. 'Tom?'

'Mm.'

'You look sad.' She drew his grizzled head down to her soft bosom. 'Would you like a cuddle?'

'Yes please.' He kissed her. She smelt sweetly of fresh toothpaste and the baby lotion she used as a moisturizer. He felt a sudden overwhelming rush of gratitude. Today and every day, however dark the working hours, come nightfall he touched home base. He stroked her hair, adding, 'And not just because I'm sad.'

Chapter Nine

It was a lovely day for a wedding. Falls of hops entwined with summer jasmine were attached to the stone arches; old-fashioned nosegays starred the end of every pew. The altar rails were covered with tuberoses. The bride stood, a glittering column of frosty satin and foaming lace, incomparably lovely. The groom wheeled his chair down the aisle. As he came to a halt at the chancel steps the bride turned and stared at him, her face gradually becoming transformed into a mask of horror. Set square on his immaculate shoulders was a grinning skull. The vicar said, 'Dearly beloved . . .' The congregation smiled. No one seemed to notice anything amiss. The bells rang. And rang. And rang.

Barnaby groped around on his bedside table. He turned the clock round. Half-past five, for God's sake. He tumbled the receiver off the hook. 'Barmby.' He listened and was wide awake. 'Christ almighty . . . have you called Bullard? . . . No . . . I'll be in straight away.'

Joyce turned over. 'Darling . . . what's the matter?'

He was out of bed, dressing. 'I have to go . . . don't get up.'

She struggled to sit, rearranging the pillows. 'You'll want some breakfast.'

'The canteen opens at six. I'll get something there.'

* * *

'How long do you think she's been dead?'

Doctor Bullard placed the blanket over Phyllis Cadell's marmoreal profile. 'Ohh . . . two . . . three hours. Early morning some time.'

Barnaby sat down heavily on the lavatory, the only other piece of furniture in the cell. 'God, George – this is all we need. A custody death.'

'Sorry.' Bullard smiled – quite cheerfully, considering the hour. 'Can't rejuvenate that one for you. Anyway from what I've heard she's better off where she is. Don't you think?'

'That's hardly the point.' Barnaby looked across at the grey flannel hump. He could see what Bullard meant. What had the dead woman to look forward to? The pain and humiliation of a public trial. Years in prison. A lonely and unloved old age. And all the while having to live with the knowledge that Henry and Katherine were alive and happy together at Tye House. All the same . . .

The custody sergeant entered Chief Inspector Barnaby's office and closed the door as tenderly as if it had been made of glass. He looked once at the figure behind the desk and once was enough. Throughout the interview he kept his eyes on the floor.

'All right, Bateman – let's have it.'

'Yes, sir. It wasn't –'

'And if you say it wasn't your fault I'll ram this filing cabinet down your gullet.'

'Sir.'

'From the beginning.'

'Well, I accepted the prisoner but before I could make out a custody record she asked to go to the toilet.'

'You didn't let her go on her own?'

Bateman cleared his throat. 'Point is, sir, Policewomen Brierley and McKinley were searching a pair of scrubbers we'd picked up on the precinct. I sent someone with the prisoner as far as the door –'

'Oh wonderful, Sergeant. Brilliant. He watched her through the wood, did he? See what she was up to?'

'No, sir.'

'No, sir. Did she take anything to the toilet with her?'

Bateman swallowed, stopped staring at the floor and stared out of the window. '. . . Handbag . . .'

'Speak up! I'm feeling deaf.'

'A handbag, sir.'

'I don't believe this.' Barnaby buried his face in his hands. 'Go on.'

'Well . . . I did the record . . . then took her down. We listed her stuff, wrote a receipt. I settled her and gave her a cup of tea. When I did my first check she was sound asleep.'

'So when did she take the tablets?'

'With the tea, I suppose. She must've palmed them when she was in the toilet. She had a cardigan with a pocket and a handkerchief. When I checked the contents of her bag' – the man started to babble in self-justification – 'there was a bottle of sleeping tablets in there with half a dozen tablets in it. She actually asked me if she could take one. She was very clever –'

'She was a damn sight cleverer than you, that's for sure.'

'If the bottle had been empty, obviously I'd have been suspicious –'

'The very fact that she'd got them in her handbag at all should have been enough to make you suspicious, man. Or do you think people take them as they go about their daily business?'

'No, sir.'

'In Sainsbury's or Boot's? Or the library?' Silence. 'When did you first discover she was dead?'

'On my third check, sir. Just before five. I noticed she

wasn't breathing. Called the police surgeon right away but it was too late.'

'Well if she wasn't breathing it bloody well would be too late wouldn't it?'

The sergeant, his face rigid with misery and mortification, muttered, 'Yes, sir.'

'You're about as much use to the force, Bateman, as a jockstrap in a nunnery.' Silence. 'I'll have your stripes for this.' Pause. 'And that's only for starters.'

'If I could —'

'You're suspended from duty. You'll be notified about the hearing. And I don't want to see your face again until you are. Now get out.'

The door had barely closed on the wretched sergeant before it reopened to admit a young constable. 'It's the prisoner in cell three, sir. He wants to make a statement about his movements yesterday afternoon.'

'Well I assume you've been with us long enough to manage that without too much nervous strain.'

'I'm sorry but he wants to talk to you.'

The prisoner in cell three was finishing his breakfast, mopping up his plate with a piece of bread. 'One star for comfort, Inspector, but definitely two for cuisine. I can't remember when I've dispatched a nicer poached egg.'

'Say what you've got to say and get on with it.'

'I'd like to go home now.'

'Don't play games with me, Lacey!' Barnaby crossed to the man on the bed and bent down so that their faces were barely an inch apart. 'I've had you up to here.' He spoke slowly and quietly but the current of anger that flowed from him was almost palpable. Lacey shrank away and turned pale. The skin graft, unchanged, stood out like a piece of stretched pink silk. 'And I should warn you,' continued Barnaby, 'that if you were lying to me yesterday you're in dead trouble.'

'Oh I wasn't . . . technically that is . . .' His speech was hurried now, not at all fluent, with an anxious edge. 'When I said I was working in the afternoon that was quite true. I was making preliminary sketches for an oil I'm going to do of Judy Lessiter. I've been thinking about it for some time and she rang up about twelve o'clock and reminded me. We worked in their garden.'

Barnaby took a deep breath, struggling to contain his rage. 'Don't you usually work at home?'

'One can sketch anywhere. And in any case she invited me for lunch. I never turn down a decent meal.'

'So when did you arrive?'

'About half one. Started work just after two, worked till around four. Stopped for some tea and cake and stuff. Worked on till around five then left.'

'And why,' said Barnaby, his voice stretched with the effort of control, 'did you not tell me all this yesterday?'

'Well . . . I don't really know.' Michael Lacey swallowed nervously. 'I suppose I was so shattered when you discovered the knife . . . then I panicked and before I knew what was happening you'd bundled me into the car and there I was . . . in one of your little grey cells.' He attempted a grin. The chief inspector did not respond. 'And somehow the longer I left it the harder it got to say anything so I thought I'd try to sleep and leave it till morning.' There was a long heavy silence and he stood up and said, a little uncertainly, 'So can I go now?'

'No, Lacey, you cannot "go now".' Barnaby moved away. 'And let me tell you that you don't know how lucky you are. I know men who would have had your head in and out between those bars half a dozen times by now if you'd messed them about like you've messed me.' He slammed the door, locked it and flung the key back on the board.

As he climbed the steps and made his way to the incident room he became aware that he was clenching and unclenching his fists with fury. He changed tack, returned to his office and stood by the window, struggling to simmer down. His brain was in a turmoil, his skin burned, there was a band of steel around his forehead and his stomach bucked like a maddened bronco. He felt almost sick with anger and frustration. But there was no disappointment. Because he had known in his heart from the moment when he saw Lacey gaping incredulously at the blood-encrusted knife that it was all too easy. Caught red handed. No problem. An open and shut case.

He sat in the chair behind his desk and closed his eyes. Gradually his pulse and heartbeat slowed down. He breathed slowly and evenly. Five long minutes crawled by and he made himself sit still for five more. By then he felt himself more or less back to normal and with normality, surprisingly, came hunger. He checked his watch. If he was quick he would have time to expose his arteries to the comfort of a quick fry-up in the canteen and still catch Judy Lessiter before she left for work.

Chapter Ten

The Lessiters were at breakfast. Trevor, who had a mouthful of bile and an aching groin, took a ferocious poke at his egg which retaliated by spouting a great gobbet of sulphur yellow all over his tie. Judy laughed. He scrubbed at the tie with his napkin, glaring at his wife who was turning the pages of the *Daily Telegraph* in the manner most calculated to annoy, i.e. with languid indifference.

She was up to her tricks again. Locked door last night and, when he'd tapped, very softly so that Judy wouldn't hear, Barbara had put her lips to the door jamb and hissed, 'Go away, you randy little man. Don't you ever think of anything else?' He had walked up and down in his room for two hours after that, torn between lust and fury, cursing Judy's presence in the house. At one moment he had even thought of dragging a ladder out of the garage, climbing up to his wife's window and breaking in. God – she'd have known about it if he had. Tears of self-pity sprang to his eyes. He recalled the time he had spent in her arms only forty-eight hours ago. Trick or treat, she'd whispered. Both had been equally enthralling. It'd been almost like the night before their wedding. He realized now what a fool he was. How she'd always used sex to lead him round, like some pathetic bull calf with a ring through his nose. Well, two could play at that game. Just wait till it was time for her next dress allowance. Or a new subscription to that rapacious health club. She could bloody well whistle for it.

Judy Lessiter stirred her coffee and stared dreamily out of the window. She wore the dress she had bought from High Wycombe the evening before. The cloth was a grey and cream harlequin pattern and the dress had a white ruff. 'Frames your face a picture,' the salesgirl had said. Judy's absurd legs were encased in new pale grey tights. She had also lashed out on some Rive Gauche and a box of eye shadows which she had applied, rather clumsily, before coming down. She was re-running, as she had done all night long, the events of yesterday afternoon.

At one o'clock it had stretched, a lonely space to be filled, until teatime. At five past one, fortified with a small sherry, she had rung Michael Lacey, reasoning that it had been over a week and he had said he wanted to paint her and what had she got to lose anyway? To her surprise and delight he had immediately agreed to come over. Even saying, 'I was just going to ring you.'

She had taken a quiche out of the freezer, popped it in the microwave, had a quick bath and scrambled in and out of three dresses. She had even experimented with some of Barbara's makeup. Michael had arrived half an hour later with a sketch pad and promptly told her to go and wash her face.

She took lunch out into the garden and he spent the next two hours drawing in a rapid but detached manner whilst she tried to keep still and refrain from looking at him all the time. He threw an awful lot of stuff away. Not angrily, screwing them up and hurling them from him, but shedding them as impersonally as a tree sheds leaves. By four o'clock there was a little sea of the stuff around his ankles and half a dozen sketches that he put in a portfolio. She had made some tea then and they had drunk it and eaten ginger cake sitting on the wooden seat that ran all round the giant cedar.

She said, 'Can I have one of these?' picking up a discarded sketch.

'No.'

'Oh but Michael' – glancing at the paper – 'it's lovely.'

'It's awful. They all are. Promise me you'll burn them. Or put them in the dustbin.'

She nodded sadly and poured out some more tea. He picked up his pad and a few minutes later handed her a sketch. 'You can keep this one.'

It was all there. The mournful curve of her lips, her beautiful eyes, clumsy fingers on the teapot, the sturdy yet submissive line of the neck. He had signed it neatly M.L. It was so precise and so cruel. She felt her throat tighten in prelude to tears and, knowing that nothing would annoy him more, blinked them away hard.

'Hey Jude . . .' he sang softly, 'don't be afraid . . .' He put his cup on the grass and touched her arm. 'You ought to get out of this place. Away from that miserable pair.'

She gulped her tea. 'Easier said than done.'

'Oh I don't know. When I start my European junketings I shall need a totally subservient dogsbody cum model. I might take you along.' And then he kissed her. Full on the lips.

Judy closed her eyes. She smelt the cedar needles and the sweetness of ginger, felt each individual moist cake crumb on her fingertips, heard a blackbird sing. The kiss lasted a millionth of a second. And a hundred years. Even as she thought I shall remember this moment all my life it was over.

'I said do you want some more coffee?'

Judy looked blankly at her stepmother. 'No thank you.'

'Trevor?'

No reply. Barbara poured a second cup for herself, unrolled the latest edition of Country Life, then pushed it aside in disgust. Much more of that and she'd be into hairy stockings and lace-up walking drawers. No one read the thing anyway. It went straight into the waiting room. She decided to cancel it and place an order for something a bit more spicy. That'd gee up the golden oldies' blood pressure. She nibbled a buttered soldier and glanced slyly at her husband's tie. What with that and Judy looking like something out of a McDonald's ad the day was off to a flying start. And there were only (eyes down to the diamond-studded wristwatch) six hours to go to nookie time. The doorbell rang.

'Who the hell is that at this hour of the morning?'

'I'll go.' Barbara sauntered out to return with Chief Inspector Barnaby.

'What time of day do you call this?' asked the doctor angrily.

'Miss Lessiter?'

'Yes?' Judy scrambled to her feet like a schoolgirl. 'What is it?'

'Just one or two questions about yesterday afternoon if you would? Your whereabouts –'

'We had someone here last night asking about all that,' snapped Lessiter.

'That's all right,' said Judy, 'I don't mind going through it again. I was here all the time. I had the afternoon off. And my friend Michael . . . Michael Lacey was here too. He was doing some preliminary sketches for a painting he's hoping to start soon.'

'Could you tell me when this was arranged?'

'Well I rang him up . . .' Barbara Lessiter covered a smile with her hand, but carelessly. 'Although actually the first thing he said was "Oh – I was just going to ring you".' She stared at the two people sitting at the table. She looked defiant and vulnerable. 'Why is it so important?'

'Someone has stated that they saw Mr Lacey enter the Rainbird house around four p.m.'

'No!' Judy cried out in horror. 'It isn't true. It can't be. He was with me. Why is everyone always picking on him? Trying to get him into trouble.'

This time Barbara did not even try to conceal her smile. Judy wheeled round and pointed at her stepmother. 'It's her you want to talk to! Why don't you ask her a few questions?'

'Me?' Amused and amazed.

'Ask her where her fur coat is. And why she's trying to find five thousand pounds. Ask her why she's being blackmailed!'

With a shout of rage Barbara Lessiter leapt up and flung her coffee in her stepdaughter's face. Judy screamed, 'My dress . . . my dress!' Doctor Lessiter seized his wife, holding her arms by her sides. Judy ran from the room. Her father hurried after her. Barbara, suddenly released, flopped into the nearest chair. There was a long silence.

'Well, Mrs Lessiter?' asked Barnaby. 'Why are you being blackmailed?'

'It's absolute nonsense. I don't know where the silly cow even got such an idea.'

'Perhaps I should tell you that we have removed a good many files, copies of letters and documents, from the dead woman's house.' This time the silence was even longer. 'Would you prefer to come to the station –'

'Christ, no. Hang on . . .' She crossed to a Welsh dresser, shook out a cigarette with shaky fingers and lit up. 'I had a letter from her about a week ago.'

'Signed?'

'That's right. Your friend Iris Rainbird. On her horrible lilac writing paper that stinks of dead flowers. It just said that they knew what was going on and if I didn't want my husband to hear all the juicy details it'd cost me five thousand quid. She'd give me a week to raise it then be in touch again.'

'And what was going on?'

'Me and David Whiteley.'

'I see.' Barnaby's mind back-tracked. She could have been the woman in the woods (no checkable alibi). And David Whiteley the man (Ditto.) At the time Miss Simpson was killed she was vaguely driving round. And she could, just about, have squeezed through the larder window. He hesitated and was wondering how most delicately to phrase his next question when she answered it for him.

'We used to use his car. The seats let down. He'd tell me where he was working. I'd drive there. Hide my car behind a hedge or some trees and we'd climb into the estate for half an hour.'

One up for Sergeant Troy, thought Barnaby. 'And you think that one of the Rainbirds must have seen you?'

'Oh no.' She shook her head. 'Impossible. But there was one occasion . . . we were supposed to meet around three and Henry kept him all afternoon at the office. And when five o'clock came and I knew he'd be home I drove round.' Barnaby remembered the notebook. Mrs L drove into the W garage. And the red star.

'It was something we agreed I'd never do because of the risk but I couldn't wait, you see. I had to have him.' She stared at Barnaby defiantly. 'I suppose that shocks you?' Barnaby managed a look of mild reproach. 'And he was just as bad. He didn't even let me get out of the car. Then we went upstairs and started all over again.'

There was nothing amative in the description. She did not even use that consoling euphemism 'making love'. Love, as Barnaby understood the word, probably didn't enter into the arrangement at all. He asked if they had spent any time together yesterday afternoon.

'Yes. We met about half-past three. He was shifting the combine so he didn't have the Citroën. We managed in the front seat of my Honda. We were together for about an hour, I suppose.'

'Well, thank you for being so cooperative, Mrs Lessiter.' Barnaby turned to leave. 'I may need to talk to you again.'

'Well, you know where to find me.' She turned also, then stopped, staring over his shoulder. Her husband was standing in the doorway. Barnaby glanced at the man as he left. Rage and triumph struggled for supremacy on the doctor's features.

When the door had closed behind the chief inspector Trevor Lessiter said, 'I shouldn't be too sure about that.'

'How much did you hear?'

'More than enough.' The rage and triumph dissolved into a look of intense satisfaction. He gazed at her, a close and rewarding scrutiny. She had started coming down to breakfast without what she called her warpaint. Something she would never have done when they were first married. And her age really showed. She wouldn't find another mug like him in a hurry. But maybe she wouldn't have to. If she came to heel. Did as she was told. She had too much time on her hands, that was her trouble. Too much time and too much money. Her allowance could go for a start. So could the car. And Mrs Holland. Keeping a house this size clean and in order, cooking for three, gardening, the ordinary duties of a doctor's wife should keep Barbara occupied. And at night there'd be other duties. And he'd make damn sure he wasn't sold short there, either. Once a night every night and more if he felt like it. Then there were lots of little variations he had picked up at the Casa Nova. She could learn all those just to be going on with. He'd still go to the club of course (couldn't disappoint little Krystal) but not nearly so often. At the thought of the money he had spent there over the last couple of years while his wife had been . . . He remembered his blood pressure and tried to take it all more calmly. Yes, the bitch had a lot to make up for (every locked door, every headache, every cutting remark) but make up for them she would or out she'd go. He recalled the tasteless tatty hole where she'd been living when they first met. That should have told him something about her for a start. She'd do anything before she'd sink back to that. She'd dance to his tune all right. He visualized a future rosy with sensual delights and started to explain the situation to his wife.

Barbara listened to him droning on. Every now and again he'd rise to the balls of his feet, cradling his pot belly with splayed fingers. She was to do this. She was to do that. She was to be a loving mother to that stumpy boss-eyed little mixer Judy. And to listen and look charitably on his bug-infested patients when they started whingeing. Poxy four-course meals were mentioned.

She thought of the blackmail money in her bag upstairs. Four thousand. And she still hadn't sold her watch. She could scrape up enough for a deposit on a house. But what sort of house would it be? A terraced hovel like the one her parents, if they were alive, were probably still living in. Back to square bloody one with a vengeance. And how would she pay off a mortgage? What sort of job would she be able to get at her age? Of course once you had a property rooms could be let. With optional extras if need be. But if she was going to spend the rest of her life wrestling between the sheets why not do it here in comfort? She could always lie back and think of Capri. Or Ibiza. Or the Côte d'Azur.

She gazed out of the window. At the green sweet grass sparkling under the hypnotic sprinklers. At the flowering trees and the terrace with its tables and umbrellas and urns brimming with flowers. Then her eyes roamed around the room. Thick Chinese rugs and puffy sofas and onyx tables, nesting slabs of green and gold. And all she had to do was pretend. She should be able to manage that. After all she'd been doing it all her life.

She looked at him. He was really getting into his stride.

Shredded rhubarb eyeballs staring, a frothy tic of malice tweaking at his lips. She would have to manage without a car. Three in one household was ridiculous. Mrs Holland would be given notice. The gardener's hours drastically revised. It wouldn't hurt Barbara to find out what a hard day's work was like. Or a hard night's work come to that. The days of freeloading were over. Ah – that had reached her. At last it had sunk in which side the bread was buttered. She was coming over now, a tender smile on her face. She reached out a hand and laid it gently on his arm.

'Fuck off, Pookie,' she said.

Chapter Eleven

Barnaby sat in the Orion at the end of Church Lane. The windows were open and the sun was warming his face. He was thinking.

Lacey's alibi was, as he had expected it to be, confirmed. The man was innocent of the murder of Iris Rainbird. Yet he had made a run for it. Why? Had he really just panicked? Sensed a frame-up? The first folds of a net falling around him cast by an unknown hand? It was feasible enough, Barnaby knew. He had seen people bolt more than once on a lot less provocation. Lacey had set off running like the wind yet Troy, who had to pick himself up from the floor before setting off in pursuit, had caught the man and brought him down before he had covered more than a few yards.

Barnaby recalled the scene, superimposing Lacey's face on his mind's eye. Amazement first. Then panic. And something else. They had looked at each other for a moment just before Lacey had been bundled into the back of the car and Barnaby had been aware of a third emotion behind the eyes. Unexpected and out of place. What was it? Barnaby found himself sweating as he struggled to recall precisely those few seconds, so fleeting and imprecise.

And then he had it. The third emotion was relief. Now, holding on to this new realization, he replayed the scene for a second time. Lacey running; Lacey getting caught almost certainly before he needed to have done; Lacey relieved. And when exactly had he started running? Not, as would have been expected, when the knife was produced. But minutes later, when Barnaby was about to turn back into the studio. That must be it. They had found something in Holly Cottage. *But they had not found what Lacey was afraid they would find.*

Barnaby got out of the car and crossed the road. His mouth was dry and he could feel his heart thumping in his breast. As he walked he recalled the studio. Neat. Professional. Trestle tables. Brushes and paints. Nothing out of the ordinary, but as he hurried down the dirt track he became more and more convinced that his sudden perception was correct.

Holly Cottage, no longer basking in the sun, looked cold and grey once more. Barnaby opened the front door, calling 'Miss Lacey' up the stairs. He thought it unlikely that she had slept there last night but, just in case, did not want to alarm her. There was no reply. He stepped through the doorless opening into the studio.

Everything looked exactly the same. He picked up all the jars, tubes and tins; opened and sniffed. They seemed to contain nothing unorthodox. The brushes were just brushes. There were lots of paperbacks and art catalogues in a corner cupboard. He opened them and shook the pages. No incriminating letter fell to the floor. There was a jar of clean spirit, one paint-muddied, and a few rags, some clean and neatly folded, some stained and crumpled. The windowsill was bare. Barnaby turned his attention to the paintings.

He wasn't sure what he expected. Iris Rainbird had called them ugly, violent things. Barnaby was aware that this remark had started an ignoble hope in his own breast, once he had met the man, that Lacey had no talent. A hope now rudely shattered.

The first canvas he picked up was the portrait of Dennis

Rainbird, and it was stunning. The paint glistened as if still fresh. A combination of grey and yellow ochre reminded Barnaby of a newly turned lump of sticky clay. Close to, the painting looked unfinished, almost crude, but put upon the windowsill a few feet away it leapt into instant complicated life. Dennis was wearing an open-necked shirt the outline of which, like his hands, was blurred, fading into a shadowy background. The bones at the base of his throat showed through the fine skin clear and fragile like those of a small bird. The planes of his face were thick yellow slabs of paint which miraculously managed to suggest the subtle living tissue of real flesh with all its tides and secrets. The mouth was very tightly controlled and the gaze turned inwards reflecting the sitter's personal thoughts. His eyes showed loneliness and sorrow. The painter had understood and realized on canvas much more than Dennis Rainbird's physical appearance. He had exposed the man's secret heart. No wonder his mother had hated it.

Another portrait. An old woman holding a bunch of violets. Her eyes were sunken in a withered brown face. Her expression held all the gravity of the old yet her lips smiled with youthful lightness and grace. The violets retained a faint rime of silver where dew still clung to them. There were some abstracts and several landscapes and Barnaby, quite against his will, felt a rush of admiration as he turned these face outwards. No wonder Lacey didn't give a damn for his surroundings with all this going on in his head.

Cornfields with poppies, a bank carpeted with wild flowers, two which could have been Miss Simpson's garden. All a million miles removed from the careful discreet naturalism aimed for by Barnaby's own art club. Here were brazen skies arched over endless almost colourless beaches; buildings shimmering in heat; gardens engorged with vivid plants and flowers, everything bathed in golden light. He propped them against the wainscot and the sunshine seemed to spill out of the canvases, forming lustrous puddles on the wooden floor.

The abstracts were very large and plain. Thick white paint and, in one corner, an imploding star. Galactic rings of ever-deepening colour shrank to a kernel of tar-black flame. Next to these was a portfolio. Barnaby opened it and pulled out a sheaf of drawings. Sketches of Judy Lessiter, quickly done but full of animation. Seeing these brought Barnaby back to the moment and to why he was there.

He looked closely at all the paintings again. There seemed to be nothing revelatory about them. Nothing to indicate why they should be sealed away behind locked doors. Stepping back, he collided with the easel. It tipped to one side and the old shirt covering it fell off. Barnaby righted the easel and replaced the cloth. It made a squarish shape supported by the two cross bars. But it was a different shape from the one he had seen yesterday. Less solid. He was quite sure that yesterday there had been a largish canvas on that easel. Which meant that, between that time and now, someone had entered the cottage and taken it away.

'Get Lacey up here.'

'*Yes, sir*,' cried Sergeant Troy italically, leaving the incident room at a brisk trot and clattering down to the basement. 'Come on you.' He unlocked the cell door and jerked a thumb in Lacey's direction. 'Get off your backside. The chief inspector wants a word.' He watched the prisoner pick up his jacket. 'And you needn't bother with that,' he continued, 'you're not going anywhere.'

Michael Lacey ignored the sergeant, pushing past and hurrying up the stone steps. Troy caught up with him and resentfully tried to regain the dominant position. He had been brought up to date by Policewoman Brierley as to the main dramatic disaster of the night but as yet knew nothing of Lacey's alibi, and his confidence was absolute. 'Just bloody well watch it, that's all.'

The prisoner sat down in front of Barnaby's desk without being asked and looked around with interest at the equipment and activity. At the bank of telephones, wheels of cards and television screens.

'So this is where it all goes on. Most impressive.' He gave Barnaby a smile, perky and sardonic. 'I shall sleep more easily in my bed tonight. I assume that's where I shall be sleeping?'

'Well, Mr Lacey, your alibi has certainly been confirmed.'

The man got up. 'So I'm free to go?'

'Just a moment.' He sat down again. 'I returned to the cottage this morning to continue my search.' No reaction. No fear. No alarm. Not even nervousness. Sod his hide, thought Barnaby. 'I believe at the time when you were detained there was quite a large canvas, covered with a cloth, on the easel in your studio.'

'I doubt it. I was just starting on a portrait of Judy Lessiter, as you know. I never work on two things at the same time.'

'Nevertheless that was my impression.'

'Then your impression was incorrect, Chief Inspector. Did you enjoy looking round? What did you think of it all?' Then, before Barnaby could reply he continued, 'I'll tell you, shall I? You don't know anything about art but you know what you like.'

Stung by this patronizing assumption that he was nothing more than a flat-footed clodhopping philistine, Barnaby retorted, 'On the contrary. I know quite a lot about art and I think you have a most remarkable talent.'

He watched Lacey as he spoke. Watched his face change. All the pugnacity and superciliousness faded. A look of the most intense pleasure spread across his face. He said, 'Yes, I have, haven't I?' But there was no arrogance in his voice. Just happiness laced with the merest thread of uncertainty.

'Your technique is very assured. Have you been to an art school or college?'

'What?' He gave a shout of laughter. 'For one term . . . that was enough. Load of pretentious wankers. There's only one way to learn and that's to sit at the feet of the masters.' The sincerity in his voice robbed the phrase of all pretension. 'I shall go to the Prado. The Uffizi. To Vienna and Paris and Rome and New York. And learn my craft.' There was a long pause then he said, 'Is anything the matter, Inspector? You look quite . . . well . . . put out.' Then, when Barnaby still did not reply he got up. 'So . . . is it all right for me to go now?'

'What? Oh' – Barnaby got up – 'yes . . . you can go.'

Michael Lacey strolled over to the door, saying, 'Excuse me,' to Sergeant Troy and adding, 'you really should close your mouth, Sergeant. You could catch something very nasty.'

Troy snapped his jaws together and glared at the closing door. 'Why the hell are you letting him go, sir?'

'He was with the Lessiter girl all yesterday afternoon.'

'But . . . Mrs Quine saw him.'

'She saw someone, I've no doubt. Someone wearing clothes and a cap very like those that Lacey wore. Now the point is,' murmured Barnaby, 'if the murderer was so keen to incriminate Lacey why didn't he make a thorough job of it and dump the clothes at the cottage as well?' Troy, understanding that these questions were self-addressed, kept silent. 'Well, they can't be far. Whoever it was was pushed for time. With a bit of luck the search should turn them up today. I'm just going over to Forensic to see what's new. I'll be back in ten minutes. Sort a car out, would you? And your bucket and spade.' Troy's jaws parted company again. Barnaby turned in the doorway and smiled grimly. 'We're going to the seaside.'

Chapter Twelve

Troy took the A21 (Hastings and Saint Leonards) at Tunbridge Wells and re-opened the conversation that had been temporarily abandoned whilst he had negotiated unfamiliar roundabouts and watched for exit signs. He and Barnaby had been discussing the latest analysis reports from the Forensic department.

'But if these ... filaments ... these bits of nylon were under her nails doesn't that mean she must've scratched the murderer's face?'

'Not necessarily. If you pull a pair of tights over your head only a small section would cover your face. That means there's quite a bit of stuff left over. She may have grabbed at that.' He leaned back and closed his eyes, picturing – not for the first time – the terrible moment when Mrs Rainbird's visitor disappeared from the sitting room, perhaps after asking to use the loo, to re-emerge moments later, features squashed out of all recognition, wielding a sharp knife. The fact that he now knew who that figure was added an extra gloss of horror to the scene. Troy moved on to the findings in the garden shed.

'Must be the rug, sir ... the black and green fibres they found.'

'Almost certainly.'

'I suppose whoever it was thought dumping it in water would be safer than trying to burn it? Less conspicuous.'

'Expect so. I've got a feeling it was in the pond in the woods near the cottage. And that the clothes might well be in there too.'

'And one or the other of the Rainbirds got wind of it and tried to put the bite on?'

'I think so. They were right out of their league, of course. The quickness and efficiency of Miss Simpson's dispatch should have told them that. "Murder being once done," Troy.'

'That Jane Austen again is it, sir?' asked the sergeant, zipping through Lamberhurst. 'Shan't be long now. That rug must have weighed something to cart away.'

'Yes. I expect they had a plastic bag, probably a bin liner. And the clothes went in as well.'

'All a bit risky. Broad daylight and everything.'

'Ah – but it's panic stations now. Things are starting to go wrong for them, Troy. Time's running out . . . time's running out fast.' Out of the corner of his eye he saw the sergeant turn his head.

'What . . . ? You mean you know who committed the murders?'

'Oh yes.'

'What . . . both of them?'

'All three of them.'

'But . . . I don't understand . . .'

'Watch what you're doing, man!'

'Sorry, sir.' Troy stared carefully at the road ahead for a few moments then continued, 'Surely Phyllis Cadell killed Mrs Trace.'

'I think not.'

'But . . . she's confessed. God – she even took her own life.'

Barnaby did not reply. His silence lasted until they entered Saint Leonards. Nearing the sea front he asked the sergeant to stop and asked the way to De Montfort Close of an old gentleman stiffly adorned with salt-caked whiskers. Troy followed his directions and drew up outside Sea Breeze, a white bungalow with a neat front garden indistinguishable from a thousand others. Barnaby got out but stopped Troy as he made to follow.

'Won't you want me, sir? For a statement?'

'I doubt it. This is just background. I'll call you if I do.'

Left alone, the sergeant turned Barnaby's cryptic remarks over and over in his mind. They didn't make sense from where Troy stood. No sense at all. It must have been Lacey. The Lessiter girl was covering up. Easy to see she was mad about him. Instead of letting Lacey go Barnaby should have arrested her as an accessory. That's what he, Troy, would have done. Because who the hell else could it have been? Dennis was out at work, Lessiter was screwing away at the Casa Nova, Mrs L and David Whiteley ditto in her Honda, Katherine was with Henry. And if the same person committed both murders that ruled out Phyllis Cadell who couldn't have been the woman in the woods and so had no reason for knocking off Miss Simpson. And in any case (here Troy was inclined to agree with Barnaby) her denial had the ring of truth. After all, if you're confessing to one murder there's not a lot of point in lying to cover up a second.

And she must have murdered Bella Trace. Troy struggled to recall the newspaper report. No one in the party could have fired the shot, that was made plain at the inquest. Katherine was back at the house making sandwiches so Phyllis Cadell was the only – Wait a minute! Troy's thoughts swarmed madly in all directions like disturbed ants. There was one of the current suspects still unaccounted for on that day. *Where was Barbara Lessiter*? Not out shooting (that would have been a sight to wonder at) yet with no definite alibi. Now *she* could have killed Miss Simpson. And Mrs

Rainbird. She wasn't all that precise about the time she was in her car with Whiteley. And keeping their affair secret would have been a strong enough motive in both cases. But Bella Trace, for heaven's sake? What would be the point in that? On the other hand why should Phyllis Cadell confess to something she hadn't done? It didn't make sense.

Troy sat grinding his teeth. He had been with Barnaby all along the line in this case. Heard all the interviews, had access to forensic results. What Barnaby saw and knew he, Troy, saw and knew. And it infuriated him to hear his chief speak with such easy certainty of conclusions reached. Troy slammed his fist at the dashboard and winced with pain. Where had he gone astray? Was he looking at things from completely the wrong angle? That might be it. A spot of lateral thinking; try a new slant. He would do a bit of Chinese breathing, go calmly back to the beginning and start again.

Barnaby stood square in the centre of the cardinal-red polished step, lifted the tail of the mermaid knocker and let it drop. An old lady opened the door. She looked at him, over his shoulder at the car and back at his face again. She looked immeasurably sad and very tired.

Barnaby said, 'Mrs Sharpe?'

'Come in,' she said, turning her face away. 'I've been expecting you.'

PART FOUR

CONCLUSION

Chapter One

As the car sped along through the pallid genteel streets and out into the Sussex countryside Barnaby reviewed what, in spite of the number of deaths, he would always think of as the Simpson case. He had arrived at a solution which he knew must be the true one and the puzzle was complete but for one small segment. He recalled the scene in question. He remembered it so vividly, almost word for word. The trouble with this small segment was that it made nonsense of his conclusions. Yet he could not ignore the scene or pretend that it had never happened. Somehow or other it must be made to fit.

Troy eased up a little as they re-entered Tunbridge Wells. The man really drove very well, thought Barnaby. For all his occasional reprimands about his sergeant's dashing over-exuberant style Barnaby acknowledged Troy's skill and road sense. Watching now, noting how frequently he checked the road behind; mirror to road, road to mirror, mirror to –

'But that's it!'

'Sir?' Troy's eyes slid, for a fraction of a second, over to his chief. Barnaby did not reply. Troy, whose Chinese breathing and circumvolutions had got him absolutely nowhere, did not pursue the matter. He was determined not to give the old devil the satisfaction of responding with wide-eyed and eager questions. No doubt all would be revealed when he judged the time to be right. Till then, thought Troy, his brilliant deductions could stew in their own juice. 'Straight to Causton is it?'

'No,' replied Barnaby. 'I've been up since half-past five and I'm starving. We'll stop off at Reading for some lunch. There's no hurry now.'

He remembered those words afterwards and for a very long time to come. But he had no way of knowing that, in the town they had so recently left behind, an old lady was lifting a telephone and, with tears streaming down her face, dialling a number at Badger's Drift.

The marquee was the size of a barrage balloon. It billowed and flapped whilst half a dozen men struggled with pegs and hammers to tether it down. Two dozen crates of champagne and twelve trestle tables stood nearby together with a tottery mountain of interlocking bentwood chairs. Under the canvas the exquisitely nurtured aristocratic green, trampled by heavy boots, was already giving off that enclosed warm smell redolent of a thousand refreshment tents – a scent of tea urns and sweet hay and freshly cut bread.

As Barnaby walked down the terrace steps for the last time he saw Henry Trace wheeling himself between florists and caterers; nodding, smiling, pointing, getting in the way. Even from a distance of several feet his happiness was tangible. Barnaby looked around for Katherine Lacey.

'Why, Chief Inspector.' Henry propelled himself skilfully across the flagstones. 'How nice. Have you come to wish us joy?' His smile faded as he saw the policeman's face. He stopped his chair some little distance away as if this gap might somehow mitigate whatever tidings Barnaby had brought.

'I'm very sorry, Mr Trace, but I have some bad news.'

'Is it about Phyllis? I already know . . . they rang up. I'm afraid it looks a bit insensitive going ahead here but everything was so advanced' – he gestured across the lawn –

'that I decided . . .' His voice ran down. There was a long pause whilst he stared at the two men, dread gathering in his eyes.

Barnaby spoke for a few moments, gently, knowing there was no way to make the cruel words merciful. Troy, who had always hoped that one day he would be in a position to see a member of the upper crust getting their comeuppance, found himself looking away from the shrunken figure in the wheelchair.

'Can you give me any idea of Miss Lacey's whereabouts?' Barnaby waited, repeated his question and waited again. He was about to ask it a third time when Henry Trace said, 'She's gone over to the cottage . . .' His voice was unrecognizable. 'Someone rang up . . .'

'What! Did she say who it was?'

'No. I took the call . . . it was a woman . . . in some distress I think. She sounded very old.'

'Jesus!' Even as he spoke Barnaby started to move. Troy ran alongside. 'Leave the car . . . quicker through the spinney.'

They cut through the garden of Tranquillada, past the startled constable, and crashed through the hedge to the spinney. Barnaby tore at the hazels and forced his way through into the woods. He ran like the wind, kicking sticks and everything else out of his way savagely. Troy heard him mutter, 'Bloody fool . . . *bloody bloody fool*.' And, not knowing who or what Barnaby meant, felt himself caught up in the slipstream of urgency engendered by the other man's flight.

Back on the terrace Henry Trace slumped in the chair. The bustling continued around him unabated. Boxes of champagne flutes went by and a hamper of napery. A pretty girl in a pink overall was wiring white carnations into an arch over the door. She was singing. Henry closed his eyes and braced himself for another wave of pain. It came in quietly but in no time was tearing at him with vicious ferocity.

'Excuse me, sir . . . ?' Pause. 'Sir?'

'Yes?'

'I'm just going to do the gypsophila. I thought it'd look rather pretty wound through the balustrades then sort of tumbling down the steps . . . ?'

He looked at her, then across at the marquee which was now gaily decorated with bunting. People were hurrying about, calling to each other. The mountain of chairs was being dismantled and carried into the tent. He must do something to stop the momentum. Even as he prayed there was some mistake he knew there was no mistake. Everything Barnaby had told him fitted. Everything must be true. But what could he say to the girl? He looked at her kind smiling face.

'Yes,' he said, turning his chair to go indoors, 'tumbling down the steps will be fine.'

Chapter Two

'Take the kitchen,' cried Barnaby, 'I'll check upstairs.'

All three bedrooms were empty and looked just as they had before: the little single bed still straining pristinely for effect, the double a tangled mess. Barnaby checked the wardrobe and was just opening a large trunk on the landing when he heard Troy cry out. He flew down the stairs and found his sergeant standing in the studio in front of the easel. He looked completely stupefied.

'But . . .' he gaped at Barnaby. 'Who is it?'

Barnaby glanced at the canvas. Resting on the rim of the easel was an envelope addressed 'To Whom It May Concern'. He snatched it up and walked quickly out of the room. Troy, his face the colour of a boiled lobster, followed.

In the hallway Barnaby tore open the envelope, glancing rapidly over the pages. Then he hurried into the kitchen. Something which looked very like parsley was strewn all over the table. And there was a musty smell in the air. Like mice.

Troy stood watching his chief uncertainly. The man looked poleaxed. He sat down and shook his head from side to side as if to escape tormenting thoughts or an insect stinging. Then he got up and looked round him in a dazed manner. He stuffed the letter into his pocket and hurried from the room. He said nothing to his companion. Indeed Troy felt that Barnaby had forgotten he was there at all. Nevertheless he followed the other man as he hurried round the side of the house and immediately plunged deep into the woods. Troy, uncomfortably aware of the effect the painting had had on him, stumbled behind.

Barnaby twisted and turned, back-tracked and turned again. Too late, too late was all he could think as he wheeled round and round in circles while the unforgiving seconds ran through his fingers like silver sand. Images in his mind: a television screen with a square inset ticking off fractions of a second almost faster than the eye could see; banked computers and a nasal voice counting 'Five. Four. Three. Two. One. Zero.' An hour glass, the last grains tumbling through. And, over and above everything, himself and Troy relaxing in the Copper Kettle. A starter, a main course. Cheese and biscuits as well as a pudding. Coffee. And a refill, sir? Why not? There's no hurry. All the time in the world.

Where the hell was the place? He tried to remember if there was anything special about it. Any landmark. Only the ghost orchid which started the whole thing and the stick with the red bow which would have been removed days ago. So there was nothing . . .

God – he'd seen those scabby parasols on that tree trunk before. He'd been running around in bloody circles. He stopped, vaguely aware that Troy had crashed to a halt beside him. Only now was he aware that every beat of his heart was causing the most intense pain. That his jacket was black with sweat and snagged, like the skin on his face, with brambles. That he was opening his mouth wide and sucking in air like a drowning man. He stood very still, willing himself to think calmly.

And it was then he saw the hellebores. And knew why the scabby parasols looked familiar. A few feet away were the tightly latticed branches which made a screen that curved. He walked alongside the partition, his footsteps silent in the thick leaf mould, until he came to the end.

He was facing a hollow. Quite a large piece of the ground was flattened; bluebells and bracken folded backwards and crushed. Katherine Lacey lay in her lover's arms. They rested heart to heart for comfort, like children lost in the wild wood. A single glass lay inches from his lifeless hand. She wore her bridal gown, stiff folds of ivory satin and a veil held in place by a circle of wild flowers. The veil, thickly embroidered and encrusted with seed pearls and diamante, streamed away from her body and seeped, a spangled luminous pool, into the surrounding dark. Her remarkable beauty was undimmed even in death. As Barnaby, bereft of speech, stood silently by, a large leaf drifted down and settled on her face, glowing richly against the waxen skin and covering her sightless eyes.

Chapter Three

'It was very good of you to come and see me, Chief Inspector.'

Barnaby sat back in the tapestry wing chair, a large slice of plum cake and a double Teachers at his elbow. 'Not at all, Miss Bellringer. If it weren't for you – as you remarked, I remember, quite early on in the proceedings – I would not have had a case at all.'

'I always suspected the Lacey girl, you know.'

'Yes,' Barnaby nodded, 'one is inclined to reject the very obvious solution. But it is so often the correct one.'

'And of course once you realized she wasn't working alone . . .'

'Exactly. It then became clear how all three murders could have been committed.'

'I feel so distressed about Phyllis Cadell. A terrible business. But I still don't quite understand all the ramifications. Why on earth would she confess to something she hadn't done?'

'It is quite complicated.' Barnaby took a sip of his Teachers. 'And I'll have to go back a few years to start explaining. Back to the Laceys' childhood in fact. Do you remember Mrs Sharpe?'

'The nanny? Yes, I do. Poor woman. They led her quite a dance, I believe.'

'So Mrs Rainbird told me. Apparently the children were as thick as thieves when they were little, always plotting,

260

planning, fiercely protective, always covering up for each other, then when they were older everything changed. Nothing but rows which got to such a pitch that, as soon as they were old enough to cope alone, old Nanny Sharpe left for a bit of peace and quiet by the seaside. I accepted this story at face value simply because I had no reason to doubt it. And the behaviour of the Laceys certainly bore it out. I overheard an extremely bitter quarrel between them myself. But my conversation with Mrs Sharpe gave me an entirely different picture.'

He took a bite of the excellent plum cake, stiff and black with fruit, and a swig of Teachers. In his mind he sat again on the unyielding Rexine sofa overlooked by a constellation of smiling Laceys. Mrs Lacey as a child and young woman, wedding photographs, christenings. The children growing up, so alike and watchful; always close.

'She was the strong one,' said Mrs Sharpe. 'Took after her father.'

'Not an easy man, I understand?'

'He was wicked!' Mrs Sharpe's thin face flushed. 'I don't go in for all this modern understanding-what-makes-people-tick rubbish. There are some people just born wicked and he was one of them. He broke my poor girl's heart and drove her to her death. She was a lovely creature too . . . so gentle. And other women . . . he was supposed to have met this smart piece he went abroad with after Madelaine died. Well I've never believed that and I never will. He was carrying on with her all along, to my way of thinking.'

'The boy was more like his mother, then?'

'He worshipped her. I felt so sorry for him. He tried to be brave . . . to protect her, but he was no match for his father. Gerald was a very violent man . . . once he threw an iron at Madelaine and Michael jumped in between them and got it full in the face. That's how he got that mark, you know.'

Barnaby shook his head. 'I didn't know.'

'But Katherine was all for her father. And he went off and left her without a backward glance. It would have damaged a weaker person for good and all but she . . . well . . . she was a chip off the old block all right. She didn't seem much like him on the surface. He was flamboyant, always showing off . . . she'd draw into herself more, but in their hearts they were a dead spit. Fiery tempers and a cast-iron will. And when he'd gone she turned all her attention to Michael. And he, poor boy, with his mother dead, clung to her in desperation. You'd never have thought he was the elder. She was mother, father, sister, everything to him. Sometimes I wondered what I was doing there at all except there had to be somebody while they were still under age.

'Michael started painting when he was about fourteen. Seriously, I mean. He'd always been good at art at school and they kept on at him to go to college. He went for a bit then walked out. Said they were a load of rubbish. And Katherine encouraged him. Told him he'd be better off travelling round Europe, going to galleries, museums and suchlike. That's what painters always did, she said. Anyway, that's how things stood till just before Katherine was seventeen. Michael'd had his eighteenth birthday a couple of months before and that's when the rows started. Adolescent rows as I saw it. Picking fault with each other all the time, every day a slanging match. She'd scream at him, he'd fling himself out of the house. And yet, Inspector' – she leaned forward and her voice became very quiet – 'all the time this was going on I felt there was something wrong. I could sense the undercurrent of their feelings for each other as strong as ever. The rows seemed . . . forced somehow . . . unnatural.

'Then, one night, I couldn't sleep. I tossed and turned for hours till at three o'clock I gave up and decided to go downstairs and make some tea. I was walking past

Katherine's door when I heard sounds . . . little cries. I thought she was having a nightmare so I opened the door and . . . looked in.' Her face burned with the memory and she covered it with her hands. 'I couldn't stay after that. I gave the excuse to the Traces that the children – I still thought of them like that, you understand – were simply too much for me and I wanted to retire. My sister had died a few months before and left me this bungalow. My last couple of weeks at the cottage were as different again. No need to stage any more rows to put me off the scent. They didn't bother to conceal how they felt. Didn't even seem to think there was anything wrong. It was so natural for them, you see . . . just an extension of their close feelings. They couldn't understand why I had to leave. Why I wasn't happy for them both. I did try once or twice considering the possibility of staying on . . . they were still my babies in a way and I had promised their mother I'd look after them, but then one day Katherine started talking about their European tour. Oh they were going here . . . they were going there . . . I don't know where they weren't going. I asked then, "Who's paying for all this?" And she said, "Henry, of course." And Michael said, "Kate can get Henry to do anything."

'They were standing together at the time behind the kitchen table, arms around each other's waists. And I suddenly realized how strong they were . . . They fed off each other. You could almost see it . . . energy flowing to and fro between them . . . doubling . . . doubling in strength. And I felt afraid. I thought, there'll be no stopping them. Whatever they want . . .

'Someone sent me the paper with the inquest on Mrs Trace. It seemed an accident clear enough. But then there was the engagement and when I heard Miss Simpson had died I couldn't help wondering . . . Perhaps if I'd got in touch with the police the third death might not have happened. But I didn't *know*, you see . . . it was just a feeling. And how could I have betrayed them? I loved them, you see . . . Madelaine's children.'

There was a long pause. Miss Bellringer nodded gravely. 'I begin to understand.' She poured herself a little more whisky and continued, 'But I still don't see how Bella could have been killed by either of them.'

'Neither did I at first. I read the report until I knew it by heart. And it tallied so perfectly with Phyllis Cadell's confession that there seemed to be little reason to look further. And yet there was something about it that didn't quite fit and it nagged at me for days before I realized what it was. Now, I'm not a sporting man but it seems to me that the place for a beater is ahead of the guns. *So why were Michael Lacey and Mrs Trace together?* Come to that what was he doing out there in the first place? He told me some story about earning money but this couldn't have been further from the truth. He was there to peel Mrs Trace off from the rest of the party. To isolate her so that she became a very clear target indeed; a sitting duck, in other words. Katherine was in the undergrowth – don't forget we only have her brother's word for it that she was in the kitchen at Tye House – and at a prearranged time, no doubt with a certain amount of leeway on either side, the murder was committed.'

'Just like that?'

'Both the Laceys were experienced shots. Mrs Rainbird told me so. And of course with all the kerfuffle with the dogs and everyone racing about she just slipped quietly away through the trees. And Michael, all eagerness to help, went racing off to phone for an ambulance. And now comes the second thing that struck me as odd. Surely, in an emergency, you dash up the nearest driveway and bang on the door, but Lacey went to Tye House. Almost as far as you could get from the spot where the accident occurred. Why did he not go to the first house in Church Lane? Or Holly Cottage, which would have been even nearer? There can only be one reason. Because he wished to delay the ambulance as long as possible. The last thing they wanted was an efficient team on the spot in no time, perhaps saving Bella's life.'

'Yes . . . I can see that it could well have been that way . . .' So enthralling had Miss Bellringer found Barnaby's recital that she had frozen into attention with a square of plum cake halfway between her plate and her mouth. She now popped the cake in and continued, whilst munching, 'But then . . . why Phyllis?'

'Well, not surprisingly, considering the terrible emotional pressure she was under, her lack of practice with a gun coupled with the vodka she'd consumed, Miss Cadell missed. By half a mile I shouldn't wonder. But by one of those dreadful coincidences that sometimes happen and change our lives by doing so, Bella stumbled over a tree root as Phyllis fired. Lessiter mentioned at the inquest that Mrs Trace had already fallen once. There can be no other explanation.'

'But . . . if Dennis saw what happened he must have seen Bella get up again. After Phyllis ran away, I mean.'

'I should imagine so. That's something we shall find out when he's fit to be questioned. But I wouldn't put it past either of them to bleed someone white, knowing them to be innocent.'

'How absolutely appalling.' Miss Bellringer looked anxiously around her exuberant room as if testing it for pregnability. She bent down and picked up Wellington, holding him to her flat chest like a charm. Four resentful feet stuck stiffly out. 'And Bella's murder . . . was this the first step in some grand design?'

'Certainly. They left a letter. Everything clearly explained.' Bold black writing boiling with anger. The only word of sorrow or regret in the whole seven pages was that they had not been able to deny themselves a brief visit to their secret place that fatal Friday afternoon. No point in wounding his elderly companion by repeating the names they called her innocent friend. 'I believe it was you, Miss Bellringer, who used the term "bad blood". I remember thinking at the time how melodramatic it sounded. As if wickedness could be passed on genetically, like blue eyes or red hair. But now . . . I'm not so sure. It's all so reminiscent of the father's behaviour. Using people with absolute callousness and then walking away from the pain and unhappiness to the next mark.'

'Mark?'

'Sorry . . . victim. They needed money, you see. Lots and lots and lots of money. It wasn't enough to live quietly until Michael succeeded with his painting, which I have absolutely no doubt eventually he would have done. He was remarkably gifted. No, they had to travel. The Grand Tour. Venice, Florence, Amsterdam, Rome. For as long as Michael needed to soak up the artistic atmosphere. Then they planned to settle abroad, probably living as man and wife.'

'And Henry?'

'Ah . . . poor Henry. I'm afraid his demise would not have been long delayed. It's my belief that he had already imbibed a certain amount of the substance that killed your friend. It surely cannot be a coincidence that on the evening of her death he fell conveniently into a doze after dinner. And it wasn't just on that occasion either. What Henry actually said to me was, "I must have dropped off after dinner. *I often do these days.*"'

'I can see why it would have been necessary for her to get out of the house, Chief Inspector. But I still don't understand about the dog.'

'It's quite simple. She walked to the post box with her

letter to Notcutts, posted it, carried on to the bottom of the lane, met Michael on the path by Holly Cottage and handed the dog over to him. He took it home with him and Katherine called on your friend, with what result we already know.'

'She must've stayed quite a while to . . . to make sure . . .' Her face crumpled with distress. 'I'm sorry . . . all these details . . . it makes it so real . . .'

'Are you sure you want me to continue?'

'Quite sure. But perhaps a little fortification . . .' She put Wellington down and unscrewed the Teachers, pouring a little into her glass. 'And two . . . um . . . fingers isn't it . . . for yourself?'

'Thank you, no. To return to Beehive Cottage. Katherine needed to stay only until Miss Simpson had drunk the poisoned wine. Then she walked back to Holly Cottage and collected the dog, and Michael took over. No doubt there was the pretence that they both needed to speak to her. What they said we shall never know. Pleas for silence, for understanding. Perhaps even a feigned suggestion that the relationship would come to an end. They were both wonderful actors.' His voice hardened as he remembered Katherine's tearful display over Benjy's slow demise.

'How she would have hated that conversation. Emily, I mean. She was so fastidious. So it was Michael who . . . ?'

'Yes. He stayed until she lost consciousness, then closed the sitting-room door so Benjy wouldn't see his mistress and raise the alarm. He washed up Katherine's glass but left Miss Simpson's. Of course they both hoped that it would pass off as a natural death but in the unlikely event of an investigation a single glass with only her fingerprints and with a residue of poison would be found. Or rather would have been found . . .'

Miss Bellringer blushed. 'So the Shakespeare was just an added pointer? In case.'

'Yes. There it was open. He was probably looking around whilst he was waiting. The speech must have caught his eye and seemed propitious. Out with the 6B pencil. Which one of them climbed through the larder window is something they don't mention. What did become clear as I read the letter was that the Lessiter girl had a very lucky escape.'

'Judy? I don't understand.'

'She went to the cottage whilst Katherine was with your friend. She actually saw Michael through the window. What she couldn't have known was that he had a dog with him. If she'd knocked and the dog had barked . . .'

'Poor child. I'm afraid she was born for unhappiness. Some people are, you know.'

'Yes.' Barnaby nodded. 'She was made use of by the Laceys as was anyone else who came into their orbit. It was important for instance that Michael spent the afternoon of the Rainbird murder with her. I remember my sergeant remarking at the time, "Lucky he had an alibi". On the contrary – luck had nothing to do with it. It was a crucial part of the plan that he should have an alibi. The knife was planted at Holly Cottage not, as I first thought, to incriminate Lacey, but to direct suspicion away from the guilty party on to someone whom the murderer knew to be innocent. *And who could be proved to be innocent.*

'Even if Judy hadn't contacted Michael Lacey he would have been in touch with her, as his first words "I was just going to ring you" imply. And of course he had to work at the Lessiters' so that the cottage would be empty for the knife to be planted. Then, according again to the letter, there was to be an anonymous tip-off suggesting we search the cottage. But Mrs Quine beat them to it.'

'What a chance to take. Walking round in her brother's clothes in broad daylight.'

'Well, of course she came straight from the cottage

through the wood and into the spinney. I've no doubt that if she'd met someone face to face the whole plan would have been abandoned but, seen from a distance, hair piled up under her cap, she would simply be mistaken for Michael.'

'Who had an unbreakable alibi?'

'Precisely. There was a fair amount of risk involved but Mrs Rainbird had only given them till the wedding to come up with the first payment.'

'Before she blew the gaff?'

Barnaby smiled. He was going to miss Lucy Bellringer. 'More or less.'

'But surely Dennis wouldn't have kept quiet? Especially after what happened to his mother. What were they going to do about him?'

'Michael was to dispose of Dennis. In fact his life was saved only because he came home half an hour earlier than usual. We met Lacey in the spinney behind the bungalow. He pretended he was on his way to the pub but we now know that his real intention was to make sure the Rainbird boy did not survive his mother.'

'They must have been frantic.'

'Yes indeed. If they hadn't been they would have realized that if Katherine was spotted, even from a distance, it would give the game away. Who else amongst our small ring of suspects was of a build and height to be mistaken for Michael Lacey?'

'But surely she took care to have an alibi?'

'Of a sort. She said she'd been picking mushrooms. There was a basket of them on the kitchen table with some in. And they were fresh. I sniffed them. Certainly she would not have had time to pick them, commit the murder, shower, change clothes and so on. But if they had been gathered earlier that day by Michael and left at Holly Cottage ready . . .'

'Ahhhh.' Miss Bellringer nodded. 'That must be the explanation.'

'After cleaning herself up' (in a flash of memory Barnaby saw the girl, dazzlingly, ironically pure in her snow-white dress) 'she slipped out of the bungalow, no doubt checking the road carefully first, by the front door and then knocked, quite loudly, to draw attention to herself. Mrs Sweeney, hearing the knock and seeing her put the mushrooms on the step and walk away, naturally assumed, as anyone would, that she had also walked *up* the path.'

'But the clothes . . . the cap and everything. And you said something about a rug. Do you know what happened to that?'

'Oh yes . . . the rug was rolled up by the back garden hedge. Michael collected it after he left the Lessiters' and returned it to the pond. The clothes were simply taken away in the mushroom basket. It was a very large basket and, when I saw it in the kitchen, barely half full, so there was plenty of room to spare. She then walked down to Holly Cottage, hid the murder weapon, rather too successfully as things turned out, dumped the bloodstained clothing temporarily in the woods, and returned to Tye House.'

'What does that mean? Your remark about the murder weapon?'

'Well, we had a warrant to search the house. Now, if she had planted the knife in the kitchen drawer or in his bedroom we might not have entered the studio, a room that proved to be crucial, until later.'

'Surely they thought you would search everywhere, Chief Inspector? As a matter of course?'

'Normally yes, but Lacey made a bolt for it simply, as I realized later, to get us out of the house. And I'd had a quick look around the studio. It seemed perfectly in order. But as we drove away from the village Katherine saw the car. When her brother made a square around his face and shouted "I've been framed" I took this as a mere gesture of bravado. In fact it was a message that couldn't have been clearer. What does a frame enclose but a painting? And why, when the cottage held so much that was valuable to him, namely all his work to date, did he leave the door open? Why did he pretend it was never locked? Because something in the studio had to be removed and if this was done when the place was locked up the culprit, as the only other person to have a key, would have to be Katherine. Unlocked, it could have been anyone.'

'Yes . . . I can see that. But what had to be removed? Was it a picture? Why was it so important?'

Barnaby drained his Teachers and sat back in his chair, wondering how best to word his reply. He saw the painting again, heard Troy cry – 'But who is it?' Felt once more the almost physical blow to his solar plexus that had struck as he gazed at the easel. He understood fully Troy's bewilderment. For Katherine Lacey was practically unrecognizable. It was the most erotic nude he had ever seen. She was sprawled on the double bed and although there was something post-coital about the positioning of her limbs there was nothing relaxed or reflective in the work. It was riven with power. Her skin was pearly with sweat; her legs and arms throbbed with energy, seeming almost to move on the canvas. There was something rapacious about them. And something faintly sinister. Barnaby was reminded of a praying mantis, alluring and deadly. She looked bigger in every way than the woman he had known. Her neck was thick and powerful, her breasts large, her belly richly curved.

But it was the face that had brought forth Troy's cry of disbelief. It was the face of a maenad. Wet red lips were drawn back into a fierce smile: greedy, lustful and cruel. Her eyes glittered with an unholy satisfaction. Only her hair was recognizable and even that seemed to have a life of its own, twisting and turning like a nest of snakes. Barnaby felt that any minute she would spring out of the canvas and devour him.

Miss Bellringer repeated her question. Barnaby, aware that his reminiscences had left his face heavily flushed, replied, 'It was a portrait of his sister which left little doubt as to the truth of their relationship.' No wonder, he thought, the little single bed always looked so pristine and newly made. She probably hadn't slept in it since Mrs Sharpe left. And now he knew why Katherine hadn't moved into the vacant bedroom which was so much larger than her own.

'How clever they have been. And to what a terrible end.'

'Yes. Oddly enough my sergeant said something quite early on in the case which could have been a pointer if only I'd had the wit to see it. He noticed Mrs Lessiter never missed an opportunity to have a dig at Lacey and said, "It wouldn't be the first time a married woman's pretended to dislike her lover in public to put people off the scent."'

'They were certainly convincing.'

'Mm. There was one episode that I had great difficulty with. Troy and I –'

'I still don't like that man.'

Barnaby smiled noncommittally and continued, 'We were walking along the path to Holly Cottage and heard the Laceys in the midst of the most terrible row. Later, when I had decided they were guilty, I simply couldn't fit this scene into my puzzle. Why continue to act out in private a charade that is purely for public consumption? It didn't make sense. In fact I'm afraid overhearing them made me slower to reach my final conclusion than I would otherwise have been. And then, returning home from Saint Leonards, and noticing my sergeant's constant attention to his driving mirror, I realized that the whole scene had been set up for my benefit. Because although we were behind a tall hedge and could not see them they would have had a very clear view of our approach in the mirror placed near the opening where the motorist turned round.'

There was a long pause, then Miss Bellringer said, 'So . . . that's it then . . . ? The final piece slips into place.'

Barnaby drained his glass and pressed the remaining delicious crumbs of cake into a neat ball. He thought it seemed much longer than two weeks since his companion had first sat in his office rooting in her capacious bag and fixing him with her glittering eye. What had she just said? The final piece? Yes, it must be. The vague feeling he had of one more loose end must simply be his natural inability to believe in life's tidiness.

There was nothing more to say. He rose to his feet. Lucy got up too and held out her hand. 'Well, goodbye, Chief Inspector. It's been most stimulating working with you. How I shall settle down again to the normal dull routine I just don't know.'

Barnaby shook hands and said, with absolute sincerity, 'I can't imagine anything being dull for long in your presence.'

As he walked towards the layby where he had parked the Orion he passed the churchyard, hesitated, then turned in. He made his way around the building through a gate in the box hedge to where the newest graves showed, rectangular strips of cold clay, in the lumpy greensward.

One was heaped with wreaths, the flowers still glowing and vibrant; on the other the tributes had been removed, leaving only a vase of dark red, sweetly scented roses. A plain stone was already in place. It read:

EMILY SIMPSON
A Dear Friend
1906–1987

Barnaby stood in the shade of the dark yew trees and listened to the kaah-kaah of the rooks for a long moment, then turned and walked quickly away.

Dinner was almost finished. Cully had provided assorted dips with crudités. Chicken chasseur. Broccoli. New potatoes. Watercress. A wedge of double Gloucester and lemon chiffon pie. And there was a little box of florentines to nibble with their coffee. Barnaby's stomach, torn between disbelief and excitement, muttered gently. Cully poured the last drops from the second bottle of Côtes de Gascogne and lifted her glass.

'Merde in your eye, folks.'

'I was going to drink to Beatrice,' replied Barnaby. His daughter was in the last week of rehearsals for *Much Ado*, happy to stay in Cambridge, even in the long vacation, if it meant getting her teeth into a good part.

Sartorially she seemed to have quietened down a bit whilst still looking definitely pantomimic. She wore a man's tailored three-piece suit in grey and white chalk stripes dating from the early fifties and her hair, the colour of sloe gin, was cut in an Eton crop. There was a monocle pinned to her lapel. She looked aggressive, sexy and, because of her youth, rather touching. Barnaby thought she was softening up a bit. He had not discussed the dénouement of the Simpson case with Joyce, waiting until Cully was home, saving it for their first long meal together. And she had listened courteously, intent and thoughtful to the very end. Joyce now returned briefly to the subject.

'I always thought that . . . um . . . that sort of thing . . . you know . . . only went on in . . . well . . . poorer families.'

'Oh Ma, don't be so mealy mouthed. If you mean working class why on earth don't you say so? In any case not true. There are lots of examples, fact and fiction, of upper-class siblings having it off.' Cully nibbled a florentine. 'Just like poor Annabella.'

'What?' said Barnaby, placing his cup in his saucer with extreme care.

'Pardon, dear, not what.'

'Annabella. You know . . . in *Tis Pity*.'

'No, I don't know. Enlighten me.'

'Honestly, Dad . . . I worked my guts out on that thing . . . it was the first big part I had . . . *Tis Pity She's a Whore* . . . at the ADC. You came up to see it and now you don't even remember.'

Yes, he remembered now. A dark stage lit with sudden flares of light from torches. Rich brocades and painted faces swirling out of the shadows. Terrible images of blood and death. His daughter in a white gown drenched with blood; daggers plunged again and again into living flesh; a heart held aloft at knife point. Horror upon horror, scenes prefiguring the death and destruction he had so recently beheld at Tranquillada. And, over and above all, the tragic pitiful incestuous passion of Annabella and her brother Giovanni. Barnaby saw again the little piecrust table in Beehive Cottage with the pile of books. *The Adventurous Gardener*, Shakespeare, *A Golden Treasury*. And the copy of Jacobean plays.

Cully spoke dreamily, her husky voice brimming with untold sadness, 'One soul, one flesh, one love, one heart, one all . . .'

Barnaby gazed at her with fatherly pride and admiration. He picked up his cup again. 'Yes,' he said, 'that's about the size of it.'

THRILLINGLY GOOD BOOKS
FROM CRIMINALLY
GOOD WRITERS

CRIME FILES BRINGS YOU THE LATEST RELEASES FROM TOP CRIME AND THRILLER AUTHORS.

SIGN UP ONLINE FOR OUR MONTHLY NEWSLETTER AND BE THE FIRST TO KNOW ABOUT OUR COMPETITIONS, NEW BOOKS AND MORE.